BROADVIEW PUBLIC LIBRARY DISTR
2226 S. 16TH AVENUE
BROADVIEW, IL 60155-4000
(708) 345-1325

Married To His Lies

BY MZ. ROBINSON

Copyright© 2010 By MZ. ROBINSON
Published by:
G Street Chronicles
P.O. Box 490082
College Park, GA 30349
www.gstreetchronicles.com
fans@gstreetchronicles.com

This work is a work of fiction. The events and characters described herein are imaginary and are not intended to refer to specific places or living persons.

All rights reserved. No part of this book may be reproduced or transmitted in any form or by any means, electronic or mechanical, including photocopying and recording, or by any information storage and retrieval system, without permission in writing from the publisher.

Typesetting: G&S Typesetting & Ebook Conversions
www.gstypesetting.com

Library of Congress-in-Publication Data
Library of Congress Control Number: 2010923725

ISBN: 978-0-9826543-6-1

Join us on Facebook G Street Chronicles Fan Page

Dedication

"A man is known for his words but remembered by his actions."
Mz. R

This book is dedicated to my father, Ray. Daddy, you were the first on the scene, ready to hustle and promote for me. Thank you! For every encouraging word, the tears you wiped from my eyes, and every time you came to my rescue, thank you. I will never forget all that you've done. Also, thank you for teaching me that loving another person does not constitute forgetting who I am. I love you!

Smooches

First, giving all the honor and glory to my loving Savior Jesus Christ, I said it once and I will say it again, "I am nothing without you."

To my beautiful mother, Shirley, Mommy, thank you for getting out there and promoting your baby. You are truly the best mom in the world. I love you! To Michael, please remember Philippians 4:13. I love you. To my partner in crime, Banita Brooks, thank you for listening to me vent, making me laugh, and knowing how to keep a secret. You are one of the realest women I know. To my cousin, Kenyetta Hewlett- Ashford, I love you sweetie! I also want to thank you for forgiving me when I was MIA. To Ms. Joann, thank you for the love and support, I'm proud to claim you as my adoptive Mother. To George Sherman Hudson and the GSH team, thank you. I will never be able to express my gratitude. I have much love and respect for you. To Valerie Ann Williams, I love you girl. Thank you for the encouragement and getting the word out. You are truly a beautiful and bad chick! To my Uncle JT, thank you for always being there to offer a kind word and a helping hand. I love you. To LaVonda Howard, of cup cake creative studio, thank you for creating one hot cover after another. To Anita Shari-Peterson with Catawba Publishing, thank you for all that you do.

Most of all, thank you for your patience. To Doris, I hope you enjoy and thank you for the support. To all the readers out there, thank you...thank you...thank you. To everyone who stayed down and remained true, thank you.

Last but definitely not least to my Lord and Savior again. For you are the first and the last. My beginning and the only man who controls my end.

Mz R

CHAPTER 1

"I'm sorry, baby," Kenny said, kissing my forehead. "I promise it'll be just the two of us next weekend.

"You've been saying that for the last month," I said annoyed.

"What am I suppose to do, Shontay?"

Stepping back, I put some distance between the two of us. "Why don't you try telling Alicia that we've had Kiya for the last four weekends, and this weekend, we'd like to spend some time alone?"

Frowning, Kenny rubbed his hand back and forth across the stubble on his face. "Alicia is trying to get her cosmetology license," he said. "She works through the week, so that only leaves the weekends for her to go to classes."

I couldn't believe my ears. Not only was he canceling our plans for another Saturday alone, but he also wanted me to support his ghetto-tramp baby's mama in her educational endeavors. I had put my own education on hold to support him and our marriage, and not once did I get a thank you. Now he had the audacity to support Alicia's trifling ass.

"Maybe she should have thought about that before she decided to lay up with someone else's man," I snapped. "Besides, I thought you told me Kiya was going to be with her grandmother this weekend."

"She was, but Alicia's mom decided to go to Tunica," he said.

"She didn't tell Alicia until this morning."

Rolling my eyes, I threw my hands up in frustration. I was defeated, and arguing about the subject wasn't going to change a thing. Sitting down on the edge of the bed, I exhaled. "I'll think of something for the three of us to do together," I said.

"Thanks, baby," he said smiling.

***

Scanning over the selection of paperback and hardcover books, I searched for something to take home and read. I was spending a beautiful Saturday afternoon in Barnes and Nobles alone. After thirty minutes with Kenny and Kiya, I decided I needed a break. I pulled out a paperback titled *G-Spot* by Noire, and began to read the back cover.

"That's a hot piece," I heard someone say.

I looked up and found myself staring into a pair of gray cat-like eyes. The eyes complimented thick eyebrows and a pair of succulent-full lips. The man they belonged to had smooth, flawless skin, the color of pecans. I nonchalantly lowered my eyes, and glanced over his wide built frame. Even in the dirt-covered overalls he was wearing, I could tell he had large biceps and an athletic physique. He was wearing a dingy black bandana that hid his hair, and cement covered leather steel toe boots. *Sexy, even covered in dirt*, I thought. I redirected my attention back to his eyes, and asked, "Excuse me?"

He smiled, revealing a set of straight white teeth. "*G-Spot*," he said. His voice was deep and sexy. He had the type of voice that was perfect for phone sex. "It's a hot piece," he said. His thick tongue rolled along the edge of his bottom lip, causing heat to surge through the seat of my panties.

I shifted my weight from one leg to the other, and asked, "You've read it?"

His eyes traveled from my face down to my low cut tank top, then back up again. "Yes," he said, "it's one of my favorites."

"Thanks." I said, giving him a small smile. As I turned around to walk away, I could feel his eyes burning a hole in my ass through my denim Capri pants.

"So, you're just going to take my suggestion and run?" he asked.

I turned around slowly, and my eyes locked with his. There was something so sexual about the way he looked at me. For a brief second I could have sworn I saw "Let's fuck", spelled out in his corneas.

"You could at least tell me your name," he said seductively.

Trying to control the flutters in my stomach, and keep my hardened nipples from poking a hole in my shirt, I crossed my arms across my breasts.

"Thanks again," I said, instead of telling him my name. "Have a nice day."

I quickly walked up the aisle to the checkout. I was practically running to get away from him, not because I thought he was a psycho or a rapist. But because, in less than five minutes, he had accomplished what my husband hadn't been able to do in weeks; he managed to make my pussy wet.

After making my purchase, I sat in my car watching the front doors of the store. After five minutes, he walked out carrying a large bag. He walked with his head held high, and this air of confidence. The brother was fine. I'm talking fine with a capital F, as in "fuck me fine". I stalked him until he climbed into a white Ford F150 with SB Building & Construction painted in bright red letters on the door, started the engine, and pulled out of the parking lot.

I reclined the driver's seat of my Honda Accord and unbuttoned the top of my pants. The dark tint on my windows prevented anyone from seeing inside. That was a good thing, because I sat there in broad daylight with my AC blowing and my fingers inside my panties, stroking my throbbing clit. I closed my eyes, and a vivid picture of the stranger filled my head. I massaged and played with my clit until I came. The entire time I had been daydreaming that he was down on his knees with his face in between my legs.

***

I walked through the doorway of my home and cursed. My living room was a mess. "Damnit," I muttered under my breath.

I tripped over a bikini clad black Barbie, and kicked the doll across the floor. I looked around the room. There were dolls and building blocks everywhere. The room looked like a toy factory.

Why can't he make her pick-up after herself?

Kicking my way through the toys to the kitchen, I contemplated on cleaning up my stepdaughter's mess, but then decided against it. I had been playing Kenny's maid for the last eight years, I was not about to do the same for his daughter.

Before Kenny and I got married two years ago, we had dated for six years. He was the first man I ever trusted; that's where I made my mistake. I thought he could do no wrong. I put his ass on a pedestal, and damn near kissed the ground he walked on. In return, he made a fool of me by running from motel to motel with woman after woman after woman. It's not that Kenny isn't a good man; he just has a big problem keeping his dick to himself.

He cheated more times than I can count, and probably more than I care to know. Before we got married, there were several occasions my best friend and I busted him with other women. It was never a difficult task to catch Kenny, because he was never good at covering his tracks.

Whenever there was a new female in his life, he would start acting real shady. He'd come in at the wee hours in the morning, stumbling over his explanation of where he was and what he had been doing. He even walked around the house with his cell phone, like it was glued to his hip. If he went into the kitchen to get a glass of water, he carried his cell. When he got up to change the TV, he had his cell. Even when he went into the bathroom to take a piss, he had that damn phone. Kenny carried his phone around like it was his second dick. So, it was quite obvious when he was cheating on me.

I have to give him some credit; he managed to keep his daughter a secret for the two years of our marriage. I found out about Kiya, courtesy of three-way calling. To make a long story short, I checked his cell phone call history online, and discovered he had been calling this one particular number several times a day. I had my girl, Octavia, call the number on three-way, and the two of us were greeted by the sweet voice of a little girl. When her father took the phone from her, his voice sent my heart straight to my toes. The little girl was Kiya Janai Green, and her father was my husband.

I kicked Kenny out of our home that day. I was hurt beyond

words. Looking back now, I don't know if my heart felt more pain from his keeping his daughter a secret from me, or more so because another woman had given him the one thing I couldn't. My right to conceive and bare children was stolen from me at an early age.

Anyway, after two weeks of Kenny begging to come home, and my suffering through unbearable loneliness, I let him move back in. I swallowed what little pride I had left, and agreed to try and make our extended family work.

The sound of the door unlocking caught my attention. I sighed loudly, preparing myself for Kiya to come running into the room.

"Hey baby," Kenny said, walking through the doorway alone. He pulled out the chair next to me and sat down.

"Where's Kiya?" I asked.

"I took her to my mom's crib," Kenny said.

"How is Etta?"

"Good," he said smiling. "She asked about you."

I gave him my "yeah right" look, and rolled my eyes. Kenny's mother had no love for me whatsoever. I overheard her telling him once that I was holding him back. Imagine that. I have my Bachelor's in Elementary Education, a decent job as Assistant Director at a daycare, and good credit. Kenny worked for the City of Huntsville cutting grass, only had his GED because I helped him study for the exam, and he couldn't get a glass of water on credit without me co-signing. He wasn't even providing a roof over my head. The house we lived in also belonged to me.

My grandmother, Martha, God rest her beautiful soul, bought the three bedroom house for me before she died. To top it off, the 2000 Mitsubishi Eclipse he drove was in my name. Etta either had too much faith in her son, or she was plain delusional. I was not holding her son back, I was carrying his ass.

"I'm serious, she asked about you," he said unconvincingly.

I studied his facial features, while pretending to listen to him ramble on and on about Etta's garden. I loved Kenny, but he had nothing on the brother from the bookstore. Kenny is dark skinned, with high cheekbones and wide dark eyes. He isn't what most women would consider handsome, but he oozes with self-confidence.

His self-confidence gave him a certain sex appeal.

I stood up, leaned over and kissed his lips. I parted his lips with my tongue, while running my fingers through the low-cut waves in his hair. Standing up, he placed both of his hands on my ass.

"How you feeling?" he asked, in between kisses. That was his way of asking if I wanted to make love.

I grabbed the hardness in his pants, and gave it a gentle squeeze. "Give me five minutes to start the shower." I said seductively.

"I'll be waiting," he said, rubbing his hands up and down my backside.

***

Ten minutes later, I stood wrapped in a thick terry cloth bath towel. I was dripping wet from my warm shower, the shower I had anticipated on sharing with my husband. I walked into the bedroom and looked at him, as disappointment ran through my body. Kenny was stretched out across the bed, sleeping like a newborn baby.

He slept for the rest of the night, so I crawled up with my new book, and ended up reading it from beginning to end. The brother from the store was right, it was a hot piece. In fact, it was so hot that my fingers were deep inside my pussy, while Kenny lay beside me snoring.

CHAPTER 2

I hoped that the two of us could make up for last night, but Etta stopped that show when she called, whining about her dishwasher overflowing again.

"She put dishwashing liquid in it again," Kenny explained.

You'd think, after the first ten times, the sixty year old woman would understand that dishwashing detergent and dishwasher detergent are two completely different things. There were times that I was convinced she was doing it on purpose.

I knew that Etta would find some other petty task for Kenny to complete, so I showered and put on my Baby Phat denim shorts, red Baby Phat tank top, and climbed into my car. I drove outside of the city to the Monrovia District to visit my homegirl and my goddaughter at their home.

Octavia opened the front door of her personal mansion wearing a shimmering pink bikini top and a sheer sarong that covered her matching bikini bottom. Her body didn't have an ounce of fat on it. I stared at her double Ds, thinking that they now looked like triple Ds. She looked great from head to toe. It was hard to believe that she had given birth three months ago.

"Hey girl!" I said.

"Hey!" Octavia said.

The two of us exchanged a friendly hug, before I followed her through her foyer into the kitchen.

"Where's my goddaughter?" I asked.

Putting her hands on her hips, she cocked her head to one side. Her movements caused her long spiral curls to bounce from one side of her head to the other. "Damn, I'm fine, and you!" she said, sucking her teeth.

"My bad!" I said sarcastically. "How are you?" I asked sweetly.

"I'm fine," she said smiling.

"Now, where's my goddaughter?"

"Out back with her father."

"Daddy's little girl," I said laughing.

"You know it."

I watched her as she removed a glass pitcher of lemonade from the refrigerator shelf and sat it on a wooden tray on the counter. She removed four tall crystal glasses from the cabinet and sat them on the tray.

"How are Kenny and Kiya?" she asked.

"Fine," I said nonchalantly.

"What's up?" she asked, staring at me.

I wanted to tell her that lately I had become more and more unsatisfied with my marriage, my job, and my life in general, but I didn't. Instead, I lied and said, "Nothing."

"You sure?" she asked.

"Positive." I said smiling. "And today I don't want to do anything but relax with my girls and my favorite brother-in-law."

"Well, if you do want to talk, I'm here for you."

I smiled at my best friend, who had been more like a sister to me. "I know," I said.

Picking up the tray, she rolled her eyes at me. "Let's go see your goddaughter. I know she's the one you *really* came to see."

Laughing, I followed her through the glass French doors that led outside to her large patio. The scent of smoke and mesquite filled my nostrils, causing my stomach to rumble.

"Damon's on the grill?" I asked.

"Yep, he's giving Jasmine her first BBQ lesson."

The outdoor stereo system was on with Al Green's *Love and Happiness* blasting from the speakers. Damon stood at the outdoor kitchen wearing denim shorts, with the receiver to the baby monitor clipped to his waist. The white tank T-shirt he had on exposed his huge biceps. He was flipping burgers and singing along with Al.

"Love will make you do wrong!" he sang. "Love will make you do right!"

"Hey brother-in-law," I said, trying not to laugh.

"What's up, Tay?" he asked, his dark brown eyes beaming. He gave me a big bear hug, then turned to his wife and kissed her on the cheek.

Octavia and Damon made the perfect couple. They were sexy, successful and ambitious. If they were in Hollywood, they would be considered the ultimate "power couple".

Is Kenny going to join us today?" Damon asked.

I watched while he brushed barbecue sauce on the row of chicken leg quarters he had cooking on the grill.

"Not today," I said, trying to hide my disappointment. "Today it will be just the four of us."

"Not a problem," Damon said smiling. "Just make sure you take some of this food home to him."

"Don't worry," I said, rubbing my stomach, "you know the Holloway family loves to eat, and I'll do anything to get out of cooking!"

"Cooo," Jasmine's soft voice came through the receiver.

The outdoor kitchen had a built-in six-inch screen that was connected to the elaborate security system Damon had wired inside of their home. The screen gave a clear view of the guesthouse where Jasmine was. Looking at the monitor I watched her lying on the bed, kicking her feet up in the air.

"Aunt Tay, you got her?" Octavia asked, looking at me. I was walking pass the huge pool to the guesthouse before she could finish her sentence. "I guess that means yes!" She laughed.

The guesthouse was more of a one bedroom apartment. It was fully equipped with a kitchen, full size bath with a garden tub, and a king size bed. I vowed that if I ever needed a quick vacation, I would just spend a week in Octavia's backyard.

I sat on the bed kissing Jasmine's soft warm cheeks. Jasmine was the most beautiful baby in the world to me. She had almond colored skin, with large, light brown eyes. She was the perfect combination of her mother and father's genes. I touched her thick, curly black hair, and felt a surge of joy fused with sadness. I found being with Octavia and her family to be bittersweet.

Whenever I saw Octavia with Damon and Jasmine, it took me to the place in the back of my mind where I stored all of my broken dreams. There was a time when I had dreamt of having children of my own, but I knew that would never happen naturally. I was even willing to adopt. However, Kenny said he didn't want to raise another man's flesh and blood.

Jasmine had her small hand wrapped around my index finger, as I held her in my arms. Leaning down, I kissed her pudgy nose. She smiled.

"Are you two okay?" Octavia asked, sticking her head in the door.

"Yeah," I said halfheartedly.

Octavia's facial expression told me that she knew I was lying. In the five years we had been friends, we knew each other well enough to know when something was wrong.

"Is the food ready?" I asked.

"Almost," she said." I actually came to get you because there is someone I want you to meet."

"Who is it?" I asked, following her out of the guesthouse with Jasmine in my arms.

"Damon's friend, Savoy," Octavia said.

"Savoy?"

"Damon hired him to start construction on Ambiance 2," she said smiling.

The Ambiance is the upscale restaurant and jazz club Octavia owned before she and Damon got married. For their one year anniversary, Damon purchased property to build her Ambiance 2.

"How are things coming along?" I asked.

"Great," she said proudly. "If all goes well, we'll have construction completed by this fall."

"I'm happy for you," I said sincerely.

Damon was still standing by the grill singing, only this time it was *Family Affair* by Mary J. Blige, and his friend was playing back-up singer.

"That's Savoy," Octavia whispered to me. "Girl, the man is fine."

Savoy was tall, with tiny twists in his hair. He had on a pair of denim shorts that showed off his nicely toned calf muscles, and a short sleeve T-shirt that showed his solid biceps. If the rest of him looked as good as his profile from the back, then Octavia was right.

"Please stop hurting Mary's song!" Octavia said loudly. They turned around, and my eyes locked with his. "Savoy Breedwell," Octavia said, "this is my girl, Shontay Holloway."

"It's nice to see you again," he said, a small smile creeping across his face.

I felt a small vibration in the hot spot between my thighs. He was even finer than I had remembered.

"Again?" Octavia asked, looking confused.

"We met at the bookstore." I explained, never taking my eyes off of Savoy.

"Are you enjoying the book?" he asked.

"I enjoyed the book," I said.

"You finished it already?" he asked surprised.

"Yeah, last night."

"What book?" Octavia asked, staring at me with raised eyebrows.

"G-*Spot,*" he said seductively. The word sounded so good coming from his mouth.

"Sounds interesting," Damon said, removing the meat from the grill.

"Sounds a little freaky," Octavia said, taking Jasmine from my arms. "Bring it by so I can read it. I'm going to take Jazz in," she said, looking from me to Savoy. "Dame, why don't we move everything inside, it looks like it's going to rain."

About an hour later, a heavy downpour watered everything in sight. After stuffing ourselves with the meal Damon had prepared, the four of us settled down in the in-home theater, in the Italian leather sectional to watch *Ray* on DVD. Although Jamie Foxx gave an outstanding performance, I found it hard to concentrate on the movie with Savoy sitting so close to me. Whenever his leg or arm accidentally touched my body, I felt a tingling in my pussy.

"What's up with these women who continue to allow themselves to be played?" Savoy asked, as we watched the credits roll on the 60-inch Plasma screen.

"Love," Damon answered. "When you love someone, you're willing to compromise."

"What do you mean by allow?" I asked, puzzled.

Shifting in his seat, Savoy gave me a look that said the answer was obvious. "Permit," he said. "Keep giving them the opportunity."

"It's almost as if you're saying it's the woman's fault," I stated.

"That's exactly what I'm saying," he said seriously.

There is no way that someone this fine can be so ignorant, I thought to myself. "Why do you say that?" I asked, waiting for his logical explanation.

"Most men *and* women cheat because there is something lacking in their relationship," he stated. "It's a proven fact that what you won't do someone else will."

"That's the oldest and stupidest excuse in history," I said, offended.

"What about those who do all they can, and they still get cheated on?" I asked, crossing my arms across my breasts. "You expect us to believe that's still their fault?"

"Yes," he said, without hesitation. "If you allow someone to continue to disrespect you, it's nobody's fault but your own."

"What if you don't know?" Octavia asked.

"That's different," Savoy said, looking at her. "I'm talking about when you do know, and you continue to subject yourself to the other person's bullshit."

"I still think it boils down to love," Damon said, stroking Octavia's hair. "People compromise themselves and their beliefs for love."

"He's right," Octavia agreed. "People do and allow things they normally wouldn't when they're in love."

"There's a difference in compromising the type of orange juice you drink or which side of the bed you sleep on," Savoy stated, "and compromising the person you are. If being in love with someone means you lose sight of who you are and what you deserve," he threw his hands up in the air, "then I say it's better to be by yourself."

Octavia and Damon appeared to be in tune with what Savoy was saying, but I wasn't buying it.

"Well, if a man's unhappy, then why doesn't he just leave?" I asked.

If Savoy was such an expert on relationships, then maybe he could shed some light on that question.

"I said a man *or* woman," he said, looking at me. "But since you want to make this whole conversation about men," he gave me a quizzing look, "then why is it that the female doesn't leave?" he asked.

"Love!" Octavia and Damon said in unison.

"Well, love yourself more and settle for less," Savoy said. "The bad part is that women settle all the time. Then they complain when a brother turns out to be a dog. To make matters worse, they make all kind of excuses for staying with the man. Oh, he is so fine!" he said, mimicking a woman's voice. "He has sooo much potential! Girl, his dick is soooo big!"

Laughing, Damon shook his head. "Boy, you crazy!" he said.

"I'm serious." Savoy laughed.

"Men settle too," I said, slightly pissed off.

"No doubt," Savoy said, still laughing. "But we settle to get sex!" Everyone laughed, except for me.

The sound of Jasmine crying came through the baby monitor sitting on the glass coffee table.

"I got her," Damon said, kissing Octavia on her forehead.

"She's probably hungry again," Octavia told him. "I'll get her bottle."

The two of them left Savoy and me sitting in the room alone. The strong sexual attraction I felt for him earlier had dwindled when he expressed his fucked up opinion on relationships. I knew it wasn't Savoy's fault, but I had taken his comments personally.

"So, what's up with you?" he asked, his eyes scanning over my body.

"What do you mean?" I asked.

"Why are you so angry?"

"I'm not."

"I offended you," he said.

"What makes you say that?" I asked, pretending not to know what he was talking about.

"Because you were defensive," he said, staring at me.

"I wasn't defensive," I lied.

"You're lying to me." There was something about the way he was looking at me that made me feel naked. It made goose bumps form on my skin. "I make you nervous," he stated, licking his lips.

Hell yeah, you do, I said to myself.

"You are so arrogant," I said, rolling my eyes.

"Don't try and change the subject." He moved closer to me on the sofa. "I make you nervous," he said again, touching my arm with his fingertips. The warmth of his touch sent heat from my arm to my toes. "Have dinner with me," he said.

"I'm married." I held up my hand to display the gold band I had on.

"That's stating the obvious," he said, laughing lightly.

"So you make a habit of asking out married women?"

"Only the ones as sexy as you," he said smiling.

If he was trying to flatter me, it was working. My kitty was purring like she had never been touched by a man.

"I only go on dates with my husband," I said, standing up.

"You can bring him, but he's paying his own way," he said, standing in front of me.

"You are trippin'?"

Savoy stared at me with lust in his eyes. "Something tells me you'd rather it be just the two of us," he said. I was at a loss for words.

The man was sexy and arrogant. He was also reading me like the pages of a Zane novel. I couldn't deny that I wanted some time alone with Savoy, and the wetness in my panties told me I wanted more than just dinner.

Octavia strolled into the room just as the tension between the two of us was becoming too thick for me to handle. "Well, lil mama is full and fast asleep," she said. "A woman's work is never done." She sighed.

I continued to stare into Savoy's eyes, while giving thanks to God that Octavia had returned when she did. One more moment alone with him, and I would have been handing him my panties on a platter.

"I should be going," I said. I tore my eyes away from Savoy, turned and gave Octavia a quick hug. "I have to get to work early in the morning."

Before either of them could respond, I grabbed my purse, and told Octavia to kiss Jasmine and Damon for me. I walked what felt like sixty miles a second out the front door.

CHAPTER 3

Smiling, I stared at the vase of twelve long stem yellow roses. Savoy had them delivered to the daycare earlier. Tucked amongst the roses was a plain white greeting card. Inside the card, he had signed his name and left his phone number. Even the man's signature was sexy.

My thoughts of Savoy had me on a natural high. Even though I had no intentions of cheating on my husband with Savoy, or anyone else for that matter, I was still intrigued. I decided to give him a call, just to thank him for the roses, nothing else.

"Savoy Breedwell," he said, answering his phone.

"Do you make it a habit of sending married women flowers?" I asked jokingly.

"Only the ones as sexy as you," he replied.

I smiled this stupid schoolgirl grin. "They're beautiful," I said.

"I'm glad you like them."

"How did you know where I work?" I hadn't mentioned it the night before, and I was almost positive Octavia didn't tell him.

"Octavia," he said, laughing slyly. "I indirectly asked her a few questions about you."

"Like what?" I asked.

"That doesn't matter. Just know I asked enough to know where to find you."

I was flattered that he had put forth a little effort, but I wasn't about to let him know it.

"You're stalking me?" I asked.

"Nah, I'm just trying to get to know you better."

I switched the phone from my right ear to my left. "Why do you want to know me?"

"Because, since the moment I first saw you, I haven't been able to get you out of my head."

The feeling was mutual. Savoy had inadvertently invaded my inner thoughts. Hearing that I had done the same to him made me feel so desirable.

"Are you there?" he asked.

"Yes," I answered smiling.

"Have dinner with me," he said.

I stared at the polished gold band on my finger. "I can't," I said. *Why did I have to be so damn loyal?*

"Thank you again for the roses."

"You're welcome."

"Goodbye Savoy," I said.

"Goodbye," he said.

***

I was still on my natural high when I walked through the front door of my home. That soon changed when I saw Kiya's toys scattered all over the living room floor.

"Tay!" Kiya screamed, throwing her arms around my leg.

"Hey munchkin." I lifted her up into my arms and gave her a big hug.

At first it took me some time to get use to the idea that Kenny had a daughter, but after spending time with Kiya, I had grown fond of her. I had to remind myself that it wasn't her fault she was in the middle of the triangle shared between her parents and me. Although there were times when I wanted to have my husband to myself, I understood the importance of him bonding with his daughter. I grew up without a father, and that's something no child should ever have to do.

"Where's Daddy?" I asked, putting her down.

"Mad." She ran back to the stack of toys she had been playing with.

"Kiya, take your toys to your room," I said.

"No!" She pouted, folding her arms across her chest.

It was amazing how much she looked like Kenny. They had the same dark skin and big eyes. They even had the same stubborn attitude.

"Yes, now," I said firmly.

"Otay!" she said.

I would never spank another person's child, but I would definitely threaten them. I had made several threats to Kiya, so it wasn't hard to get her to do what I asked. All I had to do is give her my "try me" look.

I walked into the bedroom and found Kenny sitting on the edge of the bed. He looked like he was going to explode with anger.

"What's wrong?" I asked.

"I picked Kiya up from school, and guess what they said," he stated.

"What?"

"Alicia hasn't paid them in three weeks!" he said, raising his voice. "I had to shell out three hundred damn dollars to keep them from dropping Kiya."

Kenny and Alicia had a verbal agreement that, in addition to child support, he would pay half of Kiya's daycare cost.

"Did you ask her about it?"

"I called her cell, but she didn't answer. But please believe she better have a damn good answer for what she did with my money."

The doorbell rang, and I knew there was going to be drama. I followed Kenny, as he marched to the front door. I looked around the living room, and smiled when I saw Kiya had put away all of her toys. She was now sitting in front of the TV watching *SpongeBob*.

Kenny swung the door open, pointed his finger directly in Alicia's face, and yelled, "Why ain't you paid the daycare?"

Alicia didn't say a word, she just stood there staring back at him with her eyes wide. I looked at the fresh sixteen-inch ponytail she had attached to her head. I immediately concluded that she had spent part of the money on getting her weave done. The rest was most likely spent on her clawlike fake nails, and the low-cut black skank hoe dress she was wearing. I turned my nose up, like I had suddenly smelled something funky.

I don't know what he was thinking when he laid up with this ghetto bitch.

Alicia was not a pretty woman. In fact, the only thing she had going for her was her big ass and small waist. She had zero class, and didn't pretend to be a lady. Alicia was the definition of a Hoochie Mama. Her hair was dyed platinum blond, even though she was dark as coal. Her clothes always looked like she went bargain shopping at the girl's lockers of one of the local strip clubs. When I first saw her, I thought she was a prostitute. She looked, dressed, and acted like one.

"Mommeee!" Kiya cheered, running over to the door.

"Kiya, stay inside," Kenny ordered, stepping outside and slamming the door.

Kiya ran back to her spot on the floor in front of the TV. I started to place my ear to the door so that I could hear what was being said, but decided against it. I figured whatever was said Kenny would tell me later.

After dinner, I asked Kenny what Alicia had done with the money.

"She said she used it for the down payment on her classes," he said.

"And that's okay with you?" I asked.

"It's too late to argue about it now."

I was tempted to tell him Alicia was full of shit. I doubted that she was even in school. But I kept my comments to myself. The situation was between the two of them. Kenny knew what he was getting into when he made the decision to sleep with Alicia. And since he didn't take the time to strap up, now he was getting pimped. My saying goes, "You get fleas when you lie down with dogs, you get pimped when you lie down with hoes."

Chapter 4

Octavia failed to mention that Savoy was staying with them. It wasn't until I stopped by for a visit that I found out he was their houseguest.

Savoy and Damon were sitting in front of the TV watching major league baseball. The two of them were engaged in a friendly debate over one of the player's batting average, while Jasmine sat on her father's lap, making baby sounds. I stepped in the room and gave Damon a quick hug, before leaning down to kiss Jasmine on her cheek.

"How is everyone?" I asked, making eye contact with Savoy.

"Fine. And you?" Damon said.

"I'm great." I spoke to Damon, but I was still looking at Savoy.

"What's up Shontay?" Savoy asked, flirtatiously.

"Nothing much." I scanned his body. He was wearing denim shorts with a short sleeve button front shirt. The first two buttons were open, revealing just a peek of his toned chest. *Damn, he is fine,* I said to myself.

"Man, did you see that?" Damon asked, practically yelling. "Your boy hit it out the park!"

Savoy and I hadn't caught any of what Damon was referring to. The two of us were too busy watching each other. The sexual tension was back. I felt the heat seeping from between my legs. I decided that was my cue to leave. I finally managed to tear my eyes away from Savoy, and left to join Octavia on the second floor balcony.

***

"How long has Damon known Savoy?" I asked Octavia.

"For at least ten years," she replied.

The two of us were stretched out on the matching chaises, enjoying the beautiful summer day. It was June, but the weather was perfect. The heat index wasn't too high, and the wind was blowing just enough to keep us cool.

"How did they meet?" I asked.

"They were both going with the same girl," she said.

"At the same time?"

"Yep." She laughed, looking over at me. "Some chick named Taliyah."

"How did they find out about each other?"

I listened intently, while Octavia explained that Savoy was supposed to be out of town when Taliyah had Damon over one night. The two of them had been watching movies and kicking it the whole night. Damon ran out to get the two of them dinner, when he returned, he noticed Savoy walking up the sidewalk towards Taliyah's building.

"Damon assumed Savoy was going to see the girl that lived next door," Octavia said.

" Well, they both ended up on Taliyah's doorstep," She continued.

"Savoy knocked, then Damon knocked. Damon was holding the take-out bag in his hands, so Savoy assumed he was making a delivery." We both laughed. "Savoy said he pulled out his money and asked Damon how much the food cost. Damon told him fourteen-fifty. Savoy handed him a twenty and told him to keep the change."

"You're lying." I laughed, picturing the two of them having that conversation.

"Nope, Damon said that by the time Taliyah opened the door, the two of them had figured it all out."

"What did ole girl do when she saw the two of them standing there?" I asked.

"They said she didn't even try to explain. Savoy said she invited them both in for a threesome."

"Damn!"

"Um hum."

"Do you think they did it?" I asked, still laughing.

"That's something I'll never know." She laughed. "But they claim they didn't."

We looked at each other, and nodded our heads. "They did!" we said together.

"Well, after that night they've been cool ever since," she said. "When we started construction on the Ambiance, Damon insisted on contracting Savoy."

"Everything happens for a reason," I said.

"True."

"I bet the two of them have some stories to tell." I could only imagine some of the things the two of them had done over the course of their ten year friendship.

"Girl, they do. They keep me laughing. I'll admit, at first I was skeptical about having Savoy stay here," she said." I knew nothing about him, but now I know he's good people."

"He's staying here?" I asked.

"Yeah, in the guesthouse," she said.

The thought of seeing Savoy often excited and disturbed me. I was excited because I was feeling him. I was disturbed because I was feeling him. It was a no win situation with my mixed emotions.

"Sorry to interrupt," Savoy said, walking out onto the balcony. "But Damon and I kinda got the diaper thing jammed again."

Octavia shook her head, causing her ponytail to swing back and forth. "You can design and build million dollar mansions with popsicle sticks and clay," she exaggerated. "Damon can make million dollar trades and deals with a penny and a dream. But the two of you can't figure out how to operate something as simple as a diaper genie!"

"Hey, we can't be good at everything," he said sweetly.

"I'll be right back." She laughed.

I shifted on the chaise, pretending not to notice Savoy stretching out on the chaise next to me.

"So, are you still thinking about having dinner with me?" he asked.

"As I recollect, I told you no," I said.

"But you're still thinking about it, right?"

"No, I'm not." I laughed. "I've already given you my answer."

He got up and walked over to where I was sitting. He sat down on the edge of the chaise, next to my feet. I pulled my legs up under my butt and looked at him.

"I don't bite," he said.

"Well I do!" I threatened.

"I might like that," he said laughing.

I shook my head then looked away, I had to. For some reason I was picturing my toes in between his thick, luscious lips.

"I'm serious," he said. "Let's practice, bite me right here." Looking at him, I saw he was holding his head back, pointing to a spot on his neck. "Please be gentle," he moaned.

"You have issues." I said laughing.

"But you like me," he said, his gray eyes shining.

"You're alright." I teased, smacking my lips.

"Alright?" he asked, his eyes wide. "I'm giving you some of my best stuff, and I'm just alright."

"You call this your best stuff?" I asked.

He gave me a sexy grin. "Actually, my best is yet to come," he said. "Just wait and see."

There was something about the way he said it, that told me he was telling the truth. The bad thing was that if Savoy pursued me any harder, I was going to be in a whole lot of trouble.

Chapter 5

"Shontay, your man should teach a class in Romance 101." My co-worker, Michelle, sniffed the bouquet of sunflowers sitting on the desk.

First he would have to take one. The flowers were from Savoy again. He had sent me a different bouquet every day for the last five days. Yesterday he sent me Lilies, the day before Tulips. The day before that, he sent Carnations. Before that, he sent me Daisies, and before that Roses.

"Tell me what you're doing at home to get all this special treatment," Michelle said. She stared at me over the top of her wire rim glasses.

"I don't know," I said, fighting the urge to push her glasses up on her nose. "I guess sometimes men just surprise you."

What she didn't know was that my husband hadn't done anything remotely romantic for me since we got married. He hadn't given me as much as a compliment lately.

"Well, all I know is y'all must have a banging marriage, because don't none of the men I know do this much to show their wives they love them." She blew a bubble with the gum she had been smacking on, then strolled out of the room.

Michelle was cool, but she got on my nerves from time to time.

She was one of those women who wanted to know and told everyone's business. If she devoted as much time in her appearance, as she did getting into other people's business, she would be halfway decent to look at. Michelle took no pride in her looks whatsoever. Her hair was short like mine, but never combed.

"I'm going for the natural look," she would say.

That would have been good if her hair wasn't so kinky. I knew I didn't have "good hair", so I kept mine relaxed. It wasn't just her hair that was out of control, but Michelle always came to work looking like she had just rolled out of bed. She had stank breath, and the eye crud to go along with it. When you're a size 26, the last thing you need to slip up on is your personal hygiene.

"Savoy Breedwell," he said, answering his phone.

"I got the flowers," I said.

"Which ones?" he asked.

"All of them," I said smiling. "They're all beautiful."

"You're beautiful."

"Thank you, but you have to stop sending them."

"Why?" he asked.

"Because our office looks like a florist." I looked around the room at all the arrangements.

"I wanted to get your attention."

"You got my attention, and the attention of every other woman I work with."

"Are they jealous?" he asked laughing.

"Yes!" I smiled even harder. Everyone likes to be envied every once and awhile, just as long as it doesn't turn into full blown haterism.

"So are you calling to say yes to dinner?" he asked.

"Why do you keep asking me that?"

"Because you keep saying no."

"I keep saying no because you keep asking."

"Just give me one chance," he said. "I promise you won't regret it."

"Savoy, I..."

"Just think about it," he said, cutting me off. "One night...dinner...no strings." He hung up before I could respond. I was relieved that he had, because I wasn't sure how I was going to turn him down, or even if I wanted to.

After the children in my class had their naps, I got them up for their afternoon snack, and then gathered them on the circular globe rug for music time. Buzzing Baby allowed each teacher to develop their own lesson plan, as long as it included the basic curriculum requirements issued out by the State. Unlike many of the other teachers at the daycare, my lesson plan consisted of reading and basic math in the mornings, followed by art and science after lunch. After lunch we had playtime, then naps. The other instructors started their days off with music and art, followed by their lesson plan, then lunch and naps. After their naps they had playtime. I didn't feel it was good for children to lie down after eating, no matter what age. In my opinion, that's one of the reasons why so many children and adults are overweight. We eat then sleep, causing our metabolism to slow down.

***

I came home and found Kenny looking good in his Phat Farm jeans, knit Phat Farm T-shirt, and all white leather tennis shoes. He had gotten a fresh hair cut and trim, and smelled of Curve for Men. I smiled, because I was hoping the two of us could go out and spend some time together. It had been a long time since we had been on a date, and I missed the time we shared together.

"You look good, Boo," I said.

"Thanks," he said smiling. "I was waiting for you to get home."

"Traffic was backed up on Interstate 65."

"It's all good."

"I'm going to go hop in the shower," I said. "I'll be out in a second."

"Go ahead, I'll see you later," he said.

"Where you going?" I asked surprised.

"Me and some of the fellas from work are going to go have a couple of beers."

"I was hoping the two of us could do something," I said, disappointed.

"Not tonight, but maybe we'll try for this weekend."

I was upset, but I wanted to remain calm. I was convinced that with some reasoning he would see things my way. "We've been trying that for the last month," I reminded him. "Just tell the guys you'll meet them some other time."

"Tay, I don't say a damn thing when you go over to your girl's crib," he said, referring to Octavia.

"It's not like I don't ask you!" I snapped. "You never want to go!"

"You and I both know she doesn't like me."

"Whose fault is that?" I asked.

"Yours," he said, sucking his teeth. "You're the one who is always telling her our business."

"I wouldn't have to, if I could talk to you!"

"Whatever," he said, walking to the door. "I'll see you when I get back."

He walked out, leaving me fuming mad. I couldn't understand how or why he refused to see the situation my way.

***

"Fuck me!" I moaned, wrapping my legs around Savoy's waist. He pushed deeper inside my pussy, while sucking on my neck.

"Is this what you want?" he asked, whispering in my ear.

"Yessss," was all I could mutter. Savoy was giving me exactly what I wanted, some of the best sex I had ever had in my life, and I loved every moment of it.

"Turn over," he said.

I flipped on my stomach, up on my knees. Savoy dove inside me from the back, causing my body to thrust forward.

"I like that!" I screamed, as he grabbed my shoulders, pulling me back against him.

His balls slapped hard against my ass as he penetrated me deeper. I felt that long awaited sensation in the pit of my stomach, indicating that I was on the verge of having an orgasm.

"I'm cumming," I moaned.

"Cum for me, baby!" he said.

"Yessss!" I said.

I sat up in the bed with my eyes wide open. I had been sweating so hard my oversize pajama top was sticking to my skin. I looked over to Kenny's side of the bed to see if I had disturbed him during my dream. He wasn't there, and the sheets were still in tact. I looked at the clock radio sitting on the nightstand beside the bed. It flashed 2:15 in bold red numbers. I tried not to think the worst, as I threw the covers back and climbed out of bed.

After walking from room to room, only to discover Kenny was nowhere to be found, I picked up the phone and called his cell. It rang several times until his voicemail picked up. A hundred different scenarios ran through my mind, as I attempted to call him again and again and again. I finally gave up and slammed the phone down.

I was completely pissed off when Kenny walked through the door at 3:56 am. "Where the fuck have you been?" I immediately asked him.

He walked over to the couch and plopped down. "I ain't in the mood," he said.

I watched as he emptied his pockets, dropping loose change, his cell phone, and his driver's license on the coffee table.

"You ain't in the mood!" I yelled, standing over him. "You walk your ass up in here at damn near four in the morning, and you ain't in the mood!" I crossed my arms across my breasts, waiting for him to respond. He didn't. "I tell you what," I said, glaring at him, "the next time you decide to stay out all night, don't come home."

He looked at me with raised eyebrows, before leaving the room. A few seconds later, I heard the shower running. I knew there was a possibility that Kenny had been out with his friends, but there was an even greater possibility that he had been with another female. I picked up his phone and checked the last numbers dialed. There were no outgoing calls made that morning or the previous night. I should have left well enough alone, but I had to check his incoming call list. There were five missed calls from me, two from Etta, one from his homeboy Steve, then Alicia, Alicia, Alicia and Alicia. The calls went from five minutes to sixty. I looked at the times they were received, and they were all around the times Kenny had his breaks and lunches at work. The most recent call had been at 1 am that morning.

When Kenny opened the bathroom door I jumped in his face. “Are you fucking Alicia again?” He had this dumbfounded look on his face as he stared at me.

“What you talking about?” he asked.

“These calls!” I yelled, holding the phone up in his face. “The two of you talking four and five times a day!”

“Why you going through my phone?” he asked, pissed off.

“Are you fucking her?”

“No!” he yelled, looking into my eyes.

I stepped back. What came out of his mouth didn’t equal to what I saw in his eyes. His eyes spoke the truth, what had come out of his mouth was a lie.

The eyes say what the mouth is afraid to, Grandma would always say.

I took a step back, shaking my head. “You are a liar.” I said, throwing the phone at him.

“Shontay, I ain’t...”

“Save it!” I screamed, furious. “I’m not in the mood!”

CHAPTER 6

I ended up giving Kenny the silent treatment for days. Along with the treatment, came a dose of I ain't cooking, cleaning, or washing shit. Kenny seemed to think that sex was still an option, but he soon found out otherwise.

When we were lying in bed one night, he reached under my gown and grabbed my naked breast. I responded by subtly twisting his fingers back until I heard his knuckles crack. After that, he got the idea and refrained from touching me. I wasn't about to give him any of my kitty, considering I was convinced he was getting some from his daughter's mother. The decision to cut off sex was rather hard for me. I was so horny, my shower massager became my new friend.

"What the hell are you doing in there?" Kenny yelled, banging on the bathroom door.

My morning showers went from fifteen minutes to forty-five minutes. What made things worst was that I had been dreaming about Savoy on a regular basis. The dreams weren't just about us fucking in every position known to man, they were deeper than that. In my dreams, we shared a certain intimacy that could only come from a genuine connection. They left my panties wet and my mind wondering. The flowers had stopped coming, and I was somewhat disappointed. It felt good having a man pursue me. So good, that when Kenny decided to start going out three times a week, I decided it was time for me to step out and have some fun of my own.

Wednesday nights was ladies night at Club Hydro, and they let ladies in for free from eight until eleven. I've never been a club hopper, but I figured if I could get my dance on and save myself fifteen dollars on the cover charge, then why not do the damn thang.

I stepped in the club wearing my gold backless tie around the neck satin top, black flat front wide leg pants, and gold open toe heels. The club had a large enough crowd for the dance floor to be packed, but not to the point that there were so many people it was elbow to elbow.

I found a seat at the bar and ordered myself a Gin and Coke. I bobbed my head to TI's *I'ma King*, while sipping on my drink. I hadn't been in a club in more than a year, and back then it was with Octavia. I felt a little out of place, but I was determined to make the best of my night. I had been in my seat for less than five minutes when a tall brother, who resembled Chris Rock, approached me.

"How you doing?" He had beads of sweat glistening across his forehead. I presumed it because he was burning up in the three-piece suit he was wearing. Club Hydro enforced a strict dress code; no jeans, ball caps or tennis shoes, but it wasn't that deep.

"I'm fine. And you?" I replied.

"Good, good." He wiped the sweat from his face with his hand. "I'm Tony," he said, extending his hand to me.

No he didn't! He could have at least wiped his funk off his hand! I picked up a napkin from the dispenser and handed it to him. "Shontay," I said.

"Thanks." He smiled, wiping his face again. He crumbled up the napkin and threw it on the bar. *Disgusting!* "It's hot in here." He smiled. I hadn't noticed before, but he had a gold cap in his mouth. I don't know which was more unattractive, the sweat popping off of him or that gold cap. "So what do you do?" he asked, leaning against the bar.

"I'm a pre-school teacher," I said.

"Cool." I continued to sip on my drink. "I'm in the music industry." I checked him with my eyes.

Fake Figaro around his neck. Cubic Zirconia studs hanging from ears. Gold plated link watch. Cheap suit. Cheap shoes. Music industry my ass!

"What are you, a singer?" I asked.

"Oh no." He laughed, reaching inside his jacket pocket. "I'm a producer." He pulled out a white business card, and handed it to me. The card was a plain computer printed card with T & T Productions and a cell phone number on the front.

"So who have you worked with?" I knew he was a fake, much like his business card, but decided to indulge him anyway. His expression was an indication that I had caught him off guard with my question.

"Well...ummm...mostly local artists," he stuttered. "You ever heard of Black Don?"

"No," I said.

"Infrared?"

"No."

"Jheez...Big Ant...Lowdown?"

"Nope, no, and hell no." He smiled, probably thinking he had pulled one over on me.

"Damn, baby, you need to get out more often," he said.

"I guess so." I laughed.

"How would you like to come back to the studio with me?" he asked.

I knew sooner or later the conversation would head in that direction. I was willing to bet anything his studio was in his basement. I gave him the once over with my eyes again. Correction, his mama's basement. I finished my drink then ordered another one.

"Thanks, but no thanks," I finally said.

"Alright," he said, leaning close to me. "Well, why we don't go back to my place for drinks."

"I tell you what," I smiled sweetly, "why don't you buy me a drink here."

"Then what?" he asked, his eyes bright with anticipation.

"And then I'll say thank you," I said.

"How about I leave you alone?" He walked off through the crowd, leaving me smiling with my drink in hand.

Not long after Tony left, I was approached by a cute Puerto Rican brother, who told me his name was Alberto. He bought me another drink, then proceeded to monopolize my time. Why do brothers assume after they buy you a drink, they reserve the right to harass you for the rest of the night? I had a five minute maximum per drink, and his five minutes were up.

"Excuse me," I said, climbing off my chair.

"What, you wanna dance?" Alberto asked.

"Maybe later." I smiled, walking away.

I left Alberto hanging, while I shook my ass on the dance floor. I dropped it like it was hot with brother after brother after brother. When the music changed up, and Ray J's *One Wish* came on, I decided to have a seat. I excused myself, and took a seat an empty table close to the bar.

I sat relaxing, scoping out the scene, when I saw someone who caught my eye. He was way finer than all the men who had approached me. He sat at the bar, surrounded by two females who looked like they were of Latin descent. They were extremely beautiful, and looked like they could have been models.

One of them had long jet black hair that stopped at the top of her ass, and the biggest fake titties I had ever seen. She looked like a size 2, but her falsies had to at least be a set of Es. The other had long wavy hair, and a slim petite build. I watched them as they hung all over Savoy, and seemed to hang on his every word. The two of them appeared to be into each other just as much as they were into Savoy.

They were touching each other and playing with each other's hair. Savoy sat in between them, grinning like the cream filling in between a lesbian sandwich. I watched the women running their fingers through Savoy's twist and whispering in his ear, feeling a little jealous.

"Ms Falsies" slipped Savoy a card, kissed his cheek, then reached for her girlfriend's hand. The two of them walked hand in hand to the dance floor and began to bump and grind. I watched Savoy slip the card in his pocket before he continued to sip on his drink.

I flagged the waitress over, and instructed her to take Savoy another drink. When she pointed in my direction to let him know who had sent him the drink, his eyes lit up. He smiled as he got up from his seat and started to walk towards me. I licked my lips while watching him. He looked delicious in his creased khakis and button down Ralph Lauren shirt.

"Do you always buy single men drinks?" he asked smiling.

"Only the ones as fine as you," I said flirting.

His eyes traveled over my body, as he sat down beside me. "You look hot tonight," he said.

"Thank you."

"So, are you here alone, or do I need to be concerned about your husband?"

"I'm here alone, but I saw you with your playmates earlier. Should I be concerned?" I teased.

"Not at all." He laughed. "They were just being friendly."

"They seem real friendly." I pointed to the two women on the dance floor, who were grinding their hips against each other.

"Damn!" He laughed, watching the women.

"Your kind of girls?" I asked.

"Uh...um...nah," he stuttered, never taking his eyes off of them.

"Yeah right," I said.

"No seriously." He laughed, looking at me. "Women like that have a little too much going on for me. I don't need that many women in one bed."

"Scared you can't hang?" I teased.

"Trust me, I can handle two and then some," he said, lowering his eyes at me. "But you only need one if she does it right."

"What about you?" I asked. "Can you do her right?" My pussy was throbbing just thinking about the things Savoy could do to me.

"I can do anything she wants, and a few things she never expected," he said.

"Talk is cheap."

"Yeah, but I can back mine up."

I smiled, trying to disguise the fact that I was fantasizing about the two of us doing all the things I had been dreaming about.

"Let's dance," he said, standing up.

"You think you can hang?" I asked, smiling at him.

"I'll try."

On the dance floor, I bounced my ass against Savoy like I was a stripper in Phat Cats and he was throwing Benjamins. Savoy had his hands on my hips, grinding with me. I was shameless, as the two of us moved with erotic rhythm. I backed my ass up against his crotch, leaning my back into his chest. I could feel Savoy's heart beating rapidly, as a bulge developed in his pants.

"You feel good," he whispered in my ear.

I tried to remind myself that I couldn't give into the feelings I had been feeling since I met Savoy.

"Eight years…""I do…""Love, honor and cherish…" were thoughts that went through my mind.

Savoy pressed his lips in the fold behind my ear.

"Lies…""Monica…Tonya…Latrice…Stephanie…Desiree…Alicia…" were more thoughts going through my mind.

He wrapped his arms around me tightly.

"Love, honor, and cherish.."

"I do…"

"But not tonight!" I turned in his arms, wrapping my arms around his neck.

"Do you want to go somewhere a little quieter?" I asked him.

"I'd like that." He smiled. "You want to go grab something to eat?" he asked.

"No," I said.

"What do you have in mind?"

"Let's get a room."

He looked at me with his eyes buck. "A room?" he asked, not believing his ears.

"Yes" I said, rubbing his face with my fingertips, "as in hotel."

He looked at me to see if I was serious. My expression told him that I was.

"Let's go," he said.

I pushed Savoy against the door, while kissing him hard on the lips. He responded by grabbing my face with his hands, and slipping his tongue in my mouth. I struggled to unbutton his shirt.

"Slow down, baby," he said, looking at me seductively. I took his hand and pressed it in between my legs. I wanted him to feel what was waiting for him.

"I don't want to slow down." I said, staring at him. I grabbed him by his neck, kissing him again.

He lifted me up around his waist, and carried me over to the bed. I had only been with two men in my whole life. The first one I tried hard to forget. The second was the man I married. As Savoy reached behind my neck to untie my shirt, my past ran across my mind, sending a wave of insecurity through my body.

"You are so sexy." Savoy's eyes traveled down from my face to my naked breasts.

My head felt like it had waves of water rolling through it. I was coming down off of my alcohol high, and the realty of what I was about to do was setting in.

"Savoy," I whispered. He continued sucking my earlobe gently, while attempting to unbutton my pants. "Savoy, wait."

"What's wrong?" he asked, finally getting my pants open.

"I can't," I said.

He rose up, looking completely confused. "What's wrong?" he asked.

"Please get off me," I said, unable to look him in the eyes.

Savoy stroked my cheek gently. "Did I do something wrong?" he asked.

"Get off me." I mumbled again, trying to fight back the tears welling up in my eyes.

"Shontay," he said.

I looked at him with the tears rolling down the sides of my face. He looked so concerned, but he was still on top of me.

"Get off of me!" I said once again, but with more force.

I put both hands on his chest, shoving him backwards. I sat up quickly, and buttoned my pants. I could feel Savoy's eyes on me as I pulled up my shirt and tied it behind my neck.

"Baby, are you okay?" he asked.

I was practically choking on my tears, as I grabbed my purse and hurried out the door, leaving Savoy behind calling my name.

Chapter 7

I felt like shit the next day. I had a terrible headache, but the main brunt of my pain came from the flashbacks of the night before. I had come on to Savoy hard and strong, then when he was ready to give me what I wanted, I pushed him away. I hadn't given any explanation for my behavior, even though he had begged me for one. I had behaved like a crazy bitch. I was convinced that Savoy thought I was a dick tease, or worse, a hoe. I was almost positive he would never speak to me again, but I was wrong.

To my surprise, FTD delivered me two dozen long stem yellow and white roses, along with a note that said:

Shontay,
I don't know what I did to upset you but I am sorry.
Please know that I would never do anything to hurt you.
Your Friend,
Savoy

He was apologizing for something that had nothing to do with him. The truth was that I had issues. I knew I couldn't tell Savoy the truth, but I couldn't pretend that the entire night never happened. I picked up the phone to call Savoy, hoping to explain myself.

"Savoy Breedwell," he said, answering his phone.

The sound of his voice caused my stomach to flutter. I held the phone, trying to get my words together.

"Hello," I said.

"Hi, Shontay," he said.

"Savoy, I..."

"Listen," he said, cutting me off, "I shouldn't have gone there last night. I thought we both wanted...anyway, we both had a little too much to drink."

"Savoy, I'm sorry about last night," I said, feeling guilty. "It wasn't you...I just couldn't."

"I understand," he said, sounding sincere. "Today is a new day."

"The roses are beautiful," I said.

"I'm glad you like them."

"How has your day been?"

"Hectic." He sighed." But it's much better now."

Savoy reacted way better than I had expected him to. I felt relieved that he wasn't pressing the issue of what had happened at the hotel. I knew a lot of men would have cursed me out, and hung up in my ear. My phone beeped, indicating I had a text message waiting.

"Thank you for being so understanding," I said sincerely. "I'll see you around."

"Take care, Shontay," he said.

"You too." I pressed the end call button and relaxed in my chair.

The message indicator light on my phone reminded me that I had an unread text message. I pressed the menu button on my phone and went to my inbox. The message was from Kenny, informing me that he would be home late. He claimed he was taking his mother to Birmingham to see her sister. I deleted the message without replying. Even though the two of us weren't on good terms, I needed his attention. After what happened with Savoy, I was prepared to end my strike at home just to get some affection, but now I was pissed off all over again. I picked up the phone, and called Savoy again.

"Have dinner with me," I blurted out, before Savoy could say hello.

"When?" he asked.

"Tonight," I said.

"Where?" he asked.

"Humphries down town," I said. "Eight o'clock."

"I'll be there."

***

I walked into Humphries wearing a red, off the shoulder, short sleeve light knit sweater, wide leg khaki pants, and red wedge sandals. My outfit was casual, but sexy enough to show off my curves. I smiled when I saw Savoy sitting in a booth near the back of the pub. He was wearing a green short sleeve shirt and khaki pants, looking as fine as ever. He smiled as I approached the table.

"You look great," he said, standing.

"So do you." I inhaled the enticing scent of his cologne, as I slid into the booth across from him.

The two of us sat discussing the weather and current events, while waiting for our meals. After we received our orders, we kept our conversation to a minimum, as we ate our Shrimp Alfredo and Caesar salads. There were times when there was nothing but silence between us, but it wasn't uncomfortable, it was peaceful and refreshing.

"So, who is Savoy Breedwell?" I asked.

"I'm thirty-one," he said, placing both hands on the table, "and I'm the owner of Savoy Breedwell Building and Construction."

"Where did you go to school?"

"I graduated from the Savannah College of Arts and Design," he said, "with my Master's in Architecture."

"Did you always want to be an architect?"

Rubbing his hands together he frowned. "No, I graduated from high school with a four year basketball scholarship to the University of Tennessee. I played for them for a year, then decided to move back home to Atlanta."

"What position did you play?" I was genuinely interested.

"Point Guard," he said proudly. "I was the man on the court. I even received an offer to play in the NBA from the Los Angeles Lakers," he said.

"So why did you give it all up?"

"My family," he said, looking down at his hands.

"What happened?" I asked.

He looked at me with sad eyes. "My father died," he said softly, "and my mama needed me." There was a certain pain in his eyes, pain that flowed across the table to my heart. Reaching across the table, I placed my hands on top of his.

"I'm sorry," I said sincerely.

"Family should always come first," he said, stroking the inside of my wrists with his thumbs. "So I gave up that dream, but ended up finding my passion."

"Designing homes?" I asked.

"Yeah," he said smiling. "I love what I do."

"So, is there a special lady in your life?" I asked, giving him a look that dared him to lie.

He nodded his head, laughed, and said, "Yeah, my mama."

"Anyone else?"

"Not anymore," he said. "There was someone, but we broke up a year ago."

"What did you do?"

He stopped stroking my wrists, folded his hands together, and asked, "Why do you assume it was my fault?"

"It normally is the man's fault."

"I was with that woman for two years," he said. "For those two years, I didn't even kiss another woman. I thought she was my soul mate. She was smart, beautiful, and an aspiring actress. We were engaged to get married."

"What happened?" I asked, curious.

"I came home and found her in bed bumping and grinding with another woman."

I wasn't expecting that one. I looked at him, waiting for him to laugh, but he didn't.

"Oh." I said, at a loss for words.

"Yeah, I was in love with a lesbian," he said, sadly.

"Technically she was bi-sexual," I said, correcting him. "If she was with you, she obviously liked men too." We both laughed.

"Yeah, but she liked my sister more."

"She was doing your sister?" I asked, in disbelief.

"Yep," he said.

"Damn!"

"I know." He laughed. "It was some real Jerry Springer type shit."

I nodded my head, agreeing with him. I had seen plenty of women I thought were beautiful, but I couldn't imagine giving up the ding-a-ling for another coochie.

"Are they together now?" I asked.

"No, my sister dumped her about a month later."

"For a man?"

"No, another woman."

"So, what happened to your ex-fiancée?"

"She's a star now," he said, shrugging his shoulders." From what I hear, she's on the DL."

"So women aren't the only ones dealing with the down low."

"Definitely not," he said. "There are probably just as many sisters on the DL as there are brothers."

"Society is just more accepting of two women together," I said. "Hell, most men dream about it."

"I used to be one of those men, but seeing my wife to be with my sister killed that dream." We laughed. "So who is Shontay Holloway?" he asked.

"I'm twenty-eight," I said, "and the Assistant Director at the Buzzing Baby Daycare. I graduated from the University of Alabama, with my Bachelor's in Elementary Education."

"Are you a native of Huntsville?" he asked.

"No, I'm originally from Baltimore."

"So what brought you here?"

A thousand memories flooded my head. Memories of growing up on 12th Avenue, in a small butter cream house with mint green shutters. Memories of happier times shared with my mother. The two of us drinking cherry flavored Kool-Aid and eating Frito pies. I drifted back to the days when I was my mother's daughter, and she was my mom. They were good memories, but all of those were drowned out by one disturbing memory. The memory of what happened to me thirteen years ago.

I was fifteen again, sitting on the front porch of my home watching the cars go by. I remember it was warm that day. I was wearing a short floral print sundress and flip flops. My mother, Josephine, was out doing her thing. That's what she called it when she would leave for hours at a time with no explanation of her whereabouts. My grandmother later explained to me that Mama's thing was gambling.

"Your mama's fix is gambling," she said. "Some people have booze, others have crack. Your mama has the card tables."

Like any other junkie, Mama had to support her habit. Her $9.50 an hour job as a nursing assistant wasn't enough, so Mama had plenty of unpaid debts. By the time I learned this it was too late.

The big body Cadillac pulled up in the front of our house and stopped. I watched as Pete James stepped out in a dark blue three-piece suit, and a pair of blue Gators. Pete always looked good. I never saw him in anything but a suit and Gators. I thought he was so handsome back then. Pete was tall, with skin the color of deep dark chocolate, a baldhead, and a pair of straight white teeth. Whenever I asked Mama about her relationship with Pete, she would say he was "just a friend". I always thought there was more between them, but I never pressed the subject.

"Where's Josephine?" Pete asked, stepping up on the porch.

"Out," I replied.

Pete looked at me for a brief moment, then smiled. "I'm a little thirsty," he said. "Do you have anything to drink?"

"Yeah."

I went inside, with Pete following behind me. I had never had any reason to feel uncomfortable around him, so I thought nothing of it when he locked the door behind us. He stood in the doorway of the kitchen watching me as I poured him a glass of lemonade.

"Here you go." I smiled, handing him the glass. There was something about the way he was looking at me that just wasn't right. Suddenly I felt uneasy as he gulped down the drink while staring at me.

"Thank you," he said, handing me the empty glass. I watched Pete pacing back and forth across the wooden floor. "How long has your mama been gone?" he asked.

"About an hour," I responded.

"Who'd she leave with?"

"I don't kn..." The phone rang, interrupting me. It was Mama on the other end.

I remember her sounding paranoid when I told her that Pete was there, just before he told me to give him the phone. I did as he said, and went into the living room.

"I want my money!" he yelled into the phone. "You playin' wit me, Josie? I'm leavin' here wit somethin'! Oh, there's somethin' here foe me...and I'm bout to get it!"

When Pete came out of the kitchen, he had fire in his eyes. He walked over to the small stereo we had sitting on a shelf above the TV. *Damn, he's gonna take our stereo,* I thought. Pete turned on the radio as loud as it would go, before walking over to the couch where I was sitting.

"Your mama got somethin' that belongs to me," he said, taking off his jacket. "She took somethin' that's mine, and now I'ma have to take somethin' that's hers."

It hit me at that moment that Pete wasn't going to take anything that had monetary value. I struggled to get off the couch, but I was too little too late. He pinned me down and pushed my dress up around my waist. I screamed and kicked as he pulled my panties aside, then jabbed his fingers inside me. I felt indescribable pain, but nothing compared to the feeling I felt when he unzipped his pants and rammed himself inside of me. I felt my skin ripping, as Pete raped me for what felt like hours.

When he was finished my body was numb, and I was hoarse from crying and screaming. Pete left after he had finished violating my body and mind. That was the last time I saw him. When Mama made it home, I was sitting in the same spot, my dress ripped and blood running down the inside of my legs.

"He raped me!" I screamed, staring at her. "He raped me!" She didn't say anything, as she pulled me up from the couch and dragged me to the bathroom.

"Let's get you cleaned up," she said, with her arm around my shoulder. "Then I'm going to make us a Frito pie." Mama stood in the shower with me, washing away all the physical evidence of what

Pete did to me. She warned me that I couldn't tell anyone what had happened to me. "Pete will kill us," she said. "He'll kill us." I hated her for putting me in that situation, but loved her enough to believe that if I did tell, Pete might hurt her. "Besides, ain't nobody gonna believe us," she said. "We ain't got proof."

It was eight weeks later that Mama was proven wrong. After throwing up anything I put in my mouth, and the sudden disappearance of my period, Mama finally bought me a home pregnancy test, which turned out to be positive.

"You can't have this baby," she insisted, staring at the two pink lines on the plastic stick.

"What?" I hadn't had time to process the information.

"I know someone," she said, tossing the stick in the trash. "I'll call him tomorrow."

"But what if I don't want to have an abortion?" I asked.

She looked at me with cold dark eyes. "You ain't having this baby, Shontay!" she yelled.

"But I..."

"But what?" she asked, standing with her hands on her hips. "What you think, you can raise this baby alone?"

"You raised me by yourself," I pleaded, with tears in my eyes. "I can get a job and..."

"You want to have the baby of a man who raped you?" She looked furious.

"This baby is a part of me too, Mama!" I screamed. "And I can't kill a part of me!"

"You're not keeping this baby," she said sternly. "Case closed."

The next day, I cried all the way to Mama's friend's office. I was scared and confused, but I knew there was no changing Mama's mind. It turned out that her friend was actually a doctor that had his licenses revoked. His office was in the basement of what looked like an abandoned building. I later found out that she met him through Pete. Mama paid him $50.00 to perform the procedure.

I lay on my back strapped down, with my legs spread, screaming at the top of my lungs. It felt like he was pulling my insides out of me. Mama stood beside me holding my hand, telling me everything would be alright and that I would be fine. She was wrong again.

After the basement abortion, I ended up with a severe infection that led to me developing Pelvic Inflammatory Disease. The disease left my fallopian tubes scared beyond repair, because Mama didn't get me the proper medical treatment. She knew that if she had taken me to a real doctor, they would have held her accountable for the chop shop abortion she had forced me to get. When I was finally able to get to a real gynecologist it was too late. I would never be able to get pregnant again. According to my physician, I was lucky the disease and infection hadn't cost me my life.

"A nickel for your thoughts." Savoy was staring at me from across the table. I had zoned out, thinking about my past.

"Isn't that supposed to be a penny?" I asked, shaking off my memories.

"Yeah, but I'm willing to pay five times that to get into your head."

"Why?" I asked, looking into his soft eyes. "We both know there could never be anything between us."

His eyes narrowed to small slits. "Do we really know that?" he asked.

"I think we do," I said.

Smiling, he leaned against the table. "When can I see you again?" he asked.

"Savoy, I can't see you again."

"Don't say can't," he said. "You can, but the question is do you want to?"

There was no doubt in mind that I wanted to see more of Savoy. The question I was asking myself, was how I was going to keep our interaction non-sexual? How was I going to keep my pussy from throbbing every time I saw him? I pushed all of my questions and doubts out of my mind. I would deal with all of those things later.

"Yes, I want to see you again." I smiled.

"Good," he said, smiling too.

After having dinner with Savoy, I felt irresistible. He had a way of looking at me that made me feel like I was the only woman in the room. The entire time we were together, Savoy's attention and eyes remained on me.

"God gave us eyes to look," Kenny would say whenever I caught him staring at other women.

Kenny made it his business to gawk at every big ass and set of titties that passed by. His wondering eyes only made me more insecure about our relationship. The way he behaved made me feel inadequate. I would find myself comparing myself to every woman he looked at. If they were smaller than me, then I would vow to lose weight to try and get down to their size. I had been on so many yo-yo diets it was unbelievable.

On top of that, I was convinced my size was the reason Kenny cheated. All of the women I caught him with were smaller than me in size. I'm a size 16. I stand at 5'6", and weigh 160 pounds, with wide hips, a nice round ass, and D cup breasts. The majority of the women Kenny cheated with were no bigger than a size 8. For years, I subjected myself to unhealthy weight loss gimmicks. I had finally decided enough was enough. I was going to lose weight, but for myself, not for Kenny.

I returned home, after having dinner with Savoy, to an empty house. On any other night this would have bothered me, but after being in Savoy's presence, there was nothing that could bring me down. I slipped into one of my silk teddies, and slid in between my satin sheets. Before my eyes closed, thoughts of Savoy filled my head. I sat up against the wooden headboard, unable to sleep. I wanted to hear his voice. I grabbed the cordless phone off the night stand and dialed his number.

"Savoy Breedwell," he said.

"Do you ever say hello?" I teased.

"Hello beautiful," he said, happy to hear my voice.

I smiled. "Did I disturb you?"

"No, I was just thinking about you." My smile grew wider hearing that. "I love your smile," he said.

"Thank you," I said sincerely, "for everything."

"Thank you for having dinner with me," he said.

The two of us laughed and talked until my eyelids became

heavy. I learned that Savoy was the third born and only son out of a family of five children. He told me that he loved all types of music, was an avid reader, and a lover of the performing arts.

"Get some rest, beautiful," he said softly, after we had talked for over an hour.

"You too," I said, fighting back a yawn.

"Yeah, I have to get up at four in the morning," he said.

"Why so early?" I asked.

"For my morning run," he said.

"Where are you going for your run?"

"Octavia suggested the park downtown."

The little light bulb in my head went off. I don't know if it was because I was sleepy, or because I was so anxious to see him again.

"Can I join you?" I asked.

"Yes," he answered quickly. This time I felt his smile through the phone.

Chapter 8

After Savoy and I completed our two mile run, my legs felt like they had been stretched beyond their limit. I hadn't run since high school, and it showed in the first fifteen minutes. I was panting and breathing like a dog in the desert. Savoy didn't seem to mind. He slowed down whenever he noticed I was dragging behind. He even walked with me when I needed to slow down my pace. I was so out of shape, it was a damn shame.

"It takes time," he said, walking beside me. "You've already made the first step by trying this morning." He obviously was unaware that asking to run with him was just an excuse to see him. An excuse I planned to use three times a week.

After our run, I drove back across town to shower and get dressed for work. Kenny was sitting on the sofa wearing his uniform, eating a bowl of Fruit Loops. The TV was on the five o'clock news.

"Where you been?" he asked, watching the TV.

I walked pass him to the kitchen. "I went for a run," I said, grabbing a cold bottle of Aquafina from the refrigerator door. I gulped down half the water, and walked back into the living room.

"A run?" he asked.

"Yeah, a run," I replied.

"When did you start running?" he asked, looking surprised.

I finished the rest of my water before answering. "Today."

"Are you cooking breakfast?" he asked.

He could have shown a little interest in what I told him. Walking away, I looked over my shoulder, and said, "Maybe this weekend."

After I showered and got dressed, I stood in the mirror trying, without success, to curl my hair. The morning humidity, mixed with my sweat, had caused my hair to draw up. It was like my perm had reverted. I was not about to walk around looking like Michelle. At that moment, I wished I still wore it long so I could just pull it up in a ponytail and go. I had made plans to run with Savoy at least three times a week, and I knew there was no way I would have the time nor patience to go through the same task each time.

After I unplugged my curling irons, I made two phone calls. The first was to my job, to let them know I would not be in. The second was to the African Hair Braiding Salon.

***

Zonda, the beautiful midnight-chocolate skinned woman that braided my hair, spoke very little English. I didn't care if she spoke no English at all, 'cause the sister could braid your hair, and make it look like the bomb. I had seen her work before at a local hair show, so I knew I was in good hands. I walked in her shop, and seven hours and two naps later, I walked out with more than a hundred pencil thin shoulder length microbraids.

It was well pass lunchtime when I left Zonda's, and my stomach was grumbling like it wanted to talk. I had been craving some Jamaican Jerk Chicken, and the Ambiance had the best in town. I knew Octavia would be in her office, so I figured I could feed my appetite and kick it with my girl at the same time.

"Good afternoon, Shontay," Amel, the floor manager said, greeting me.

"Hey Amel." I smiled.

"Your hair looks great."

"Thanks."

"Octavia's in her office. I'll buzz her to let her know you're on your way."

"Thank you."

I walked pass the tables and booths of well dressed patrons to Octavia's office. I knocked twice on the solid wood door before letting myself in. Octavia sat behind her huge maple desk, placing paperwork in a large manila folder.

"Hey you," I said, shutting the door behind me.

She looked up at me and smiled. "I love your braids!" she exclaimed.

"Thank you."

She stood and came around the desk to give me a hug. "When did you get them?" she asked, adjusting the jacket of her Versace suit.

"Just now," I said. "I went to Zonda's over on University Drive."

"Well, she did a great job," she said sincerely. "You look beautiful." I loved how Octavia always made me feel good about myself, even when my self-esteem was lower than low. "So, what's up?" she asked, looking at the diamond encrusted watch on her wrist. "And why aren't you at work?"

"I called out today," I said.

She eyed me suspiciously, before stating," The last time you called in, we ran up on Kenny at the motel with some chick."

She was right. It had been three years since I last called in, and then it was to investigate my suspicions of Kenny cheating on me.

"Well, today is all about me," I said.

"It's about damn time!" she stated, walking back around her desk. "What do you have planned for the rest of the day?"

"I was hoping to have lunch here, but you guys are packed," I said.

"Yep, it's a forty-five minute wait," she said, rearranging some of the documents on her desk.

"I love your jerk chicken." I frowned. "But not enough to endure a forty-five minute wait."

"This is not a fast food establishment." She laughed. "You want ten minutes or less, then go hit the golden arches."

"I know this ain't fast food," I said, crossing my arms across my chest. "Fast food doesn't buy Versace."

"Neither do I," she said. "This suit was a gift from my husband."

"He has good taste," I said smiling.

Putting her hands on her hips, she gave me a conceited stare. "Of course he does," she said confidently, "look who he's married to."

"Well, he made a great choice," I said, stroking her ego.

"Thank you, girl," she said.

"So, what's up for lunch?"

"El Mariachi," she said.

"Enchiladas and margaritas?" I asked.

"Si Senorita!"

El Mariachi was one of our favorite Mexican restaurants. Whenever Octavia and I went, we always shared the chicken enchilada and yellow rice platter. It was also our tradition to order a couple of frozen margaritas. They had the best ultimate margaritas, and they served them out of tall wide glasses, in the shape of fish bowls. The two of us finished off our entrée, and sat discussing the progress on Ambiance 2, while enjoying our strawberry margaritas.

"You have to see it, Savoy is doing a fantastic job," Octavia said. "The place is going to be beautiful when he finishes," she said.

The mere mention of Savoy's name made me smile like a little girl with a schoolgirl crush. Octavia's eyebrows shot up, indicating she had noticed my reaction.

"What's up with the Chester Cheetos grin?" she asked, curious.

"What?" I asked.

"What nothing!" she said, staring at me. "You know what I'm talking about."

"Nothing, I'm just excited about the progress on Ambiance 2," I said.

It wasn't a complete lie. I was happy for my girl, but at the same time, I was daydreaming about Savoy. The image of sweat glistening on his skin earlier that morning made my coochie tingle. Octavia leaned back in her chair and studied my face.

"Speaking of Savoy," she said suspiciously, "he is fine."

"That he is," I said nonchalantly.

"And rich," she said, giving me a sly grin. "He's intelligent, charming, and built like a quarterback."

"And cocky," I added, pretending not to be interested.

"Confident," she stated. "And, girl, I bet he can fuc..."

"I wouldn't know," I said quickly, cutting her off. "And really don't care."

"And why would I think you did?" she asked, her eyes shining.

"I was just saying," I said.

"I know what you're saying," she said." And your ass is lying." She had a mischievous look on her face.

"Okay, damn," I said giggling, "it has crossed my mind."

"Oh, I know that!" She laughed. "But I want to know what's up with the two of you."

"Nothing is up with us," I said.

"Please," she said, rolling her eyes. "When y'all was at my house, there was enough heat between the two of you to warm an entire continent."

"Was it that obvious?" I asked.

"Yes ma'am." She laughed.

"Tavia, he is so sexy!" I confessed. "And those bedroom eyes, umm humm!" I moaned.

"And those lick 'em like LL Cool J lips," she added.

"Girl, yes." I sighed. "And he has this way of making you feel so sexy. Last night at dinner, he..."

"What dinner?" she asked, her mouth wide open.

Damn, I had a slip of the tongue.

"Shontay," she said loudly, looking around. "Girl, you hooked up with Savoy?" I nodded my head, smiling. "Did the two of you get freaky?"

"No, just dinner," I whispered. "Then this morning..."

"This morning what?" she asked.

"Nothing," I said. "We just went for a morning run."

She gave me a look of complete disbelief, as I told her about all the flowers and my date with Savoy.

"So, what do you expect to happen between the two of you?" she asked.

"I have no expectations," I said sincerely. "I just want to spend some more time with him."

"I've never known you to have a male friend other than Kenny," she said surprised.

Octavia was right, Kenny had been the only man in my life since we started dating. I had practically isolated myself from every other man I knew after Kenny and I had our first date.

"Savoy is going to be my exception," I said. "There is something about him," I said smiling, "that makes me feel so good. It's been a long time since I felt this good."

"Are you falling for him?"

"No," I said hesitantly. "I just enjoy being around him."

My cell phone rang, interrupting our conversation. I pulled it out of my purse, and smiled when I saw Savoy's name flash across the Caller ID.

"Hello," I said.

"Hey you," he said sweetly.

"Hi," I said, looking over at Octavia.

She was giving me a pop quiz with her eyes from across the table. I shifted in my seat, pretending not to see her.

"How has your day been?" he asked.

"Great. And yours?" I asked.

"I can't complain," he said. "But there is one way you can make it better."

"What's that?"

"You can agree to go out with me tonight."

"I'd love to." I smiled brightly.

Octavia tapped her fingertips on the table impatiently. I held my index finger up to her, telling her to give me a minute. She mouthed, "Get off the damn phone."

"Great. Our first date was on your terms, and not exactly what I had in mind," he said. "I'd like to make it up to you."

"Where are we going?" I asked, curious.

"You'll see," he said.

"What should I wear?" I asked.

"Whatever you like," he said. "But here is a hint, I'm wearing a tux."

"What time should I be ready?"

"Seven," he said. "I'm sending a car for you. I just need to know where you want to be picked up."

I looked over at Octavia, giving her a small smile. "I'll be at Octavia and Damon's at seven," I said.

"Great," he said. "I'll see you then."

Before I could hang up, Octavia started interrogating me. "Was that him?" she asked. "You'll be ready at seven o'clock for what?"

"Yes," I said calmly. "And he's taking me out."

"Out where?"

"I don't know, but he's wearing a tux."

"And just what are you going to tell Kenny?"

I gave her an innocent grin. "Well..."

She rolled her eyes, then said," Let me guess, that you're with me."

"Do you mind?" I knew she didn't, but I respected our friendship, and didn't want her to feel like I was using her.

"You know I don't." She smiled.

"Thanks, because I need another favor," I said.

"What's that?"

"I need your help in finding something to wear."

"Shopping," she said smiling. "You don't even have to ask."

***

I stood in my bathroom mirror admiring my reflection. Octavia had helped me pick out a sexy red flowing silk dress that crisscrossed in the back. The dress hugged my curves just right. I brushed a little of my MAC pressed powder across my face, put on a little of my MAC lip gloss over my lips, and I was ready. I walked out of the bathroom, and stepped into my red peep toe pumps. I was sitting on the edge of the bed securing the straps around my ankles, when Kenny came in.

"Who did your hair?" he asked.

Standing, I adjusted my dress. "Zondra at the African Hair Salon," I said, walking over to the dresser. I picked up my bottle of Very Sexy, and sprayed from my neck down to my toes.

"You were off today?" Kenny asked, watching me as I put on a pair of diamond chandelier earrings.

"I called out." I secured my diamond teardrop necklace around my neck, not looking at him.

"You look nice," he said.

I turned to look at him and smiled. "Thanks, Ken."

"I would hug you, but I'm too dirty," he said, pointing to his grass covered uniform.

"That's okay." I said sweetly. "But thank you for the compliment." *It's about damn time!*

"Where are you going?" he asked.

"Octavia's hosting an event at the Museum of Arts."

"For what?" he asked.

"Publicity for her new restaurant," I lied. I was hoping by mentioning Octavia, and the fact that we were going to an Art event, that he wouldn't ask too many questions. He didn't. Kenny had no interest in art whatsoever.

"Well, have a good time," he said, watching me as I grabbed my purse.

"I will" I said smiling. "I'll see you later."

"Alright."

My heart was pounding a mile a minute as I left. I was nervous as hell lying to Kenny. I had never lied to him about anything before. I was on pins and needles as I left the house. I was also wondering if he felt any anxiety whenever he lied to me.

***

All of the anxiety I was feeling soon evaporated when I got to Octavia's. I was excited when I saw the stretch limo parked in the circular driveway. When I rang the doorbell, I had to take a deep breath. Savoy opened it, looking like a black king. He was holding a single long stem red rose, wearing a black Armani tuxedo. When he saw me his eyes lit up like stars.

"You look unbelievable," he said.

I smiled, blushing slightly. "You look handsome," I said.

"I love your hair," he said. "It really shows off your face."

"Thank you." I smiled. "Where's Octavia and Damon?" I asked, looking around.

"They're upstairs." He smiled. "Jasmine is with her grandparents. So, you know what that means." He raised his eyebrows at me.

I laughed, because I knew Octavia was making up for all those midnight feedings that normally interrupted her and Damon's playtime.

"When I saw Damon running upstairs with the whip cream, I knew what was up." He laughed. "But to tell you the truth, I ain't mad at 'em."

"I know that's right." I smiled.

The two of us stood there smiling at each other in silence. The sexual tension had returned.

"Are you ready?" he finally asked.

"Whenever you are," I replied.

Inside the limo, there was a bottle of Cristal chilling on ice, along with two crystal long stem champagne flutes. I settled in the comfort of the leather seat, while Savoy filled the glasses. He handed me one of the glasses, then settled into the seat beside me.

Raising his glass, he said, "A toast to a wonderful evening."

We clanked our glasses together and took sips, while staring into each other's eyes. The champagne bubbles tickled my nose, and his sensual stare tickled my kitty. I crossed my legs, trying to calm the storm brewing in between them.

"Now, will you tell me where we're going?" I asked.

"Nope," he said, shaking his head. "Just sit back and enjoy the ride."

I poked out my lip, pretending to be upset. The truth was I liked the mystery behind it all. It was exciting.

"I promise you'll have a good time," he said. "You're in good hands." He placed his arms on the seat behind me. "So, tell me something I don't know about you," he said.

"What would you like to know?" I asked.

"Everything."

"You ask me questions, and I'll answer," I said," But I don't volunteer information." I took another sip of my champagne.

"I see. So if I ask, you'll answer," he said smiling, "honestly."

"Yes," I said.

"What's your favorite color?"

"Red."

"Favorite food?"

"Italian."

"Favorite artist?"

"There are too many for me to narrow them down to just one."

"How long have you been married?"

"Two years."

"Why are you so unhappy?"

I paused, looking at him with wide eyes. He had caught me off guard. "What makes you think I'm unhappy?" I asked.

"You're here with me, aren't you?"

I looked away, not wanting him to see my eyes or the truth written in them. He stroked my hair gently with his hand.

"Tell me the truth," he said.

I turned and looked at him. "Where do I start?" I asked. "My job or my marriage?"

"Your career," he said, soothingly.

"It's not a career," I stated flatly. "I go in, do what's expected, then I come home. It's a job."

"You wanted to be a teacher, right?" he asked, continuing to stroke my hair.

"Yeah I did, but not in a daycare," I admitted. "I want to teach elementary school."

"So what's stopping you?" he asked.

"I didn't complete my certification."

"Why didn't you?" he asked.

"I met Kenny, my husband, and I just put it off," I said. "I guess I got caught up in living my life with him."

"You couldn't do both?" he asked. "Finish your degree and have your relationship?"

I thought about all the time I let go by, trying to keep up with where Kenny was going and who he was with, and the classes I missed time after time after time.

"It didn't work out like that," I said.

"So what's stopping you now?" he asked.

"I don't know."

He looked at me for a moment, before asking, "Why are you unhappy in your marriage?"

There were so many thoughts running through my mind, I didn't know where to begin.

"I don't know," I said. "I guess I imagined things would be different."

"Different how?"

"Different from how they are now," I said, not wanting to discuss my marriage with him.

He put his arm around my shoulder, pulling me close to him. I settled into the comfort of his arm, my shoulder resting against his chest.

"So, tell me, do you have any bad habits?" he asked. "Nose picking? Farts when you laugh?"

I laughed, shaking my head. "Uh, no," I said. "But the night is still young."

He laughed, wrapping both arms around me. "Thanks for the warning," he said. He didn't press the subject of my marriage, instead he held me in silence for the rest of our ride.

An hour later, we arrived at our destination. The driver held open the door, as Savoy assisted me out of the limo. We were in Birmingham at the Jefferson Civic Center.

"A concert?" I asked, holding his hand as we walked through the glass doors of the Center.

"Not quite," he said smiling.

We walked into the concert hall, and I noticed that we were the only ones in the room.

"We're really early," I said, while Savoy led me to the third row center stage.

"They're waiting on us," he said.

We took our seats and the lights dimmed. A young boy in an usher's uniform came up the aisle, stopping near our seats. He handed each of us a program, then said," Enjoy your show," before walking away.

"The Lion King?" I asked, looking at the program.

"An All-Star cast." Savoy smiled, looking at me. "I purchased a private showing just for you."

"Are you serious?" I asked, my eyes wide.

"Do you see anyone else up in here?" I shook my head no. "Alright, then sit back and enjoy the show," he said smiling.

I was fascinated and thrilled by the show. The all Black cast was remarkable, from the costumes, to the set, to the musical performance. Afterwards, Savoy took me backstage to met the cast and get autographs. He had thought of every little detail. He even had beautiful bouquets of long stem roses, delievered to the leading ladies. I thought that the night couldn't get any better. That was until Savoy had the chauffeur take us to a restaurant called Ocean for dinner, where we enjoyed crab cakes and stuffed lobster tails.

During the ride back to Huntsville, I sat in Savoy's arms, still beaming from the perfect evening he had created. I felt like a Queen, or better yet, a princess in one of those Disney fairytales.

"Did you have a good time tonight?" he asked.

"Tonight was unbelievable," I said, looking up at him. "Thank you so much."

"Thank you for allowing me the opportunity to spend the evening with you," he said, kissing me softly on my forehead.

I stared into his eyes, lost in a trance. I touched his lips with my fingertips, wanting to kiss him. He must have been feeling the same way.

"May I kiss you?" he asked.

"Yes," I said smiling.

He smiled, then lowered his head, pressing his lips to mine. I felt my panties getting moist, as our tongues touched and caressed each other. I cupped his face with my hands as we kissed, while he held me tightly in his arms, his hands rubbing my back.

After minutes passed, we finally pulled away from each other. I wanted so badly to spend the rest of the night with Savoy. I just wanted to be with him, have him hold me. I knew it was impossible, but I didn't want my fairytale evening to end.

When we pulled back up to Octavia's home, I felt a sudden sadness, realizing that my dream date was coming to an end. Savoy helped me out the back of the limo, and held my hand as we walked to my car. There were countless stars covering the night sky, as the two of us stood facing each other.

"I'll see you in the morning?" he asked.

"Four o'clock," I said, admiring how his eyes twinkled.

"Goodnight, Shon."

"Goodnight."

He gave me a soft kiss on the cheek before opening my car door for me.

Kenny was home in bed, and snoring so loud I could hear him when I walked through the front door. I slipped off my clothes, and got into bed next to him. My mind was still full of the memories of my evening with Savoy. As sad as it was, I laid in bed with my back to my husband, wishing that it was Savoy lying next to me.

CHAPTER 9

It's amazing how a simple change in your daily routine can make the day seem much brighter. Savoy and I had started our day off together taking our two mile run around Big Spring Park downtown. Afterwards, I felt so good I went home and cooked Kenny some breakfast. He looked like he was in paradise, as he grubbed on the scrambled eggs, bacon and French toast. I don't think he came up for air, as he wolfed down his meal. When I left him to go shower, he was filling his plate up again.

I stood under the warm water, with my braids pulled high on top of my head, singing Jill Scott's *Golden*, like the lyrics were my own. I spent a few extra minutes in the shower, with the vibrating head of my massager pulsating in between my legs. I got out the shower, dried my body off, and rubbed Shea Cocoa Butter all over my skin. Afterwards, I slipped on a pair of jeans, a T-shirt, and my white Reeboks. I secured my braids in a bun.

I arrived at the Buzzing Baby with a smile on my face, determined that I was going to have a great day.

"Claim happiness," Savoy had told me earlier that morning. "Each day you wake up claim that no matter what comes your way, you will still have a great day."

I had every intention of doing just that. I didn't care if every child in my classroom had to throw-up, or worse, the runs, I was going to have a great day.

Okay, maybe I was trippin' with my earlier thoughts, because by that afternoon, I was ready to pull every braid in my head out. For some unknown reason, every single child in my class decided they wanted to be the rugrat from hell. They were running around screaming, kicking, and throwing shit everywhere. It was like their little asses had been fed a dose of Benadyrl laced with crack. I had given so many timeouts, that I couldn't remember whose turn it was.

One of them, Samantha, a normally quiet cute little girl, with skin the color of almonds, even had the nerves to tug on my braids when I bent down to wipe up the juice she had spilled. I had to pry her chubby little fingers off of me. I took several deep breaths, and recited a quiet prayer to get myself together before I verbally disciplined her. Then I gave her twenty minutes in the timeout chair. I usually never gave more than ten minutes in timeout, but under the circumstances, I felt Sam had earned double time. That shit hurt! When she tried to play tug of war with me I almost snapped. Don't get me wrong, I would never hit Sam but I was tempted to call her mother so that she could come take the ass whippin' for her little girl.

I was a little stressed out by the end of my workday, but decided to go home with a pleasant attitude, and try to have a decent night with Kenny. I even planned to give him a little bit. I was still unhappy with the late hours he was coming in, but I figured there was no reason to keep up the little game I had been playing. I was hoping that if I made a sincere effort, he would make a sincere effort. As far as the situation with Alicia, I would deal with that later.

***

I was a happy woman until I pulled up to my home, and saw Alicia's red Kia parked in my driveway. My mood turned sour, and I was ready for whatever. I had to park by the mailbox, because she was parked in my space behind Kenny's car. This further infuriated me, because I believe trash should remain at the curb.

I walked into my home to find Alicia sitting on the couch, wearing a red spandex body dress that dipped so low in the front you could almost see her nipples. I gave her a smirk, before dropping my keys and purse on the coffee table in front of her.

"Where's Kiya?" I asked, staring at her.

"With her grandma," she said, sucking her teeth.

I wanted to slap the taste out of her mouth, but I decided to keep my cool.

"Why are you here?" I asked, folding my arms across my chest.

If her daughter wasn't with her, then she had no business in my home. She gave me a screwed up look before parting her lips to answer. Before she could, I heard footsteps coming up the hallway.

"Alicia, you better make this last," Kenny said, stomping into the room. He stopped dead in his tracks when he looked up and saw me. He was holding a few crisp twenty dollar bills in his hands. "Hey," he said, looking at me nervously. I shot a glance at the money then back up at him.

Alicia stood up, giving me a cocky grin. She walked over to Kenny, with her long ponytail swinging.

"Thanks," she said, snatching the money from his hands.

"What's going on?" I asked, staring at Kenny.

"Ken was just giving me some extra cash," Alicia said grinning.

"For what?" I asked.

"Alicia ran short this month," Kenny said lowly.

"That's right," Alicia jumped in. "And *our* daughter needs new shoes."

New shoes my ass! Kiya had a brand new pair of Nikes on the last time I saw her.

"What happened to the ones she had on last weekend?" I asked, cutting my eyes at Alicia.

"Kids grow fast," she said sarcastically. "But then that's something only a *mother* would understand."

I took a step towards her, ready to rip the weave right off the top of her head. I felt my pulse racing. I was ready to kick her ass. Kenny quickly stepped in between us.

"Look, Alicia, you need to get going," he said, looking at me. "You don't need to be late picking up Kiya."

She rolled her eyes at me, then cocked her head to the right.

"I'll be back on Saturday to drop Kiya off," she said.

"Don't bring your ass up in her without her," I said, ready to push Kenny out of my way. "If *your daughter* ain't with you, don't step foot in my house."

"Whateva," she said, turning on her plastic heels. "I'll see y'all on Saturday." She walked out the front door, slamming the door behind her. Kenny looked at me with a dumbfounded expression on his face.

"Don't stand there looking stupid," I said angrily. "How many times have you given Alicia money without me knowing about it?" I asked.

"Let's not argue about this," he said, walking around me to the couch.

"There wouldn't be anything to argue about if you put your foot down!"

"Shontay, she said Kiya needed shoes," he said, raising his voice.

"You know that was a damn lie!" I yelled. "Besides, that's what the five hundred a month is for."

Alicia had a job, plus she was riding the government, getting food stamps and Section 8. I knew women who wished they could get that much assistance for two kids. There was no possible way Alicia couldn't make it work with just one child.

"Shontay, Kiya is my daughter, and I can't change that," he said.

"Well you should've thought about that before you knocked up her trifflin' ass mama!" I snapped.

"I can't fuckin' change that Alicia is her mama!" he yelled. "Any more than I can change the fact that you're not!"

He hit me in my weakest organ with his comment. He hit me in my heart. Kenny must have immediately realized what his words had done to me, because his eyes filled with sympathy.

"Baby I..." he began.

I threw my hand up, dismissing him and the apology I knew he was attempting to give. I walked away, retreating to our bedroom, not wanting him to see my tears. I know you can't alter the truth, but that doesn't mean you want to hear it.

Chapter 10

On Saturday I was still pissed off with Kenny, but I still tried to play the role of supportive wife by spending the day with him and Kiya at Chuck E Cheese. However, that night he went his way, and I went mine with Savoy.

The spot Savoy was taking me to was three hours away in Memphis. Savoy told me the dress was casual, so I put on a pair of studded Baby Phat jeans, tan heels, and a tan spaghetti strap sheer overlay shirt. We agreed to take his truck, so I had him meet me at a parking garage down the street from the Ambiance.

I stepped out of my car just as Savoy pulled up in a baby blue 2006 Jaguar. The paint shined, and the rims were blinging. I was impressed with the car, but I was even more impressed with the man driving it. Savoy looked sensational in his jeans and white Sean John cotton shirt. He kissed me on the cheek, while he held the passenger's door open for me.

"You look great." He smiled. "I love what you did with your braids."

I had them pulled up into two pigtails, and I had curled the ends. "Thank you." I settled into the seat, inhaling the fresh new car smell. "Is this your car?" I asked, looking over at him.

"Yeah." He smiled, pulling out of the garage. "This is my baby."

I admired the leather interior and wood grain trim. "It's nice," I said.

"Thank you."

"So, tell me about the place you're taking me to."

"It's called Poetry Alley," he said. "One of my boys from college is the owner."

It had been awhile since I had been to a poetry reading, although Octavia had open mic night every Sunday at the Ambiance.

"Are you going to recite something for me?" I asked sweetly.

"I'm an avid fan of the Art," he said laughing, "but I have no skills on the mic." I laughed. "Trust me, a brother can catch hell reciting roses are red, violets are blue, up in Poetry Alley."

I found it hard to believe that Savoy was bad at anything. Lyfe Jennings *Must Be Nice* played through the Bose speakers, as we rode in silence.

"May I ask you something?" he asked.

"Anything." I answered, bobbing my head to Lyfe's voice.

"You work with children," he said, "but you don't have any of your own. Why?"

Shifting in my seat, I looked out of the window at the passing traffic.

"Did I say something wrong?"

"No," I said, looking over at him.

I had never shared the entire truth of what happened to me with anyone, other than my mother and Kenny. I knew I could talk to Octavia, but I had never been able to bring myself to do so. But there was something about Savoy that made me want to confide in him.

"I can't have children," I said softly. "Something happened to me when I was younger."

He took his eyes of the road, briefly looking at me. "What happened?" he asked, looking concerned.

"I was raped," I said.

"Shon," he reached over and put his hand on top of mine, "I'm sorry."

"It's okay," I said. "You didn't know."

"We don't have to talk about this if you don't want to," he said.

"No, I want to."

I spent the next few minutes telling him everything that had happened. He listened quietly as I poured out the awful details, along with a waterfall of tears. He looked completely blown away by the information I shared with him. After I finished, he pulled off the highway and took me in his arms. Savoy literally allowed me to cry on his shoulder.

"I'm so sorry," he whispered, kissing me on the forehead.

"Thank you," I sobbed.

My thanks were not only for his empathy, but for the comfort and tenderness he was providing me. Pulling away, I looked into his eyes. There was something so soothing in the way he looked at me. I wiped my face with my hands, and gave him a small smile.

"Thank you," I said again.

He smiled and pulled back onto the highway.

Poetry Alley was a small café located on Beale Street. The atmosphere was Neo-Soul. The walls were decorated with framed quotes from various poets, from Langston Hughes and Emily Dickinson to Nikki Giovanni, and even 2Pac.

After Savoy introduced me to Nat, the owner, we sat down at an empty table near the front of the stage.

The lights dimmed, and a tall beautiful sister with honey-colored skin walked out onto the stage. She looked like a runway model, with her long, silky black hair and small frame. She stood with her hands on her hips, dressed in a tight gold catsuit. Looking at her you would think she had no poetic skills, but her looks were deceiving.

The sister had me in awe, as she recited a piece titled *More Than Just A Pretty Face*. There was a roar of applause when she finished. She never told us what her name was. Savoy said he had seen her several times at the Alley, and she never introduced herself to the audience. It didn't matter, because I knew all you had to do is mention her work and how beautiful she was, and anyone who had ever heard her would know who you were talking about.

She was followed by a heavyset white guy, who called himself Man. Man had Savoy and myself rolling from his piece titled *I*

Have The Fever. The piece was about his crush on a black woman, and her rejection of him. After Man, there were eight other artists, and I enjoyed every one of them. Some of them were hilarious, while others were so deep they left me speechless.

After we left Poetry Alley, we had dinner at a quiet little bistro down the block, then walked back up the block to his car. The two of us strolled hand in hand, enjoying the warm summer's night breeze.

"Did you enjoy the show?" he asked.

"Yes," I said, smiling at him.

"Me too," he said, squeezing my hand.

When the two of us made it back to his Jag, I let out a small sigh. Being with Savoy had been another free pass out of my real life. I knew that, once again, my trip out of reality was coming to an end.

"A nickel for your thoughts," he said, holding the car door open for me.

I stared into his shining eyes, wondering why he was being so good to me, and why we couldn't have met years ago.

"I was just thinking about how good it feels being with you," I said. "And how much I hate for this night to end."

"It doesn't have to," he said, touching my face with his fingertips. "Spend the night with me." The thought of spending the night with Savoy sent chills of excitement down my spine. "We can do whatever you want to do," he said, stroking my cheek.

Why is this man so fine? He would be so much easier for me to reject if he didn't look so damn good!

After a brief silence, I finally said, "I can't."

"Okay," he said, with a look of disappointment on his face.

The ride back to Huntsville was quiet, with the exception of Seleena Johnson's voice coming through the speakers. When we got back to the garage, it took every ounce of strength in my body not to tell Savoy I had changed my mind about his invitation. I sat behind the wheel of my Accord, with Savoy standing in the door beside me.

"Call me to let me know you made it home safely," he said.

"I will."

There was an uncomfortable silence between the two of us, until he kneeled down to my eye level, and kissed me on the cheek.

"Talk to you later," he said.

"Okay," I said.

I started my car, while watching him as he walked back over to his. I knew that going home to my husband was the right thing to do, and that was exactly what I had planned. But first there was something I had to handle.

"Savoy!" I called, jumping out of my car.

I ran to the spot where he was standing, and threw my arms around his neck. I kissed him with urgent force, as the two of us stood in each other's arms. Our lips and tongues created the rhythm I knew our bodies could not.

To my surprise, Kenny was up waiting for me when I got home. He was sitting in the living room with all the lights on, holding the TV remote in one hand, and a bottle of Michelob in the other.

"Where you been?" he asked, his eyes red. I knew he was drunk.

"I went out," I said, stating the obvious.

"With who?" he asked, following me into the bedroom.

"With a friend," I said, stepping out of my heels.

"What friend?"

"One of the girls from work," I lied.

He stood in the doorway sipping on the half empty beer watching me undress. "Where did y'all go?" he asked.

"To a poetry reading," I said, walking into the bathroom. I turned on the shower, trying to figure out why he had all of a sudden turned into 50 Cent with the *Twenty-One Questions.*

"Till one in the morning?" he asked, leaning against the bathroom door.

I stepped in the shower, and looked at him. "Yeah," I said.

"Why didn't you answer your phone?"

"My battery ran down." I said, standing under the warm flow of water.

He watched me, as I lathered soap all over my body, sipping on the rest of his beer.

"What?" I finally asked.

Staring at my wet naked breasts, he shook his head. "Nothing," he said, before turning and walking away.

I stood in the shower rubbing and massaging my breasts, and the heated place in between my legs until the water ran cold. When I finally got out, Kenny was sprawled out on the couch sleep. I didn't bother waking him to tell him to come to bed. I had come home to him, but the truth was my mind and desire was with Savoy. If I didn't have Savoy lying next to me, I'd rather sleep alone.

I went into our bedroom and picked up my purse. I dug through the contents, searching for my cell phone, but it wasn't there. I dropped to my knees and looked under the bed, thinking I might have dropped it. It wasn't there either. I stood up, and that's when I saw it sitting on the nightstand plugged into the battery charger. I had lied when I told Kenny the battery was dead. The truth was I had turned my phone off. I got paranoid, wondering if he had checked to see if the battery was really dead, or even worse, if he had checked my call log. I finally calmed down, and figured if he had, he would have questioned me about it, and if he hadn't checked the phone, then I was worried for no reason.

I kept my promise to Savoy, by calling him to let him know I had made it home safely. Then I turned my phone off, but not until I made sure it was locked.

CHAPTER 11

I was awakened the next morning to the smell of pancakes and sausage. I thought I was dreaming at first, so I closed my eyes and tried to go back to sleep. As the aroma grew stronger, I decided to get out of bed to see if some deranged burglar had broken into my home, murdered Kenny, and decided to cook himself breakfast. It was a farfetched theory, but I knew it was more realistic then the idea that Kenny was actually cooking. I walked in the kitchen and almost fainted when I saw Kenny standing over the stove.

"Good morning," he said, looking over his shoulder.

"Morning," I mumbled, totally shocked.

"Breakfast is almost ready." I watched him flip the pancakes he had cooking on the griddle, then the sausage patties he had sizzling in the skillet. "How do you want your eggs?" he asked.

"However you're having yours," I said, rubbing my eyes.

"Scrambled it is," he said.

I watched him moving from one task to the other, wondering what was going through his head. Maybe he had checked my phone and saw the calls to and from Savoy. *And he's rewarding me with breakfast?* I shook off the thoughts, and excused myself to go take a shower.

I was still dazed and confused, as the two of us sat at the table eating the meal Kenny had prepared. I tried to remember the last time he had cooked for me, but couldn't remember him so much as cracking an egg, let alone scrambling one.

"I was thinking the two of us could spend the day together," he said, clearing our plates from the table.

"What did you have in mind?" I asked, watching him as he began to wash the dishes.

"I thought maybe we could go see that new Terrance Howard flick."

"*Hustle and Flow*," I told him.

"Yeah, *Hustle and Flow*."

"I heard he got a standing ovation at the Sundance Film Festival," I said.

"My boy Dee took his girl to see it, he said it was good."

"Judging from the previews it is."

"I'll go out and grab a paper when I finish," he said, "so we can see what time it's playing."

"Okay." I said, standing to help him with the dishes.

"I got this," he said smiling. "Go kick your feet up." I looked at him with raised eyebrows. "What?" he asked.

"Nothing," I said, and walked into the living room.

As soon as Kenny left to go get the paper, I couldn't wait to call Octavia.

"He did what?" she asked.

"Cooked breakfast," I said.

"What's gotten into him?"

"I wish I knew."

"You think he knows about your date with Savoy last night?"

"Nah," I said confidently. "He would have mentioned that already. Wait a minute, who told you?" I was curious, because I hadn't mentioned it last night to her.

"I was up feeding Jazz when he came through the gate this morning."

"How do you know he wasn't with someone else?" I asked, curious about her assumption.

"Damon is his only male friend in Huntsville," she said. "And he doesn't hang out with his employees, he says it's unprofessional."

"How do you know he wasn't with another woman?" I asked.

"Savoy's been here for a month, and I haven't heard him mention another woman." Her saying that made me smile. "So, where were the two of you?" she asked. "And what were you doing until this morning?"

"He took me to Poetry Alley," I said, reminiscing.

"Nat's place? I love that spot."

"Girl, the poets were off the chain," I said.

"I know," she said. "Dame took me there about a month ago."

"Did you see Man when you went?" I asked.

"Yes, and his ass is hilarious!"

"I know, and that female."

"The one who looks like a model?" she asked.

"Yes."

"That's a bad chick!"

"Yes she is."

We talked about the other artists, before she asked, "So, what's really going on?"

"What do you mean?"

"You know what I mean," she said. "You and Savoy."

"We're just friends."

"Well you better be careful." She laughed. "Because Savoy looks like the type of friend that'll have you butt naked on your back, screaming out his name." The thought of it made me hot. "Tay?" Octavia called from the other end of the phone. "Are you there?"

"Huh?"

"Did you have sex with him?" she asked.

"No!" I said, practically yelling.

"But you want to," she said, "and you know that could be a major problem."

"I know," I said. "But I have it under control."

"I hope so," she said, sounding unconvinced.

I had no clue Terrance Howard was so talented or so sexy. I had seen him in several other roles through the years, but none of them compared to his role in *Hustle & Flow*. Terrance was definitely one of the many brothers who wasn't getting the props he deserved.

After the movie, Kenny and I went to Backyard Burgers, where he had the mushroom Angus burger, and I had the blackened chicken. I had forgotten how much fun the two of us used to have together. There was a time when the two of us would sit and talk for hours about the most trivial subjects. We would laugh and joke, like the best of friends. In fact, the first thing that attracted me to Kenny was his sense of humor.

The day we met I was sitting in IHOP, with my nose buried in my calculus notes. I was studying for my college finals.

I was deep in thought, when I heard, "This table is for paying customers only."

I looked up, and there he was standing by the table wearing a blue baseball hat, jeans, and a leather bomber jacket.

"Well, I guess I don't have to worry about giving it up to you," I said sarcastically.

"Nope," he said. "But you do have to share it with me." I watched him sit down, thinking he had lost his mind.

"That seat is taken," I said annoyed.

"I know." He smiled. "I'm sitting in it."

"Listen, I'm trying to study...alone."

"I can help you," he said, leaning across the table. He pointed to the page I was looking at. "I'm an expert at that," he said.

Sitting back in my chair, I crossed my arms across my breasts. "Okay, Mr. Expert, explain the formula on line one." I was calling his bluff.

"Girl, I got this," he said, cracking his knuckles.

He turned my notes around and stared at the formula, like he was trying to discover the meaning of life. He had this amusing expression on his face, with his eyebrows raised and his lips twisted. He held up his fingers and started counting.

"Two plus two," he said." Add X slash Y, take away..." Shaking my head, I pulled my notebook back across the table. "I would explain it to you," he said, "but then you would never learn."

"Um-hum," I said smirking. "You got it, huh?"

"I was this close," he said, pinching his fingers together.

"I see." We both laughed.

"Seriously," he said, "girl, what are you studying to be, a Rocket Scientist?"

"Actually, I'm an Education Major." I giggled.

"What grades?" he asked.

"Elementary Education," I said proudly. "I want to teach first graders."

"I don't know any first graders who are going to know what that shit means."

I laughed because I felt the exact same way. "They don't have to." I smiled. "But I do if I want my degree."

We continued to talk and laugh until the manager came over and asked us to order something or leave. We left, but not until we had exchanged phone numbers. Three days later we went roller skating, and from that day on we were inseparable.

Kenny told me that he was raised by his mother and never knew his father. "I know his name," he said, "and that's enough."

I told him that I didn't know that much about my father, and from there we forged a bond. He accepted the fact that I wanted to wait on having sex with him, and unlike other guys I had dated, he didn't dump me because of it. I accepted that he didn't have a car, was barely working, and had no idea what he wanted to do with his future. What Kenny didn't have in material possessions and aspirations, he made up for by showing me attention. I loved that.

Four months after we met, on the night of my graduation, I confessed to him why I was afraid to have sex with him. I told him about Pete, the baby, and my inability to have children. Kenny said he didn't care about any of those things; that he just wanted to be with me. We made love that night, and I knew that I would love him for the rest of my life.

"You know what I want to do that we haven't done in a long time?" he asked, as we walked out of Backyard Burgers.

"What's that?"

"Go to The Roller Rink," he said, grinning like a little boy.

The Roller Rink on a Sunday night, with a bunch of hormone raging sixteen year olds, was no longer my idea of the perfect date with my husband, but Kenny was putting forth an effort.

"I'd like that," I said smiling.

To my surprise, Sunday nights at The Roller Rink were now Adult Night. You had to be eighteen or older to get in. There were couples, ranging from ages eighteen to fifty, on the floor. Kenny and I rocked and rolled until they announced it was time to close.

Later that night, I lay with my head on Kenny's chest. The two of us had made love when we got home. Kenny had this smile of satisfaction plastered on his face as he slept. The two of us had shared a day with no interruptions from his mother or his baby's mama. I was content and pleased, but at the same time, I was curious. I wondered why Kenny had suddenly done a three hundred and sixty degree turn around, but then figured it was what it was. I also wondered what Savoy was doing, and if he was thinking about me.

CHAPTER 12

A month had gone by, and Kenny was still playing the role of the perfect husband. We hadn't had one single disagreement, and it seemed as if the two of us were finally on the right track. The funny thing is, I thought that the lack of attention I was getting at home was the reason I was spending time with Savoy. But even though Kenny and I were on good terms, I was still seeing him.

We continued to run three times a week, and met up for lunch occasionally. There were several times when Savoy had invited me to dinner or a play, but I had turned him down. I explained to him that I was trying to make things work with Kenny. I sensed his disappointment, even though he said we were cool. I thought I had the best of both worlds. It was the perfect equation to me. I had my husband and my friend. I thought I had it all under control, but I was wrong.

Octavia had informed me that she had a hot new poet from Birmingham debuting at Open Mic Night. Kenny kindly declined my invitation to join me, so I went alone.

The upstairs lounge was packed by the time I arrived. Octavia greeted me with a hug, and instructed me to have a seat at one of the three tables marked "reserved", towards the front of the stage. I sat waiting for the show to began, watching the people entering the room.

When I spotted Savoy, I smiled instantly. He looked sexy as ever. I decided to go over and get him, but froze in my place when I saw the female hanging on his arm. It was the broad from Club Hydro, the one with the big titties. I watched them as they slid into one of the booths in the back. It was like the two of them were conjoined at the hip. She sat with her store bought breasts pressed up against Savoy's arm. It was déjà vu, but this time she didn't have her girlfriend with her. Savoy smiled, while gazing into her eyes sweetly. He seemed to be enjoying her attention. I felt a pinch of jealously as I watched the two of them.

The lights grew dim, making it hard for me to continue observing their interaction. I adjusted my chair so that my back was to them. I faced the stage, and tried to focus on the introduction Octavia was giving.

"Welcome to Open Mic Night here at the Ambiance," she said, speaking into the wireless microphone. "Tonight we will be featuring some of the hottest artists in our city and the surrounding area. But first," she said cheerfully, "I'd like to introduce our guest MC for the night. Ladies and Gentleman, let's welcome DJ Styles to the stage!"

The crowd applauded loudly, as a tall, slim light-skinned brother ran out onto the stage. Octavia gave him the microphone and a friendly hug.

"Thank you. Thank you," he said smiling. "Let's give it up for our sexy hostess." He gave Octavia the once over with his eyes. There was applause and cheers for my girl. "I tell you," he said, smiling at her, "you're wearing that dress!"

The crowd clapped and screamed, with a few of the men whistling. I clapped and yelled as well. Octavia looked great standing in the spotlight wearing a gold strapless knee length dress and four-inch heels. Her long wavy hair hung over her shoulders.

"Thank you," she said, blushing.

"Okay," DJ Styles said, looking back at the crowd, "we want everyone to sit back, relax, and enjoy the show. First up, coming straight out of Atlanta, Georgia, everybody welcome Diamond to the stage!"

Diamond did her thing, followed by four other performers, before DJ Styles announced there was going to be a short break.

"If this was TV, this would be the point where we'd air a bunch of damn commercials," he said. "Well this ain't TV, but we still got to pay the bills, so get up, order a couple of plates, then holla back at us in thirty."

The lights came back up, and people started moving around. I casually looked over my shoulder, and caught a glimpse of Savoy's date kissing him on the lips. When she pulled away, I saw the big smile on his face. Then, as if he could sense someone was watching them, he looked in my direction. The two of us made eye contact before I could look away.

We stared at each other, while his date slid out of the booth and headed towards the ladies room. Savoy got up behind her and started walking in my direction. I quickly grabbed my purse and got up from the table, walking off in the opposite direction.

"Shontay!" he called out to me.

I hurried downstairs to the restaurant, and slipped out of one of the side exits. I would call Octavia later and explain I hadn't felt well, thus explaining my disappearing act.

I was halfway to my car, when I heard Savoy yelling behind me, "Shontay, wait up!"

I stopped walking, and turned around to see him running towards me.

"What's up?" I asked calmly.

"Didn't you hear me calling you?"

"No, it was kinda loud in there," I lied.

"Didn't you see me coming over to your table?" he asked, looking at me like I was crazy.

I couldn't deny that I had, so I pretended to be in a hurry. "Look, I gotta go," I said, with false urgency.

"Alright," he said, staring at me. "I'll see you in the morning."

"Actually I have something to do in the morning," I said.

"At four am?" he asked frowning.

"Yeah." I was making up an excuse, so that I wouldn't have to face him.

"Okay, well I'll see you Wednesday."

"You know what, I don't think we should see each other anymore."

He took a step back, looking at me. "What's going on, Shon?"

I shifted my weight from one leg to the other. "Nothing,' I said, looking away. "I just think that it's better if we end our friendship."

"Better for who?" he asked.

"Everyone."

"Shon..."

"Savoy, I have to go," I said, looking away.

He took a deep breath then exhaled. "Alright," he said. "Take care of yourself."

I turned and started to walk away, when I heard a high pitch voice calling his name. "Savoy?" I turned back around, and saw Ms. Falsies standing out on the curb with her hands on her hips. "Is everything okay, papi?" she asked.

"Yeah," he said, looking back at her.

"Well, hurry up, baby, the show is starting." She gave me a small smile, then turned and walked away.

I felt that pinch of jealousy again, only this time it was more of a punch. "Go ahead," I said, "your girlfriend is waiting."

He looked at me with raised eyebrows. "My girlfriend?" he asked.

"Yeah, Ms. Barbie with the plastic titties," I said sarcastically.

"Who, Maria?" he asked.

"Yeah."

"Are you jealous?"

"Of what," I asked laughing, "you and your bi-sexual date?"

"You said it, not me," he said arrogantly. "This is what all of this is about?"

"All of what?" I asked.

"You not wanting to see me anymore."

"She has nothing to do with that."

"I think she does," he stated. "You're jealous."

We both knew he was right, but at that moment, my pride

would not let me admit it.

"Why would I be jealous?" I asked.

"I don't know," he said. "You tell me." There was silence between us. "Shon, she is just a friend," he said softly.

"So you kiss all your friends?" I asked, cutting my eyes at him.

"Actually she kissed me."

"You didn't seem to mind," I snapped.

"Why would I? She's a beautiful *single* woman."

"I have to go," I said irritated. "My *husband* is waiting."

He looked away for a moment, then stared directly into my eyes. "Are you mad because I went out with another woman," he asked coldly. "Or is it because I'm not sweating you?"

"I never asked you..."

"I want you, Shon," he said, cutting me off. "But I'm not going to run after you. If you want me, you know where I'll be." He turned and walked away, leaving me standing there with my mouth open.

I stood there thinking that at any moment he was going to come back, but he didn't. I finally made myself get in my car and drove off.

On the drive home, I thought about everything Savoy had said. I knew I was being completely selfish. I didn't want anyone else to have him, but I wasn't able to give him what he needed.

Kenny was on the couch wearing nothing but a pair of boxers and tube socks when I walked through the door.

"You're home early," he said.

"Yeah," I said sulking. My mind was still on Savoy.

"How you feelin'?" Kenny was smiling, totally oblivious to the fact that something was bothering me.

"I'm tired," I said. "I'm going to bed."

He jumped up like I had given him an invitation to join me. "Good," he said, rubbing his hands together, "because I've been thinking about that ass all night."

"Not tonight," I said, giving him a half smile.

"Come on," he said, walking over to me. He put both his hands on my ass and squeezed my cheeks. "All I need is a lil' bit."

"I'm tired," I said annoyed.

"Come on, Tay," he said, sliding his hands under my shirt and squeezing my breasts.

I pushed his hands down and stepped back. "Didn't you hear me say I was tired?" I snapped.

The smile vanished from his face. "What's wrong with you?" he asked, frowning at me.

"I just need some time to myself."

"You complain about us not spending time together," he snapped. "Then when I try to give you what you want, you say you want to be alone."

"I'm just going through something right now," I said, trying to smooth over the situation. I knew that our conversation was on the verge of becoming an argument.

"You're always going through something," he said sarcastically.

"What's that suppose to mean?" I asked him.

"Nothing," he said, walking off.

I followed him into the bedroom. He grabbed a pair of jeans and a T-shirt from the closet.

"Where are you going?" I asked.

"Out," he said, slipping on his pants. He put on his shirt, and slipped his feet into a pair of sneakers.

"Out where?" I asked.

"Does it matter?" he asked, tying his shoelaces. "You said you needed some time alone."

"Is this because I don't want to have sex?" I asked. He didn't answer. "Well, I'm sorry if I don't feel like satisfying your needs," I snapped.

"Shit, when have you ever?"

"What is that suppose to mean?" I asked, with raised eyebrows.

"Nothing," he said, walking towards the door.

I walked in front of him, blocking his path. "Say it!" I yelled. "Say exactly what's on your mind."

"I don't want to argue," he said calmly, looking at me.

"Then just tell me this," I said, in his face. "If I don't satisfy you, then why are you with me?"

He bit down on his bottom lip, like he was trying to figure out the answer. "You're a good woman," he finally said. "And I love you." There was something not quite right about his answer.

"But I don't satisfy you," I stated. I took two steps back, while running my fingers through my braids.

"Is that why you fucked all those other bitches?" I asked. "Including that bitch Alicia."

He looked at me with wide eyes. The mere mention of his baby's mama seemed to piss him off.

"Why they gotta be bitches?" he asked, defensively.

"I'm sorry, hoes. Is that better?"

"Well, those hoes were willing to do what you wouldn't," he said, pushing pass me.

"Like what!" I screamed, walking behind him.

"Like listen," he said, turning to face me. "You don't fucking listen. And you don't know how to stop feeling sorry for yourself," he added. "You've been feeling sorry for yourself for so damn long, over something you'll never have, you don't even know how to be happy. The past is the past," he said, grabbing his keys off the coffee table. "You need to accept it and move on."

He walked out the door, leaving me standing in the hallway with my mouth wide open.

Chapter 13

The past is the past. Kenny's words echoed through my head, as I pumped my arms and legs fiercely. My feet hit the smooth pavement as sweat ran over my body, causing the cotton sweats I had on to stick to my body. The sun had yet to rise, as I ran with all my might around the winding trail. I was on my third mile through the park, attempting to clear my head of the thoughts bombarding it.

After Kenny left the night before, I sat in bed thinking about everything that had been said between us. He was right, it was time for me to stop feeling sorry for myself. It was time for me to make myself happy.

I took a deep breath, slowing down my pace. Looking out of the corner of my eye, I smiled at Savoy. He was right beside me, our strides almost synchronized.

Last night, after wallowing in self-pity, I got in my car, and drove around the city aimlessly. I told myself it was to clear my head, but the truth was I was looking for Kenny. I wanted to apologize to him for the way I had behaved. After what felt like an hour, I finally spotted his car. It was parked in front of Hillside Village, the apartments where Alicia resided. I sat staring at her apartment, with my heart racing a mile a minute. The first vision that ran through my head was to knock on the door and go straight crazy. I wanted to whoop both their asses, but I didn't have the fight in me. I was tired of fighting. I drove off, ending up at Octavia's front door.

"You can stay here for as long as you want," she told me, while the two of us sat in her kitchen talking. I had just finished telling her about everything that had went down with Kenny.

"Thanks, but that's my house and I'm going home," I told her, wiping my eyes. "But just not tonight."

"You know where the guest rooms are," she said standing, leaning down to give me a hug. "Oh, and yes, he's here."

"Who?" I asked, with a confused look.

"Savoy," she said. "He left before the show was over. Dame said he dropped off ole' girl and came straight home." She started to walk away then stopped. "If it's any consolation, Dame said that nothing happened with him and that big tittie chick," she said, looking back at me.

"Girl, ain't those things ridiculous." I laughed.

"They look like damn flotation devices!" She smiled.

"Thanks, Tavia, for everything."

"You're welcome."

I sat in the kitchen alone for a while, trying to regain my composure. Once I thought I had myself together I went out to the guesthouse. I knocked on the door lightly, hoping that Savoy wouldn't hear me, partially wishing he was asleep. He wasn't. In fact, he opened the door rather quickly. He was wearing a pair of silk pajama pants with no shirt.

"Shon," he said.

The tears I promised I would not shed flowed freely. He looked at me compassionately, and pulled me through the doorway into his arms. I broke down my whole fight with Kenny, and then confessed that I had initiated the argument because I was frustrated from seeing him with Maria. I also apologized for my behavior. After our conversation, Savoy ran me a hot bath and gave me his matching pajama top to put on. When I came out of the bathroom he was stretched out on the chaise, with a pillow supporting his head. He looked at me and smiled.

"You want me to walk you back up to the house?" he asked.

I didn't answer. Instead, I climbed onto the bed, and motioned for him to come to me. We stared into each other's eyes, as he got up and walked over to the bed. He sat down beside me, looking at me like I was the most beautiful woman he had ever seen. I ran my hand over the soft hairs of his chest, up his neck, to his face. I pulled his face to mine and we kissed.

He slowly unbuttoned the shirt I was wearing, moving his lips from mine, down to my naked breasts. His mouth spread across one of my nipples, while he gently massaged the other with his fingers. He took his time, going from one breast to the other. In between my legs, there had been a slow sensational heat building. Savoy had further ignited it when he moved from my breasts down to my toes. He sucked, licked and kissed all ten of them one by one. Then he worked his way up my calves to my thighs. My kitty throbbed, because she knew that she was going to be next.

When Savoy finally made his way up to her, he sucked and ate me like he was a man on death row, and I was his last meal. I closed my eyes, arched my back, and exhaled. My body shook uncontrollably as I came, experiencing my first multiple orgasm. Savoy slipped off his pants, and I thought my eyes were going to pop out my head.

"Damn!" I blurted out.

My dreams had not done him justice. His dick was long, thick and incredible. It was big, but not that grotesque big, that would make a woman want to throw on her clothes and run. I got on my knees, determined to take all of him in my mouth. I didn't care if I was hoarse for a week, I was going to make him feel as good as he had made me feel. I wanted him to know how hungry he made me. I took my time licking my way up his shaft to the head of his dick.

"Shontay," he moaned, as his entire body shook with pleasure.

I gave Savoy what was, in my opinion, the blow job of a Porn Queen. I watched his eyes roll back in his head until he moaned for me stop. I laid on my back, waiting for him, as he retrieved a condom from his luggage. He slipped on the condom then kissed me softly. We stared into each other's eyes while he entered me, then the two of us made love like I had never made love before.

The two of us finished our run by walking along the trail to cool down. I slipped my hand in Savoy's as we walked in silence.

"I'm asking, no, I'm telling Kenny to move out," I said.

"Are you sure that's what you want to do?" Savoy asked.

"I'm positive," I said confidently.

He gave my hand a light squeeze. "Construction on the Ambiance 2 should be completed in another month," he said. "I'll be leaving to go to Atlanta for a week, and then I'll be off to Europe for a little rest and relaxation." We stopped walking, but continued to hold hands. "I want you to come with me."

"To Europe?" I asked.

"Yes," he said smiling. "But if you don't want to go to Europe, we can go anywhere you wanna go. To Africa, Montreal, Paris, Asia, Arkansas," he said.

"Okay, okay, I get it!" I said laughing.

"I don't care where we go," he said, "as long as we're together. I want to be with you, Shontay," he said seriously, "in every possible way."

I felt tears in my eyes, but they weren't tears of sadness. These tears were because Savoy touched my heart. He made me feel so good. He made me feel wanted.

"I'm in love with you, Shon," he added, touching my face.

My heart fluttered. "Are you sure?" I asked.

"I've never been so sure of anything in my life."

"But what happens when you leave to go back home?" I asked.

"I'm not going to let distance separate us," he said, pulling me into his arms.

I wrapped my arms around his waist, snuggling my face into his chest. We were both sweaty and funky, but I didn't care.

"Let me handle my business at home," I said. "Then we'll go from there."

"As far as Europe," I said, looking up into his eyes. "Let me think about it."

"Okay," he said, kissing me on the top of my head.

I was thinking that I wouldn't have to face Kenny until later that afternoon, but I was wrong. When I got home, to my surprise, he hadn't left for work yet. I took a deep breath, inserted my key in the lock, and decided now was as good of a time as any to confront him. The door flung open before I had the chance to turn my key.

"Tay," Kenny said, staring me in my eyes. He had this cold look in his eyes. "I've been calling you all morning." He stood in front of me wearing wrinkled jeans and a faded T-shirt. He looked like he hadn't gotten any sleep the night before. I presumed from screwing Alicia all night.

"We need to talk," I stated, walking pass him.

"Tay, that can wait," he said, shutting the door behind me.

"No it can't!" I snapped, spinning around to face him. "I'm sick and tired of..."

"Shontay!" he yelled, cutting me off, "the hospital called about your mother."

"Wh…who?" I stuttered, thinking I had heard him wrong.

"Your mom," he said. "Josephine."

"What did they want?" I asked, my mind reeling.

He walked towards me. "She's dying," he said gently.

My heart started beating so loud I could hear the echo in my ears. I felt my knees giving out and my feet slipping from under me. Kenny moved quickly, throwing his arms around me. He held me as we slid down to the floor. My mouth was so dry I felt dehydrated. I could feel a knot forming in the back of my throat. It was the feeling I got whenever I was going to cry. I lay in Kenny's arms, with my head resting on his shoulder, waiting for the tears to start, but they never did.

CHAPTER 14

I hadn't seen my mother in thirteen years. After everything that happened with the rape and the abortion, she sent me to Alabama to live with my grandmother and never looked back. She never called, never visited, or even sent me a damn birthday card. When my grandmother died, I expected that my mother would at least show up for the funeral. I called the same number I remember us having when I was in Baltimore, and left her a message that her mother was dead, but she didn't have the decency to return my call.

In my mind Josephine was already dead, so I couldn't understand why I took the news that she was in the hospital so hard. I guess deep down inside I knew that she was still my mother, and that as her daughter, I had a certain responsibility. Keeping that in mind, I booked the next flight out of Huntsville to Baltimore.

I got off the airplane, grabbed my luggage, and immediately picked up my rental car. Baltimore looked more like a foreign land to me, rather than my birthplace and the city where I was partially raised. I made the drive to Baltimore General in a daze. I didn't know what I was going to say when I saw my mother, or even if I was going to be able to say anything.

Kenny had practically demanded that I let him come along with me. But I knew I had to confront my past on my own, so I insisted on going alone. The combination of facing my mother and dealing with the problems in our marriage was too much for me to focus on at one time.

I walked through the corridor of the hospital feeling like I was on my way to trial. I stopped in front of the room assigned to my mother, and tried to control the nervous energy that was flowing through my body. I stood outside the door with my heart pounding and my palms sweating.

Turn and walk away, I thought. I took a deep breath then exhaled, blowing warm air out through my mouth. I knocked on the door twice.

"Come in," a voice said.

I hadn't heard that voice in years, but I immediately recognized it. It was my mother's. I pushed the door open slowly, and walked into the room. My mother sat propped up in the small hospital bed, looking like my older twin. It was unbelievable that throughout the years, besides having lost some weight, she looked exactly the same. I felt like I was looking in the mirror, staring at her dark brown eyes and heart-shaped face, with dark chocolate skin. She smiled as she watched me. I moved into the room, and sat down in the small chair, facing the bed.

"Shontay." She smiled, holding her arms open to me.

I didn't move from my place on the edge of the chair. There was a little girl inside yearning to run into her arms, but the woman that I had become refused to succumb.

"I didn't think you would come," she said, slowly dropping her arms to her side.

"Are they not giving you any medication?" I asked, noticing she was not connected to any machines.

"I refused treatment," she said, her eyes shining while she looked at me. "I've had chemo and radiation in the past. There's no need for me to continue treatment. I have cancer. I'm dying." She looked away for a brief second then looked back at me. "God has given me peace." I couldn't believe my ears. When I lived with Mama she had never acknowledged there was a higher being. "But I couldn't die without knowing I have your forgiveness."

I figured that was coming next. She was lying on her death bed, and *now* she wanted to make things right with me. What about the last fucking twelve years?

"You want me to forgive you now?" I asked sarcastically. "After thirteen years? Did you want my forgiveness when you were out there running the streets gambling, racking up debts that you knew you couldn't repay?" I stood up, crossing my arms across my chest. "Did you ask for my forgiveness after I told you that Pete raped me?" I snapped, my voice shaky. "Did you ask for my forgiveness when you drug me to a damn chop shop and let some quack sucked my baby from my body? Did you ask for my forgiveness when my insides became infected and diseased, leaving me sterile?" I looked at her, feeling the hatred pouring from my eyes. "Did you?" I screamed.

She had tears in her eyes, as she shook her head. "No," she said.

"That's right, you didn't!" I said, pacing back and forth. "So don't ask for it now!"

"I love you, Shontay," she said softly. "And I know I did some terrible things back then, but there hasn't been a day that I haven't thought about you."

"Please, I was out of sight out of mind for you," I said, sucking my teeth. "You shipped me off to Grandma Martha and didn't look back. You left her to raise your daughter. To explain to your daughter that you had a problem, and that it wasn't her fault she got caught up in your bad business. You didn't even come to pay your last respects when she died!" I stopped pacing, and stood at the foot of the bed.

"I came," she mumbled.

"What?" I asked.

"I came," she said, tears rolling down her cheeks. "You had on this beautiful black suit. The skirt was short and flared at the bottom. Your hair was different, it was short with layers." I looked at her with my mouth wide open. She was exactly right. "You read this beautiful poem," she sniffed. "*This is Not Goodbye.*"

I had forgotten all about the poem I had written after my grandmother died. I swallowed hard, trying not to cry.

"Why didn't you say anything?" I asked, lowering my eyes.

"I sent you several letters," she cried, "but you never replied. Then when I got the message you left about Mama, I figured you were just being polite. I didn't think you would even talk to me. I saw how upset you were, and I figured that you would just push me away. I hadn't done right by you or Mama," she said, "and I figured I was the last person you wanted to see."

"What letters?" I asked puzzled.

"I wrote you several times," she said, wiping her face with the back of her hands. "I sent you the letters. I called information, and you were the only Shontay Allen listed in Huntsville. At first I thought I had the wrong address, but none of them were returned."

"I...I didn't get them," I said confused. "But why didn't you call?" I asked. "If you had my address then you had my number."

"I called once," she said, "and I left a message. Then, after that I tried again, and my number had been blocked."

The anger that I had been feeling returned. I just knew she was lying, there was no way her number had been blocked.

"You're sitting up in here claiming you want my forgiveness, but yet and still you're still lying!" I said angrily. "I didn't get no damn message, and I didn't block your number!"

"Tay, I promise you..."

"Stop it!" I snapped. "Just stop it! I can't listen to this anymore." I said, turning to leave. "Goodbye."

"Please don't leave!" she begged. "Shontay, please, I can't change the past," she cried. "But just tell me what I can do to get you to forgive me."

I stopped moving, and turned to look at her. There was nothing I could think of that could rectify all of the wrongs my mother had done, but there was one thing she could do for me. She could satisfy my curiosity.

"You can tell me who my father is," I said, walking back to the foot of the bed.

She lowered her head, not looking at me. "Shontay, you don't need to know him," she said.

"You asked me what you could do," I reminded her. "That's the only thing you can do for me."

"I…I can't," she stuttered.

"Fine," I said, walking to the door.

"Tay, wait I'll tell you," she said weakly. "Please come sit down, I'll tell you."

I turned around, and saw the sadness in her eyes. There was something inside of me telling me to just leave, but I had to know. I deserved to know. I walked back to the chair and sat down. She dropped her head down into her open hands.

"Baby, I'm so sorry," she said crying. "I'm so sorry." She looked up, allowing me to see her fresh tears. "Pete is your father," she said.

The room felt like it was spinning, as I felt my heart skip a beat. I wanted to scream but I couldn't, it was like I had gone mute. I jumped up from the chair, almost falling to the floor. The memory of my father raping me played through my mind like a bad dream. I gagged as I felt my insides churning. I ran to the small bathroom in the room, fell to my knees, and with my head hanging over the toilet, I threw up. I was shaking as I cried, trying to control my breathing. I sat on the floor, crying and gagging at the same time. The thought of Pete being my father was inconceivable.

"Shontay," Josephine called, from the other room. "Baby, I'm so sorry."

I pulled myself up to the sink and splashed cold water on my face. I was still crying hysterically. I had many images of who my father might have been, but the father of my aborted baby was never one of them. I pulled myself together before going back into the room to face my mother. She had tears in her eyes as I stared at her, trying to process the new information.

"That's why I couldn't let you have the baby," she cried. "I just couldn't."

"Did he know?" I asked angrily. "Did he know when he raped me that I was his daughter?"

"No," she cried. "He didn't know until later."

"Where is he now?" I asked.

She looked away, then said, "He's dead. He was murdered three years ago. He got into an argument during a card game and was shot. He died on the spot."

I wanted to feel joy because my sick father had died a horrible death, but at the same time, I felt that once again I had been violated. I hadn't been given the opportunity to confront him. I wanted to stare him in his eyes, and yell and scream that I was his daughter. The same girl he raped and left his seed in, was his daughter.

"Why didn't you tell him before he raped me?" I asked, channeling all my anger to my mother. "Maybe if he knew, he wouldn't have done what he did!" I screamed.

"Pete was involved in all types of illegal activities," she said, wiping her face. "I thought I was protecting you."

"Protecting me?" I walked to the side of the metal bed. "You've never protected me!"

"I did the best I knew how to do!" she said defensively. "I did my best, Shontay!"

"Well your best wasn't good enough," I said, turning my back to her. There was an uncomfortable silence between the two of us. "You asked for my forgiveness," I finally said, "you have it. And now, I'm leaving."

My departure was interrupted by a knock on the door. A tall, balding older white man walked in, wearing a white lab coat and carrying a chart. "How are you, Josephine?" he asked.

"I'm fine, Dr. Weiss, and yourself?"

"Just fine." He smiled, looking at my mother. "How are you, Miss?" he asked, extending his hand to me.

"Holloway," I said, shaking his hand. "And I'm fine, Doctor."

"Dr. Weiss, this is my daughter, Shontay," Josephine said.

"I've heard so much about you." He smiled.

"I was just leaving," I said, faking a smile.

"Before you go, I'd like to speak with you," he said, following behind me.

I didn't want to converse with Dr. Weiss, or anyone else, at that moment. I wanted to get as far away from Baltimore as I could, as fast as I could. I chose to hear the doctor out anyway, because I didn't want to be rude.

"As you know, your mother has refused treatment," Dr. Weiss said, as the two of us stood outside of the room. I nodded my head. "Her cancer has spread, and to be completely honest, there is nothing left we can do for her. The only thing now is to make her as comfortable as possible. In my opinion, she would be more comfortable in her own home with her family." I exhaled deeply, because I knew what the doctor was saying and what he expected from me.

"Isn't there some home healthcare providers you can recommend?" I asked.

"There are," he said, studying my expression. "I'd be happy to make recommendations if you'd like someone to sit with her when you're out."

"I'm going back home tonight," I said firmly. "I'm not returning to Baltimore, so I'll need someone who is available 24-7."

I could tell he was trying hard not to show any emotions with his facial expressions, but I knew my comment had caught him off guard. I can't say that I blame him. The man had just told me my mother was dying and there was nothing that could be done, and my only response was that I was leaving town.

"May I speak candidly for a moment?" he asked.

"Go ahead."

"I've been Josie's physician for the last three years," he said. "She's shared a lot of things with me. I'm sure you have your reasons for leaving." I looked away, not wanting him to see the pain in my eyes. "But no one should have to spend their last days alone. Not when they have a better option."

CHAPTER 15

After my talk with Dr. Weiss, I went down to the hospital chapel and fell to my knees. There were hundreds of lit votive candles surrounding the altar while I cried, praying for the Lord's guidance. I begged Him to help me find it in my heart to forgive my mother. Then I asked Him why was Pete the sperm donor that helped bring me into the world? Why was I raped by him? Why did He allow his seed to creep into my body and create a child? Why, why, why? I screamed that I deserved better. I knew it was wrong for me to question Him, but I was in an utter moment of weakness. It was during that moment of weakness that I felt an old familiar presence.

"You can spend the rest of your life hating Josephine," Grandmother said. "But the only person who is going to suffer is you." I could feel her arms around me, comforting me. "You can't haunt the dead," she said, "and you can't make them suffer. Let it go, Tay-Tay."

When I got up off my knees, I decided to do what I could for my mother while I still had the chance. The pain and the anger was still coursing through my body, but those were not the only elements, there was also love.

It was the same butter cream house with green shutters on the outside, but the inside had been completely remodeled. The old furniture had been replaced with new contemporary pieces. The kitchen now had all new Whirlpool appliances. The hardwood floors in the kitchen had been totally redone. All the other rooms had thick plush carpet, except for the bathroom. The bathroom now had beautiful marble tile. The entire interior looked different, except for my old room. Mama had refurnished it, but all of my school awards and trophies were still in place. She had even kept the stuffed animals and dolls I had as a child.

I helped Mama get settled into her bed, and then stepped into the living room to make a few phone calls. I called the Buzzing Baby to let them know the situation, and that I didn't know when I would be returning to work. Alberta, my supervisor, expressed her empathy, and told me she would make sure she sent me the paperwork through UPS so I could apply for FMLA. She explained that I would get paid only sixty percent of my income while I was gone. I was relived, because something was definitely better than nothing.

I called Octavia next, to let her know what was going on. She knew that things had been bad between my mother and me, but I had never told her the entire story until now.

"Tay, why didn't you tell me before now?" Octavia asked.

"I don't know," I said.

"I can only imagine what you're going through," she said. "And what you've already been through."

"I don't know if I can handle all of this right now," I admitted. "It's all so overwhelming."

"I know it is, but you're stronger than you realize. I know it doesn't feel like it right not, but trust me, you are."

"Thanks," I said, letting her words sink in. "I'll call you soon."

"I love you, sis."

"I love you too."

I had received messages from both Kenny and Savoy. I decided to call Kenny back first. I figured that it was better to get what I had to say to him out of the way. I wanted to finish the conversation I had attempted to start before I left for Baltimore. He answered his cell on the first ring, immediately showing concern for my mother's condition. I gave him a quick run down on her condition before turning the conversation towards my real reason for calling.

"Kenny, I have something to tell you..."

"Before you do," he said, cutting me off, "I have something I want to say."

I didn't feel like arguing, so I decided to hear him out. "I'm listening," I said.

"Shontay, I've done you wrong more times than I can count," he confessed. "There is no excuse for why I did what I did. I guess I've never been good at expressing myself. But, Tay, I love you so much." I was quiet as he continued. "I know I haven't proven that to you, but I do." His voice was shaky. "I know this isn't the right time to tell you this, but with everything that's happened with us, and now with your mom, I realize what's important, and I know that there's no better time for me to change and try to make this, no us, right."

"What are you saying?" I asked, trying to make sense of his rambling.

"I'm saying that I hope, no, pray that you will forgive me for what I've been doing." I could tell he was crying on the other end of the phone. I had never seen or heard Kenny cry before. "I told Alicia that it's over, and that I want our marriage to work," he cried. "That is, if you'll have me." There was a pregnant pause. He had confessed what I already knew, that he was still sleeping with his baby's mama.

"I don't know if we can get pass this," I said.

"I understand why you're saying that," he said. "And I know I don't deserve you but, damnit Tay, I can't let you go. Not until I've tried to be the best man I can be for you."

I felt tears swelling in my eyes. I was on emotional overload. I had my mind made up when I called, but hearing the sincerity in his words, I was stuck.

"Kenny, I think we should at least separate," I said, trying to remain focused.

He took a deep breath. "Baby, just think about it," he said, clearing his throat. "Think about all we've been through...the good times."

"Kenny, I..."

"Please, baby," he begged, "just think about giving me one more chance, please baby."

I hesitated, before saying, "I'll think about it."

"Thank you, thank you," he said, sounding relieved. "I love you so much, and I promise you won't regret this."

"I have to go, Mama is calling me," I lied. "I'll call you later."

I hung up the phone before he had a chance to respond. I tried hard not to think about what he had said. I had heard "I'm sorry" time and time before. I wanted to believe Kenny because I loved him, but at the same time, I was tired. I called Savoy next, but instead of speaking with him, I got his voicemail.

"Hi Savoy, it's Shontay. I was just thinking about you. I'm in Baltimore with my mother right now. I don't know how long I'll be here, but I'll be in contact soon. I miss you."

CHAPTER 16

The first few days there was an awkward tension between the two of us. We rarely talked, and when we did, it was about things like the weather and current events. I think neither one of us wanted to be the first to bring up our conversation at the hospital. At the end of the week, Mama was finally the first one to break the ice.

"Shontay, can you come here for a second?" she asked.

"You okay?" I asked, sticking my head in the bedroom door.

"I'm fine." She smiled. "But I have something I want to show you." She was sitting on the edge of the bed, with a large leather photo album in her hands.

"What's that?" I asked.

"Come here," she said, patting the space next to her on the bed. I walked over and sat down beside her. "I put this together a couple of years ago." She opened the book, turning to the first page.

"Is that you?" I asked, pointing to the pretty teenage girl in the first picture.

"Um hum." She laughed. "I was something back then."

"How old were you?" I asked.

"Fifteen and I was a PYT." PYT stood for Pretty Young Thing. We both laughed as she turned the page. There was another picture of her, this time she was a little older, sitting on a park bench under a huge weeping willow. "I was seventeen here," she said.

"Was this in Alabama?" I asked, staring at the photo.

"Yep, before I hopped on a Greyhound and hightailed it to Baltimore."

"What made you leave?"

She smiled an angelic like smile before turning the page. "Mr. Ashad Remir," she said, stroking the faded picture. Ashad looked like he could have been Morris Chestnut's father. He was tall with beautiful chocolate skin and strong facial features. I could tell, even in the picture, that he had beautiful perfect white teeth. "Ashad was the finest man I had ever seen," she said sweetly. "We met at the mall, and I fell in love instantly. We had been going together for four months when he decided to move here. He had family here, and they wanted him to come help out with the family business."

"What kind of business?"

"Back in the day they owned a couple of laundry mats over on 54th Street. I wanted to be wherever Ashad was, so I packed my bags and left."

"What did Grandma say?"

"She raised hell!" she said, shaking her head. "She told me that I was too young to be running behind a man. But I wasn't even trying to hear her. I knew what I wanted, and that was Ashad. We got us a cute little one bedroom apartment." She continued. "Ashad was a good man, a hard worker. He treated me like a queen. He wanted to marry me."

"Why didn't you?"

"We were engaged," she sadly. "But he wanted to wait until he had enough money saved up to buy us our own house and to buy me a ring, but moving here did something to me."

"What?" I asked.

"I got caught up in the fast life," she said. "I saw all the women walking around with their diamonds and gold and their designer clothes. And I wanted the same thing. Then the men, there were so many ballers and big time hustlers hungry to get a taste of me, that they were throwing their money at me. I started stepping out on Ashad. I had men wining and dining me while he was hard at work. I had a nice little stack of cash I had accumulated. Plus all the gifts they were giving me."

"Didn't Ashad ask you about those things?"

"Yes, and I told him I had gotten a little housekeeping job, and that Mama was sending me all of the clothes and purses."

"How did he find out the truth?"

"One day we were walking home, when we ran into this dope dealer named Maurice that I had been spending time with, standing on the block with some of his flunkies. He started trippin', whistling at me and making all kinds of comments." She took a deep breath, exhaling through her nose. "Ashad was a peaceful man, but he wasn't a punk. He didn't start any shit, but he didn't take none either. I tried to get him to let it go, to just keep on walking, but he couldn't." Her voice went low, as tears began to surface in her eyes.

"He walked right up to Maurice and confronted him, told him not to disrespect his lady. Maurice just laughed. He called Ashad weak, told him he couldn't even take care of his own woman, told him he was a joke. Ashad looked Maurice in his eyes, and told him to stay away from me or he would regret it. The two of us started to walk off. That's when Maurice said, 'Ask your girl how good I be givin' it to her.' She looked at me with sadness in her eyes. "I'd never seen Ashad so hurt before," she said. "He rushed towards Maurice and knocked him to the ground. Ashad was beating Maurice like a madman. I knew Maurice's crew wouldn't stand by and just watch, but I had no idea…"

"What happened?" I asked, taking her hand in mine.

"They pulled Ashad off of Maurice. It was three against one. Ashad tried to fight back, but they just kept on hitting and stomping him until he stopped moving. He was bleeding from his nose and mouth. I thought he was just hurt." She squeezed my hand hard. "But he wasn't breathing. I was screaming and crying, begging for Ashad to get up, but he never did. They killed him, Tay, right there in front of me. I loved him. I promise you I did, but because of me and my mess he died."

"What happened to Maurice and his friends?" I asked.

"They got away with Ashad's murder. People were too scared to talk, including me. But they later got what was coming to them. A month later, Maurice was killed during a high speed chase with the police. The majority of his clique got sent off after a major drug bust. I presume the two that helped him beat Ashad to death were included." There was a moment of silence between the two of us.

"How did you meet Pete?" I asked.

She looked shocked that I had asked. I rubbed her hand gently, to let her know that I was okay talking about him.

"After Ashad was killed I was a wreck," she said sighing. "I held myself completely responsible. I went through this period of mourning, where I shut everyone out. I didn't want to deal with any men. But, at the same time, I didn't have Ashad around to support me either. I hadn't worked a day in my life. I had no job skills."

"What did you do?"

"I took a job at the old strip club on the Westside."

"You were a stripper?" I asked, with my eyes wide.

"No, I worked at the bar." She laughed. "But I could have been a dancer. I told you I was fine!" She turned the page, showing me a picture of herself in a body hugging denim jumper. Her hair was blown out in a beautiful Afro.

"I didn't mean it like that." I laughed. "I know you were fine."

"Okay then."

"So you started working at the bar and..."

"I was struggling, and then one night this handsome man with dark skin came in." She turned to the next page. It was a photo of her with Pete. "He reminded me so much of Ashad," she said seriously. "I don't know what it was, maybe it was the dark complexion."

"And the smiles," I suggested, seeing the resemblance.

"Yeah, and the smiles," she said. "Every night Pete would come in and sit down at the bar. He'd order a couple of drinks, and just hang out at the bar with me. The dancers would come by half naked, hanging all over him, but he wouldn't pay them no mind. He was completely focused on me. After a few weeks passed, he asked me out. At first, everything was all good between us. Pete was good to me. He had a couple of little bootleg houses that he ran numbers and held card games in. He'd take me around his spots, introduce me to his friends. Let me play on the house and keep my winnings.

"Pete was taking care of me, so I didn't have to work. I moved out of the apartment I once shared with Ashad and moved in with Pete. I thought I had finally found someone who loved me like Ashad. Pete was making good money. He opened up a few more underground spots and tripled his money. That's when his attitude slowly began to change. He became hard and impatient. He had a bad temper. It got to the point that he would push me around sometimes when we would argue."

I thought about my temper. I guess that's the one thing I inherited from Pete.

"I finally got fed up," she said. "I told him I was leaving."

"What did he say?"

"He told me to go," she said, looking at me. "So I did. I packed my things and I left. I got me another apartment, and decided to go back to school to get my nursing certification. A month passed before Pete showed up on my doorstep, apologizing and asking me to forgive him."

"And you did?" I asked.

"Yep, and he took me to Vegas to celebrate." She smiled. "Seven days later we came back, and things were once again good. That lasted about six months, before I realized that he was back to his old ways. Nothing had changed but my name."

I was completely confused by her statement. She turned to the next page in the album, and my bottom lip dropped.

"You two were married?" I asked, staring at the marriage certificate on one page, and the picture of the two of them on the other.

In the picture they were both smiling, standing in a small wedding chapel. Mama had on a plain white off the shoulder gown, and Pete wore a simple black tux and black gators.

"Yes," she said.

"For how long?"

"Thirty-two years."

"That means that the two of you were married up until..."

"He died," she said, cutting me off.

I tried to process all of the information. I had so many questions, I didn't know where to begin.

"I wanted to make it work because I loved Pete, and I thought he loved me, but he loved his money more. Then one night he came home at three in the morning with lipstick on his collar. I could deal with his hustlin', but I wasn't about to put up with him cheating on me. I confronted him, and we got into this big fight. I got in his face, and he pushed me so hard I fell through the glass table we had in our dining room. I had this big gash on my arm," she said. "I drove myself to the hospital. I ended up having to get thirty-six stitches, and that's when I found out I was pregnant with you. I was scared to death when I found out I was having a baby. I didn't know how to take care of myself, yet alone another human being. Then with the situation with Pete," she looked down at her hands then back at me, her eyes were clear and wide, "I knew that there was no way I could bring a baby into that situation," she said. "So I left him. I packed all my things and I found this place."

"Why didn't you have an abortion?"

"What?" she asked, looking insulted.

"Didn't it cross your mind?"

"I would be lying if I said that it never crossed my mind," she admitted. "I thought about it, but I was too selfish."

"What do you mean?" I asked.

"I wanted someone who would love me no matter what," she said. "I thought that no matter how I screwed up, you would be the one person who would always love me. So, I guess you could say I wanted you in this world for me."

"So you never told Pete that you were carrying his child?"

"I couldn't tell him," she said. "You were his only child, and he would have taken you from me. Pete was a very vindictive man, Tay. He was also very powerful. He had connections everywhere, from the Department of Transportation to the Federal Government. I kept my pregnancy a secret until I was in my last trimester. I didn't gain a lot of weight during my pregnancy, so it wasn't hard to conceal my secret."

She turned to the next couple of pages. The pictures were of her during her different stages of pregnancy. There was very little indication that she was pregnant. The only major change was that her nose had spread, and her face was fuller.

"When Pete did find out, I lied about my due date." She continued. "He assumed that you were another man's child. I never told him any different until after you were gone."

"What about all the money you owed him?" I asked. "Grandma said you had a gambling problem. She said when you were out 'doing your thang,' you were out gambling." She looked at me like I had lost my mind.

"When I was out doing my thang," she said, laughing a little, "I was doing what grown folks like to do." She looked at me with raised eyebrows.

"What do you mean?" I asked.

She took a deep breath before asking, "Did you ever see any men around here besides Pete?"

"No," I said.

"And when he came by he only stayed for a few minutes, right?" I nodded my head. "I know I was your mama, but I was still sexy, right?" I laughed.

"Right," I said.

"Well, when I was out, I was getting mine," she stated bluntly.

"Oh," I said, a little embarrassed. The thought of my mother getting her freak on made me uncomfortable. "But what about the money you owed Pete?"

"Like I said, Pete was very vindictive. He was also very proud. He hated to lose anything, including his women. The only money I can think of is the money he had given me when we were dating. Unless he was talking about the money he gave me for a wedding present."

"How much money did he give you?"

"All together about twenty thousand," she said. "But that was chump change to him."

"If it was chump change, then why did he come over that day looking for you?"

"A couple of days before he raped you, he had seen me out with a man I worked with," she said. "He came up and spoke, but he didn't make a scene or anything. That's why when I called home, and he asked for his money, I didn't think anything of it. He had mentioned a few times before about me paying him back for everything he had done for me, but that was usually when he was pissed off because I wouldn't agree to take him back. He never acted on any of his previous threats."

"So what he did to me was out of jealousy?" I concluded. "He wanted to hurt you, so he used me."

"Yes," she said softly. "And for that I am so sorry. I had no idea that he would do something to you. If I had, I would have killed him before he had the chance."

"I felt like you blamed me," I whispered. "I felt like you hated me."

She stroked my face gently with her hand. "I didn't blame you. I could never blame you. I was supposed to protect you. I didn't, and that was something I couldn't handle. When I sent you to Alabama, I thought that being with Mama would be so much better for you. I didn't want you to end up like me." There was an uncomfortable silence between the two of us.

"What did he say when you told him I was his daughter?" I asked.

"He started rambling on and on about me being a liar, and that he should have killed me when he had the chance," she said. "I told him to do what he had to do. He put a gun to my head and pulled the trigger, but the gun jammed. I walked away before he got the chance to try again. After that, I started re-evaluating my life and all that I had lost. I figured God allowed the gun to jam for a reason, and for that I was thankful."

The two of us sat on the bed looking at the rest of the album. We smiled and laughed at the pictures of the two of us together when I was a child. She told me more about Ashad, and the good times they shared. I asked her about Ashad's family, and how they handled his death. She explained that his parents had given her their forgiveness, but his sister, Henrietta, held her responsible and vowed that one day she would reap from the pain she had caused their family. I asked Mama when was the last time she saw her.

"Right after Ashad was killed," she said. "She came to collect Ashad's things, and that was the last I saw her."

I could understand Henrietta's pain, but at the same time, my mother had suffered enough. I realized that my mother was a victim herself. She had never met her father, and I think that played a huge role in her destructive relationships with men.

I told her about Kenny and the problems we had been having. I left out the part about him cheating on me. I think I was embarrassed to admit that he had cheated so many times, and that I was still with him. I also told her about Savoy.

"Do you love him?" my mother asked.

"I think I do," I said.

"Do you still love Kenny?"

"Yes."

"I can't tell you what to do," she said, "but I can tell you to make sure that what you're feeling for Savoy isn't based on what he has or what he can do for you."

The two of us spent the rest of the day getting reacquainted. There was so much Mama had missed out on in my life. There was so much I had missed out on in hers. We ordered Chinese for dinner, and sat in our pajamas watching *CSI* on TV. During the show I leaned over and kissed Mama on the cheek.

"What was that for?" she asked smiling.

"I love you, Mama," I said.

She had tears in her eyes, as she wrapped her arms around me. "I love you too, baby," she said.

CHAPTER 17

It was a beautiful August day, and to my surprise, Mama felt up to going out. The two of us had spent the majority of the last three weeks in the house, baking and playing board games because she had been so drained from her illness. I was ecstatic that she felt well enough to leave the house. The two of us had put our past behind us, and we had vowed to enjoy whatever time we had left together. I had even gone as far as to ask Mama to come home with me. When she happily accepted, I called and booked two one-way tickets back to Huntsville.

Kenny and I talked everyday, and I was starting to believe that this time things would change for the better. He was thrilled when I told him Mama was coming home with me. He even offered to pick us up from the airport when we arrived.

Savoy called me a few times, but each time, I intentionally sent him to voicemail. I missed him like crazy, but I wasn't one hundred percent sure that the feelings I had for him were genuine.

Mama had me drive her downtown to the law offices of John E. Waters. I sat outside in the waiting area, while she had a private meeting with her attorney. When she came out, I asked her what the meeting was about.

"Just taking care of some business before we leave," she said.

I figured whatever business she had to handle had something to do with her selling her house. She planned to put it on the market after she moved back to Alabama with me.

After we left the attorney's office we decided to go shopping. We went to the mall, where we had our pictures taken in one of those fifteen minute photo booths. Then we stopped by Zales, where Mama bought me a beautiful heart shaped diamond locket. The locket hung from an18-inch, 14 carat white gold chain. I almost passed out when the salesman told us the necklace cost $750.00. Mama, on the other hand, didn't even blink.

"We'll take it," she said.

"Mama, it's too much," I said, shaking my head.

"This is for the Birthdays, Christmases and Graduations I missed," she said.

"Mama, you don't have to make up for anything."

"I want to," she pleaded. "Please take it." I agreed.

Mama paid cash for the locket, then we had the salesman put one of the pictures of the two of us in it before I secured the chain around my neck.

The two of us had lunch at Ruby Tuesdays, and then went to the Museum of Arts. After walking around the museum for over an hour, we returned home so that Mama could get some rest. I helped her into her pajamas then tucked her into bed.

"I had a great time today," she said.

"Me too," I said, fluffing the pillows behind her back.

"You know what I want right now?"

"What's that?"

"A Frito pie."

"I'll go make us one," I said smiling.

"The cherry Kool-Aid is in the cabinet by the stove," she said, yawning.

"One Frito pie and two glasses of cherry Kool-Aid coming right up," I said, turning to walk away.

"Tay Tay," my mother called out.

"Ma'am."

"I love you."

"I love you too."

I called Octavia while I was preparing our snack, and she told me the cutest story about Jasmine's new habit of putting her toes in her mouth.

"She won't even suck her pacifier anymore," she said. "Every time I turn my back she spits it out, and instead she's sucking on her big toe."

"A lot of babies probably do that." I laughed.

"I asked Mama and she said I never did," she said, sounding paranoid. "Damon's mother said he didn't either. I thought at the most she would suck her thumb, but her toe." I laughed. "It's not funny, Tay."

I never imagined Octavia would turn into one of those paranoid mothers, but she was definitely trippin' now.

"What did her pediatrician say?" I asked.

"She told me she would grow out of it. She said that plenty of babies do it."

"I'm sure she's right."

"She better be," she said. "I can't have my baby going around being nicknamed toe jam."

"Look at it this way, the worst that can happen is that she'll grow up with a foot fetish," I said laughing.

"I don't want to even think about it."

"In the famous words of Juvenile, 'She get it from her Mama'."

"I don't do toes," she said. "But I warned Damon about that shit when I was pregnant."

"Oh, so she gets it from her Daddy." I giggled.

"Girl, yeah, and there's no telling what else she learned in the womb." We both laughed.

Before we hung up, I told her Mama was coming home with me, and that she was excited to meet all of them.

"I can't wait to meet her either," she said. "Jazz will have another Grandma."

"One more person to spoil her," I said.

"As if she's not spoiled enough," Octavia said.

"Take care, and I'll see you when we get there."

"I will. You do the same, and give Ms. Josie my love."

"Bye."

"Bye."

I walked up the hallway carrying the Frito pie and our two glasses of Kool-Aid on the wooden serving tray, giggling to myself. I walked into the bedroom and found Mama sleeping peacefully. I sat the tray down on the dresser, deciding our conversation about Jasmine would have to wait until after her nap. I couldn't help but smile as I looked at her. I knew she was sick, but she looked more beautiful than I could ever remember. She had a small smile on her face, and her skin had a shimmering glow. At that moment everything about my mother looked perfect.

I stared at the covers pulled up around her chest. They weren't moving. There was no rise and fall with every breath. I stood paralyzed by fear, as I realized that my mother was not breathing.

"Mama," I whispered. "Mama," I called, walking over to the side of the bed. I touched her face gently. Her skin was lukewarm. "Mama," I cried, easing down on the bed. "Mommy." She never answered.

I pressed my head against her chest, with tears streaming down my face. I listened for a heartbeat. I wanted to hear her heartbeat so badly. I needed to hear it, but I didn't. My mother was gone.

"I love you," I sobbed uncontrollably. I knew in my heart that she was gone to a far better place, a place where her heartaches and pain would be no more. I knew all of this, but I wanted to be selfish. I wanted her to stay in this world for me. I didn't want to let her go.

CHAPTER 18

Before she died, Mama requested that her remains be cremated. I honored her wish and brought her ashes back home with me. I planned to eventually have a memorial service, during which I would spread her ashes, but I had yet to set a date. In the meantime, her ashes would remain in a ceramic urn on the top shelf in the glass curio in my living room. As silly as it may sound, it felt like I would have her with me just a little while longer.

I had gotten my mother back, only to lose her. I was happy for the time we had together, but it was too short. In the back of my mind, I kept thinking about what could have been done differently. If I had been there for her sooner, maybe I could have encouraged her to get the proper treatment before things took a turn for the worst. The thing that really bothered me the most was that Mama said she tried to get in contact with me. I couldn't understand why she would lie to me about the letters and the phone calls, then later open up about everything else. I tried hard not to dwell on it, but I couldn't shake the feeling that something wasn't right.

I slipped on my plush house shoes, and walked into the living room to do some cleaning. The house was practically spotless thanks to Kenny, but I needed something to distract me from the question that was troubling my mind. Kenny had done an excellent job of taking care of our home while I was gone. He even stocked up the refrigerator, so I wouldn't have to worry about grocery shopping when I returned home. He was doing everything he could to show me that he was trying to make our marriage work. He was being more loving and supportive than I had ever known him to be. He held me whenever I had one of my crying spells, which was often. And he tried his best to get me to open up about my conversation with my mother. I told him that I would talk to him when I was ready, but for right now, I just needed time to deal with my emotions.

After I vacuumed the living room, dusted and polished every piece of furniture, I decided to check out Kiya's room, to make sure everything was in order. Her daybed was made up with the covers neatly in place but, as usual, there were toys scattered across the floor. I picked up the dolls and games until both my arms were full, then attempted to open the top of the toy chest with my foot. I ended up kicking the lid so hard the chest flipped over.

"Damnit!" I screamed, dropping the toys.

I dropped to my knees then pulled the chest upright. I started dropping the toys in one by one, when I noticed that the bottom of the chest looked warped. I felt along the bottom of the chest, thinking that Kiya may have poured juice or water in the bottom and gotten it wet. The wood was dry, but it was pulling away from the side panels. Kenny made the chest for Kiya when she was a baby, so it was no surprise that it was coming apart. Kenny was not the craftiest of men.

I took the few dolls that I had put in back out, and turned the chest on its side. I felt around the bottom to see if I could possibly glue it back together. The wood shifted to the left, revealing a piece of plastic. I pulled on the plastic, but I wasn't able to get it out. I got up and went to the hall closet to retrieve a screwdriver.

When I returned to Kiya's room I sat on the floor, pressing the screwdriver in between the pieces of wood. After a minor struggle, I was able to pop the loose piece out. The piece of plastic was actually a sealed Ziploc bag with envelopes in it. I knew that whatever was in the bag had been hid intentionally. Why else would Kenny have made a makeshift secret compartment? I knocked the dust from the bag then opened it. I removed the five envelopes from the bag, and turned them over. My heart beat so hard I thought it was going to jump out of my chest. I shuffled through the open envelopes; all of them were addressed to me. I looked inside each envelope, and the letters were still there. I wanted to scream.

I called once. I left a message then, after that, I called again, and my number had been blocked. My mother's words echoed through my head.

I put the chest back like I found it, minus my letters, then piled all of Kiya's toys inside. I grabbed the screwdriver and the bag, and ran into my bedroom with my letters tucked under my arm. I dropped everything on the bed, and grabbed the cordless phone off the nightstand. As soon as I heard the dial tone, I pressed #33.

"To block a number press 1," the automated recording said. "To unblock a number previously added press 2." I pressed 2. "You have one number on your list, to hear this number press 4."

I pressed 4. "The number is area code 410-555-9999. Again, the number is area code 410-555-9999." I pressed end.

Mama had been telling the truth. She had written me and had called. I tried hard to calm the rage that was building inside of me. I started dialing Kenny's cell number. I wanted to scream and curse, and ask him who gave him the fucking right to screen my calls and my mail. I stared at the letters on the bed, and hung up the phone. Kenny would have to wait. I was going to confront him, but first I needed to read my mother's letters.

April 17, 2000

Shontay,

I hope this letter reached you and finds you doing well. I know I'm probably the last person you want to hear from, and I can truly say I understand. Baby, if I could undo everything that has happened, I would. I can't, but I can try and save whatever chance or hope the two of us may have in the future. I know you probably think I sent you away because I hated you, but that's not the case. I love you so much! I just couldn't stand the coldness I saw in your eyes whenever you looked at me. Tay, you were the best thing that ever happened to me. I hate myself for hurting you. I hate Pete too. When I confronted him about what he did to you, he held a gun to my head and pulled the trigger. There are times that I think about what I allowed him to do to you, and I wish that the gun hadn't jammed. I know there is a reason God allowed me to live. I know one of them was so that I could try and make things right with you. I promise, if it's the last thing I do, I will somehow, someway make things right.

I love you,

Josephine Allen (Your Mom)

I read the next three letters, with tears rolling down my face. Mama apologized for everything she thought she did wrong. In each of them she begged for me to write her back. I clutched them to my breasts, as sadness and regret coursed through my body. I pulled the final letter from its envelope, and gently unfolded the page. The phone rang, interrupting my thoughts. I started to ignore it, but then decided to answer in case it was Kenny. I had words for him that would make a sailor blush.

"Hello," I said.

"Yes, is Ms. Allen in?" a voice asked.

"Who?"

"I'm looking for Ms. Shontay Allen."

"Who is this?" I asked frustrated.

"Are you Ms. Allen?" the voice asked.

"No, I mean I am, but its Holloway now," I rambled. "I'm Shontay Allen Holloway."

"Please excuse the error," the man said, on the other end. "Your mother didn't mention you had gotten married."

"How do you know my mother?" I asked the man.

"Mrs. Holloway, my name is John Waters." I tried to remember where I had heard that name. "I am…I was your mother's attorney." I had already forgotten taking Mama by the man's office. "Did I catch you at a bad time?" I assumed he was calling about my mother's house. I wasn't in the mood to discuss business.

"Actually you did," I said, clearing my throat.

"I apologize."

"It's okay," I said, trying to be cordial.

"When would be a good time for us to meet about your mother's will?"

"Mr. Waters, the only thing my mother had was that house, and I don't want it."

"She figured you would feel that way," he said. "So she gave me complete instructions on how to handle the selling of her home."

"Then everything should be settled," I said.

"Not exactly," he said abruptly. "There are some other things we need to discuss."

"Like what?"

"Mrs. Holloway, I'd rather not go into the details over the…"

"If this is about your fee, just send me a bill." I cut him off. I wanted to end our conversation as quickly as possible.

"Your mother paid me in advance."

"Then what else is there?" He was starting to piss me off.

"Please understand, for security purposes, I can't discuss this over the phone," he pleaded. "I'll be in your city next week, and would be happy to meet with you then."

"Fine." I exhaled.

"Thank you," he said, sounding relieved. "Is Monday good for you?"

"Monday is fine," I said, thinking the sooner the better.

The two of us agreed to meet in the lounge of the Hilton Hotel, where he was going to be staying. I didn't give much thought into what the man had said. Mama had not mentioned anything about having a will. She had no money. She probably spent her life savings on the locket hanging around my neck. I quickly dismissed the conversation I just had with John Waters, and went back to my mother's last letter.

January 1, 2002

Happy New Year, Baby!

Today is the start of a new year, and I hope to spend this year with you. If I don't get the chance, I just want you to know I love you. I hope you're spending this day with someone special. I also hope all of your dreams and wishes for this year come true. Now, I'm going to go cook me some black eye peas, bake me a ham, and pray that this lotto ticket brings me some luck. I only spent a dollar on it, but if I win, the two of us will be rich. It doesn't hurt to try! I hope to talk to you soon.

I love you,

Josephine (Your Mom)

I hid all my letters in a shoe box in the bottom of my closet, took a quick shower, and put on my gray sleeveless knit Tommy Girl dress. There was a time when the dress hugged my body, but since I had dropped twenty pounds over the last month, it hung loosely on my body. I vowed to go shopping later to get me some more clothes, but for today, the dress would have to do. I slipped my feet in a pair of open toe sandals, grabbed my purse and cell phone, and ran out the door.

"Why would he hide the letters from me? Why would he delete

her message and block her phone calls?" I asked Octavia.

Octavia sat behind her desk with a look of utter confusion on her face. Her expression had been the same when I told her about how I found the letters, and how I checked to see if Kenny had blocked my mother's number.

"I don't know, Tay," she said.

"It doesn't make any sense," I said, shaking my head. "None whatsoever."

"Maybe he thought he was protecting you," she said. "He knew about everything that you went through, maybe he thought your mom would cause you more pain."

"He should have given me a chance to make my own decision."

"I agree."

"What I don't understand is why he kept them if he knew he never planned on giving them to me?"

"Was there anything in the letters that would give him the wrong impression about your mom's intentions?"

I shook my head. "No," I said, "nothing."

Octavia shook her head. "The only way you'll know is to ask him about it."

"Something is not adding up," I said, running my fingers through my braids.

Octavia frowned, and leaned forward in her chair. "Maybe you should hint that your mom said she wrote you, just to see what he says, but don't mention that you found the letters."

"Why?" I asked confused.

"If Kenny hid the letters just to protect you, he should have no problem with admitting he got them. If he doesn't..."

"Then he's hiding something," I said, finishing her sentence.

"Exactly," she said.

"I'll do that tonight," I said, relaxing in my chair. "For his sake he better have the right answer."

Kenny and I were getting ready for bed when I brought up my conversation with Mama.

"Mama said something while I was at the hospital with her," I said, turning the sheets back.

"What did she say?" He stood on the other side of the bed looking nervous.

First mistake.

"She claimed she wrote me a few times," I said, getting into bed. "I told her I never got any letters." He sat down on the side of the bed, looking at me. "Do you think she tried and maybe had the wrong address?" I asked, staring at him.

"I hate to say this but," he said, lowering his eyes, "I think she was just lying, trying to smooth over the situation."

Second mistake.

"We both know she never tried to contact you," he said softly. "As bad as it sounds, I think she just wanted to make herself look good."

I wanted to scream that he was the liar, but I kept my cool. "I know," I said softly. "I was just hoping."

He smiled and stretched out next to me. "It's over now," he said, wrapping his arms around me. "You're home and now we can move on."

"Yeah," I said, closing my eyes, "it's over." Little did he know I was referring to our marriage.

Chapter 19

John Waters was tall, with gray hair and ocean blue eyes. He was incredibly sexy for an older man. The first thing I noticed about him when I walked into the lounge was his striking resemblance to Sean Connery. We introduced ourselves, then I gave him the once over with my eyes. He was wearing a pinstripe Armani suit, a dark silk shirt with diamond cufflinks. On his right hand, he wore a diamond three row band on his index finger. On his left wrist was a gold diamond Rolex. I wondered where Mama got the money from to pay him.

"I'm glad you came," he said smiling.

"You seemed adamant," I said.

"I ensured Josephine that I would make sure you were taken care of," he said, clasping his hands together. "I'm a man of my word."

"Taken care of how?" I asked.

"Financially, of course," he said.

"Financially?" I asked, full of confusion.

He looked at me, raised his eyebrows, and pulled a large folder out of his leather briefcase. "If you didn't look so much like your mother, I'd think you were an imposter."

"You are confusing me," I said, staring into his eyes.

He rubbed his hands across his well trimmed goatee. "Mrs.

Holloway…"

"Call me Shontay."

"Shontay, didn't you and your mother discuss her money?"

"No," I said, studying his expression. "My mother didn't have any money. I'm sure she died broke paying for this." I touched the locket around my neck.

"That couldn't have cost more than six or seven hundred," he said, looking at my neck.

"$769.75, to be exact," I said.

He laughed then shook his head. I looked at him like he had lost his mind.

"Josephine was far from broke," he said, opening the folder. "In fact, your mother died a rich woman." He pulled out a large document and slid it across the table to me. "Now that she has passed on, you are a rich woman."

"How rich?" I asked.

"20.5 million dollars."

I grabbed onto the table to keep from falling out of my chair. I looked at him waiting for him to say "April's Fools", although it was the end of August. I thought maybe John Waters had a delayed sense of humor. A sick one, but delayed. He looked dead serious.

"Wha…how…how is that possible?" I stuttered

"She won the lottery three years ago," he said, cocking his head to one side. "The jackpot."

I thought about the last letter I read, the one in which she mentioned the lotto ticket. I was speechless. I looked at the document in front of me. I quickly scanned over all the legal mumbo jumbo, until I got to the part that stated I was inheriting 20.5 million dollars.

"I have your first installment check here with me," he said, pushing the check across the table to me. "Your mother originally planned not to have your installments start for another two years, but after the two of you made amends, she decided she wanted you to start receiving your payments immediately. $250,000 now, then $35,000 a month."

I stared at the check like it was poisonous. I was afraid it might evaporate into thin air. Through my trance, I could feel John's eyes on me. I looked up to see him shaking his head.

"I'm sorry," I said, looking from him to the check. "I'm just overwhelmed right now."

"Shontay, may I ask you something?"

"Sure."

"You said you had no idea about the money, but your mother wrote..."

"She did," I said, cutting him off. "But I didn't get her letters. I mean they were delivered, but I didn't know anything about them until a couple days ago."

"Now you're confusing me," he said, frowning at me.

I took a deep breath, and then explained how I had found the letters, and that my husband had hid them from me.

"I didn't know about the letters you're referring to," he said. "The letter in question is the one that she had me send by certified mail to your home."

"I never received it," I said.

"You didn't but someone did," he said firmly. "The letter was signed for."

"What was in the letter?"

"I didn't read it because she said it was personal," he said. "But I sent it off myself. One thing is certain," he said, "I know your mother mentioned her winnings in that letter."

"So he knows about the money." I said, crossing my arms across my chest.

"That's not the only thing."

"What?"

"Against my better judgment your mother sent you a gift."

"What gift?"

"$75,000," he said.

I grabbed my head with both hands and closed my eyes. "Was the check cashed?" I asked, not looking at him.

"It was a cashier's check, but I can have it traced," he said. "I can also find out who signed for the letter."

"I already know who signed for it," I said confidently. I put both hands on the table and opened my eyes. "My future ex-husband."

"So the two of you are getting a divorce?" he asked.

"I plan to file for divorce as soon as possible."

John put his elbows up on the table. "I'm going to give you some free advice," he said.

"I'm listening."

"You've heard the saying, 'It's cheaper to keep her'?"

"Yeah, but what does that have to do with me?"

"In your case it may be cheaper to keep him."

"I don't want him!"

"Then you better get ready for a fight," he said. "Because if your husband was slick enough to keep you from communicating with your mother, I'm willing to bet he'll sue for half of your money."

They always say that which does not kill you, only makes you stronger. I was using that as my motivation to keep my front with Kenny going. I had managed to keep my game face, despite knowing that he had been playing me.

***

John called my cell two days after our original meeting, and informed me that the letter Mama sent me was signed for by Kenny. I already knew that in my heart. What threw me off is when he said that the check my mother sent had been endorsed by me. I knew my signature had been forged. John offered to start an all out criminal investigation. I told him thanks, but that I planned to handle it my way. However, I did request a copy of the cancelled check. I wanted to know if Kenny had forged my signature or if he had help. If he did have an accomplice, my number one suspect was his baby's mama.

After my conversation with John, I went to the post office and rented a post office box. I also went by the bank and opened me a new savings and checking account. I closed my old accounts and transferred all of my funds. I called John back and told him to send any paper documents to my P.O. Box, gave him my new checking information, and told him if he needed to speak with me to hit me up on my cell. I also gave him Octavia's name, number, and address for a second point of contact, just in case something happened to me. I figured if Kenny was snake enough to steal my money, he might be brave enough to try and take my life. If he did he wouldn't get shit, because immediately after my phone call with John, I called an attorney he recommended, set up a meeting that day and made myself a living will. I left everything to my goddaughter in care of Octavia. I didn't think that Kenny would try to kill me, but you never know. After all, he did get me for seventy-five grand.

CHAPTER 20

I waited for Kenny to leave for work before ripping the house apart, looking for some clue as to what he did with my money. I didn't find one clue. I even called the bank and checked his personal checking account, thinking he might have gotten sloppy and deposited the money there. I lost all hope when the automated information informed me his balance was ten dollars and fifty-six cents. I decided to search Kenny's car later that night, but for now I was going to let it go.

I had been so wrapped up in finding my money that I hadn't taken the time to spend any of the money John had handed over to me. I was going shopping.

I walked through the mall carrying an armful of bags. I had everything from New York and Company to Victoria's Secret to Dillards. The worst part about living in Huntsville was that I had to go out of town to hit up any of the major top name stores. I planned to do exactly that as soon as I got the chance. For the first time in my life I was going to hop a flight just to go shopping. I wanted to hit up Rodeo Drive, then hop another plane to hit Fifth Avenue. Thanks to my mother, I would be doing all the things I always wanted to do. Octavia and I had already made plans to fly to New York for our next "girl's day out".

I was headed towards the mall exit when I saw something in the Crown Jewelers window that caught my eye. I strolled over to the store window to admire the beautiful his and hers platinum and diamond Rolex watches. They sparkled under the fluorescent light. I walked into the store, and without a second thought, bought both of the watches. I asked the salesgirl to have the men's watch gift wrapped for me. Five minutes later, I loaded my packages in the trunk of my car and left the mall.

I walked across the plastic covered floors, trying my hardest not to get my 3-inch heels caught. The last thing I wanted to do was fall on my face in front of the group of workers staring me down in my knee length spaghetti strap silk dress. They were drilling and banging hammers while watching me. Their smiles and bug eyes told me that I looked as good as I felt. I scanned over the men, finally asking one of them for Savoy. He told me he was outside in the onsite trailer. I exited out of one of the side doors and headed for the small metal building.

"Come in," a voice said from inside.

I stepped into the building, pulling the door closed behind me. Savoy sat at a small metal desk with his back facing me, looking over a set of blueprints.

"Hi," I said.

He turned around slow and easy, like he had heard the voice of a ghost. He looked at me and smiled. His eyes were glowing.

"Shontay," he said.

I didn't realize how much I missed hearing him say my name until that second. My eyes scanned from his face to his hair, then down to his lips. Everything about him was beautiful. He stood up and walked around the desk in front of me.

"How are you?" he asked.

"I'm fine," I said, tightening my grip on the gift bag in my hand. I needed to hold on to something, otherwise I was going to have my hands all over him.

"I'm sorry to hear about your mother," he said, leaning on the edge of the desk. "I wanted to be there for you."

"Thank you," I said, embarrassed that I had left him hanging.

"I had a lot to work through. I still have a lot to work through."

"I understand," he said.

"You look great," he said, looking from my head down to my open toe shoes.

"So do you."

There was a pregnant pause between the two of us. I shifted the small bag from one hand to the other, then remembered why I had brought it.

"I just wanted to bring you something," I said, handing him the bag.

"What is it?" he asked.

"Open it and see." I watched him as he removed the wrapped box from the bag, and tore off the shiny paper and ribbon. When he finally flipped open the box his jaw dropped.

"Baby, this is banging!" he exclaimed.

I smiled because, even though he probably had several Rolex watches, he looked liked he had never seen one before.

"You like it?" I asked.

"I love it!" He smiled, while securing the links around his wrist. "This had to cost a fortune," he said, looking at me. "How did..."

"It's a gift," I said, cutting him off. "One that I can afford."

"Thank you, baby," he said.

He leaned in to kiss my cheek, but I turned my head so that his lips were on mine. From that moment the heat was on. I tried to touch his throat with my tongue, as he pulled me in his arms and started caressing my arms and back.

"I missed you so much," I moaned.

"I missed you too."

"I love you," I said.

He pulled away, searching my eyes with his. He looked confused, but relieved at the same time.

"I love you, Savoy," I said again.

"I love you too." He smiled, stroking my cheek with his fingertips. "I love you too."

I kissed him again, this time with enough heat to start a fire. He slid his hands up underneath my dress, grabbing the g-string I had on. Savoy ripped the silk material from my body, like it was a plastic wrapper and I was the chocolate candy inside. He lifted me up on the desk, pushing the blueprints to the floor. I grabbed at his belt, struggling to pry it open. I was soaking wet, and I needed to feel him inside of me.

He pushed my hands away and dropped to his knees. He spread my lips then dove into my pussy tongue first. I fell back against the cold metal, with my head hanging over the edge of the desk. My body trembled as Savoy licked and sucked my clit, pushing his tongue in and out of my wetness. I came quickly, my body shaking like I had an earthquake coursing inside of me.

Savoy stood and dropped his pants and boxers, leaving only the silk shirt and tie he was wearing on. He entered me so hard I almost flipped off the desk. I wrapped my legs around his waist, trying to pull his entire body inside of me. He kissed my lips, neck, ear lobes, and even my eyebrows as he pounded inside of me.

"Shon," he moaned, his body tensing up.

I moved my hips faster, clinching his dick with the walls of my vagina. He wrapped his arms around my shoulders then stood up, with my legs wrapped tightly around his waist. I felt light as a feather as I came again.

"Savoy!" I screamed his name, with tears rolling down my cheeks.

"I love you, Shon," he moaned, busting inside of me.

He eased me down onto the desk, kissing my tears away. In between my legs I was wet and sticky, but I didn't care. I didn't care about the $400.00 dress I was wearing that probably had cum stains all over it. I didn't care that the men working outside probably heard me screaming at the top of my lungs. I was with Savoy and I loved him.

After the two of us tried to clean ourselves with the pack of wet wipes Savoy had inside his desk, we then picked up all of his paperwork. He sat in the leather office chair, with me sitting on his lap.

"The restaurant looks great," I said, my head lying on his chest. "I can't wait to see it when you finish."

"You'll be able to in another month."

"Then you'll be leaving?" I asked sadly.

"After the grand opening," he said, rubbing my back gently, "I'll be going back to Atlanta, unless I have a reason to stay longer."

I looked into his eyes, and they told me he was waiting for my response.

"You don't have to stay," I said. "Go back to Atlanta like you planned."

"Alright," he said, a look of disappointment etched on his face. I wrapped my arms around his neck, and kissed his lips softly.

"I have some things I have to handle here," I said, staring into his sexy eyes. "But when I'm done, I'm coming to you."

***

I waited for Kenny to start snoring before slipping out of bed, wearing nothing but a silk chemise that stopped just above my knees. I slipped on my fuzzy slippers, grabbed his keys off the coffee table in the living room, and went outside to check Kenny's car. I searched the inside of the car first, starting with the front seats, then moving to the back. I checked in between the seats, under the seats, and the compartments behind the seats. I found nothing. I unlocked the dashboard and pulled it open.

The first thing I spotted was an open box of condoms. I didn't care if Kenny was fucking around anymore, the two of us hadn't had sex since I had returned from Baltimore, and in my eyes our marriage was a done deal, but I was still curious. I opened the box to see what was inside. The box was a three condom box, but there was only one condom inside. I tossed the box on the seat, and pulled all the papers inside the compartment out. I went through every piece of paper and came up with nothing. I put everything back in the compartment like I found it, and locked the dashboard. I was ready to give up, when I remembered I hadn't checked the trunk.

I hit the latch to pop open the trunk, and ran around to the back of the car. There was a black nylon gym bag in the corner. I pulled the bag out and unzipped it. There was a pair of jeans, a T-shirt, boxers, socks and tennis shoes inside. I pushed them out the way, and that's when I found what I was looking for. Kenny had several bank statements stashed under the clothes. Each of them had his name on them, but they had his mother's address. I looked over them until I found the most recent one. It was dated August 18, 2005, just two weeks ago. The ending balance was $50,489.32. I folded the statement and tucked it inside the waistband of my boy-cut panties. I had what I needed. I shut the trunk gently and ran back inside.

Kenny was still sleeping. I hid the statement in the bottom of my purse, kicked off my slippers, and climbed back into bed. I looked over at Kenny snoring, with a hint of slob dripping from the corner of his mouth. I wanted to slap his ass out of his sleep. I fought my urge and whispered, "Sweet dreams." He was going to need them, because when I got finished with him, he was going to think he was living a nightmare.

CHAPTER 21

Janet Milo was the lawyer John hooked me up with to handle my will. She was also the one I planned to use to handle my divorce. I had a feeling that Janet did not have a problem playing dirty. She was exactly who I needed on my team. I called her as soon as her office opened that morning, and arranged a meeting to start the divorce.

Two hours later I sat in her office, telling her about the letters and the one I was unable to locate. I told her that it was no coincidence, that after six years of dating, Kenny finally proposed the year he found out I would some day become a millionaire.

"If he married you just for your money then you're going to have to play it cool," she said. "Don't give him any evidence that can prove you're the bad guy in this marriage. The truth is it's more likely that the judge will award him alimony because he makes less money than you." I rolled my eyes and exhaled. "But if you can prove that he's unfaithful, then that will be another story."

Proving Kenny was cheating should not have been that hard, but the only problem was that he had been at his best since I returned home. He was sweating my ass, all up under me and wanting to go everywhere I went. The only time he left me was when he went to work. He didn't even go to Alicia's to pick up Kiya anymore. Alicia had to drop her off and pick her up at our place, and when she did, he made sure I was right there. Even his mama had to come to our house if she wanted to see him.

"I don't want to give you any reason to believe that I'm not for real about our marriage," he said, when I suggested he go out and spend some time with his boys. "I told you, I'll do anything to prove to you I want this marriage to work."

It was a load of shit, but he was sticking to it. I explained all of that to Janet during our meeting.

"He's good," she said. "But sooner or later he's bound to slip up. But until he does, you better make sure you don't." I stared at the thin blond haired woman like she was crazy.

"What do you mean?" I asked her.

"If he catches you cheating first, then you're likely to end up taking care of him for the rest of his life." The look on my face must have made her suspicious. "Do you have anything you need to tell me?" she asked.

"No," I lied, staring into her green eyes. "Nothing."

She studied my face before responding. "Listen, I'm a woman who knows what it's like to be married to a scum bag," she said. "My first ex-husband got me for eighty-five grand because I slipped up and shared one night with an old boyfriend. The funny thing is my husband had been cheating for years." She laughed, and shook her head. "But because I was the breadwinner, and he had physical evidence, the judge awarded him a sweet little settlement."

"Damn," was all I could say.

"The bottom line is," she said, leaning forward in her chair, "fuck him before he fucks you."

Janet's words rang through my head while I sat in the Bank of the South three hours later, withdrawing every dime from the savings account Kenny had set up behind my back. At first I thought the task was going to be difficult, but it turned out to be a lot easier than I anticipated.

When I called the bank that morning before my meeting with Janet, I was informed that I would not be able to receive any information due to my not being authorized on the account. I had no clue of how I was going to get Kenny to add me to his account, so I took a wild chance. I went by his job and gave an Oscar worthy performance. I told him that my mother had left me some money in her will, and that my bank would not let me deposit all of the money in one account.

"I figured since the two of us are going to be together forever that I could have them deposit some of the cash in your account," I said sweetly. "But I need you to go by the bank and tell them that I have permission to be added to your account." I could see the dollar signs in his eyes while I was speaking.

"Sure, baby," he said smiling. "I'll go on my lunch break." That's exactly what he did.

While I was meeting with Janet, he was at the bank signing a statement that gave me permission to access any of his account information and available funds. I knew there was a chance he could have only granted permission for me to have access to his checking account, but I was hoping he would slip up and grant permission for all, which he did. I figured he was too busy thinking about how much more of my money he would have access to, that he had forgotten about the money he already had.

I thanked the bank manager, David, for his help, stuck my cashier's check in my coach bag, and then left the bank smiling. I drove across town to my bank and deposited all but forty-five thousand into my account. I then stopped by the Lexus dealership, and dropped thirty-nine on a 2007 GX coupe.

The color I selected looked like a cross between candy apple red and burgundy, so my car had to be specially ordered. The salesman told me my car should be in, in two to three weeks. I told him I wanted it fully loaded with chrome twenty-inch rims, leather interior, a moon roof, navigation system, and a Bose sound system. The salesman looked like he wanted to faint when I told him that I didn't need to apply for financing, and that I would be paying with cash. I signed the paperwork, paid him, and told him to call me as soon as my car arrived.

I met Octavia at her office so that I could use her computer to create a couple of fake bank statements and two other documents I planned to use. I had to make Kenny think that money was being deposited into his account. Octavia and I scanned the statement I had taken from Kenny's gym bag then, pasted and copied the bank logo, routing number and account number onto a blank office document. After adding color, fake transaction dates, and balance information, we printed the fake statements. The statements were for back up, just in case the plan I had come up with didn't work and I needed some extra time.

"Are you sure you want to do this?" Octavia asked, when I told her what I planned to do.

"I'm positive," I said firmly. "I can't let Kenny get away with this."

"I'm not saying you should," she said, leaning back in her chair. "But are you sure you want to include *her* in your plan?"

"What other choice do I have?" I asked. "Do you want to do it?" Octavia looked like she wanted to gag from the mere mention of her participating.

"Hell naw," she said, turning her nose up. "You know I can't stand Kenny's ass long enough to be in the same room with him. I just want to know how you know you can trust this chick."

"I can't," I admitted, "but I'm counting on one thing."

"What's that?"

"That she's a gold digger."

"What if she already knows about the money, and she actually loves Kenny?"

"Then I'll have to come up with another plan," I said, hoping that I wouldn't have to change my scheme. "But right now, I'm going to take my chances."

"So, have you thought about what you're going to do once you're free from Kenny?"

"Be happy," I said, thinking of Savoy. "Get away for awhile." I smiled, while picturing the two of us traveling the world and making love in all kinds of exotic places.

"You're thinking about that man!" Octavia said, smiling at me. She knew me too well.

"I am not." I lied, blushing.

"Um huh," she said, sucking her teeth. "You have that look."

"What look?" I asked.

"That I'm in love look."

I thought for a moment. "You know the difference between Savoy and Kenny?" I asked.

"Yeah, Savoy is successful, rich, sexy, loving, and kind. And Kenny," she said, tapping her fingers on the desk, "well, Kenny is the exact opposite of all of the above." She was right, but that wasn't what I was looking for.

"True, but the difference for me is that I love Kenny," I said. Octavia looked like she wanted to reach across the desk and knock me out of the chair I was sitting in. "But," I said quickly, "I'm *in* love with Savoy."

"You love Kenny, but you're not *in love* with him?" she asked.

"I don't think I was ever *in love* with him," I admitted. "I think I was just content. But with Savoy, I feel complete."

"Wow!" she said, looking blown away by my response.

"Does that make any sense?"

"It does," she said smiling. "It makes a whole lot of sense."

CHAPTER 22

I took a deep breath in through my nose then knocked on Alicia's door. I didn't call her before I came, because I felt my chances were better face to face. She opened the door wearing a cut off tank top, and a pair of denim shorts that were so short and tight I could tell she wasn't wearing any panties. She had her traditional ghetto fabulous platinum blond hair color, only this time her hair was up in a curly ponytail.

"What's up?" she asked, standing with her hand on her hip.

"Can I come in?" I asked, trying my best to be cordial.

"For what?" she asked, looking at me from my head down to my toes.

"I need to talk to you about something."

"Who is it?" a female yelled from inside the apartment.

"Kenny's wife," Alicia said, never taking her eyes off me.

"What the hell that bitch want?" the female asked.

Bitch? I wanted to snap, but thought twice about it. I knew I was outnumbered, and the last thing I wanted was to get jumped. I could handle my own one on one, but two on one, well that's another story.

"Look, Kenny ain't here," Alicia said, crossing her arms across her breasts.

"I'm not looking for Kenny," I said. "I came to talk to you."

"About what?"

"Money," I said.

Alicia's eyes lit up like fireworks on a summer's night. "Come in," she said, stepping back to let me into her home.

The other female sat on the couch wearing a short denim dress that buttoned down the front. The first sets of buttons were open, revealing the curve of her small breasts. She was pretty in the face, with light brown eyes and high cheekbones. Unlike her friend, she had low cut hair that was texturized with light brown highlights. She looked the total opposite of how I expected one of Alicia's friends to look, but I knew they had at least their hood attitude in common. She gave me the once over with her eyes, then pulled a rolled blunt from in between the sofa cushions, picked up the lighter laying on the table in front of her, and lit the blunt up.

"Sit down," Alicia said, pointing to the chair across from the sofa.

"Thanks," I said.

Her living room was decorated with traditional style furniture and wood accents. On her walls were beautiful pieces of African American Art. She closed the door, and sat down on the couch next to her friend. Her friend took two pulls from the blunt, and then passed it to Alicia. Alicia took two long pulls and passed it back.

"This is my girl, Donna," Alicia said, taking another pull of the blunt. "Anything you got to say to me you can say in front of my girl. So what money you talking about?"

I looked from Alicia to her friend then back to Alicia. I was taking a huge risk coming to Alicia in the first place, but I knew it was an even bigger risk talking in front of a stranger.

"Maybe I should come back," I said, pulling the straps of my purse back up on my shoulder.

"It's now or never," Alicia said, with straight attitude. "If you don't want to talk now, then don't come back. Fuck it!"

"Alright," I said, crossing my legs. "I want to know what you did with my money."

"What is she talking about?" Donna asked, looking at Alicia.

"The hell if I know," Alicia said, cutting her eyes at me.

"You know what money I'm talking about!" I said, faking attitude. "My twenty thousand dollars!"

"Whatever you smoking, I want some." Alicia laughed. "You must be on some real good shit, because you are really trippin'!" Donna laughed along with her. "If I had twenty grand, I wouldn't be living here," Alicia said, taking another pull, and then letting out a light cough.

"Look Alicia," I said, raising my voice, "I know you're still fucking Kenny. I also know he split my twenty thousand dollar inheritance with you." I pulled one of the documents Octavia and I had drawn up on her computer out of my purse. "Kenny admitted that you were his accomplice," I lied, handing her the paper. "He gave a sworn statement to my lawyer."

Alicia snatched the documents from my hand. I watched as the two of them looked over the forged statements that I had personally notarized. I knew one day being a notary public would finally come in handy, I just never thought it would be for some illegal shit. Donna threw what was left of the blunt into the ashtray on the coffee table then jumped up. I stood up ready to throw blows.

"You been holding out on me!" Donna screamed, standing in front of Alicia.

"Calm down, baby," Alicia stuttered, still studying the document.

Baby? I looked from one woman to the other.

"Calm down my ass!" Donna yelled.

"He's lying!" Alicia said, throwing the papers down on the table.

"Why would he lie, huh?" Donna asked her. "You plan on leaving me for him?" My eyes got big as fifty cent pieces. I had started a lover's quarrel.

"No!" Alicia whined. For the first time since I first met her she appeared insecure. All of her ghetto arrogance was gone.

"Then you better start talking!" Donna ordered.

"I don't know anything about her money!" Alicia said, staring at me.

"Well, why did Kenny sign a confession under oath?" I asked, crossing my arms across my breasts. I looked at Donna. She looked like she was ready to pull the weave out of Alicia's head. I was wrong for lying, but I loved watching Alicia sweat. "He sold you out," I said, shaking my head dramatically.

"Hold the fuck up," Alicia said standing up, stepping back from Donna. "I don't know nothing about your money. Even if I did, Kenny wouldn't play me for you. He can't stand being married to you," she said, taking a step towards me. "The only reason he's still with you is because you're dumb enough to put up with his shit."

"Oh, and he's supposed to love you?" Donna asked, stepping back into Alicia's face.

"That's what he..." Alicia said.

"Don't be stupid, bitch!" Donna snapped, cutting her off. "The only reason he keeps running back to you is because he knows you can break his ass because of Kiya! But you're too stupid to even do that!" Donna continued. "You will never learn!"

Alicia looked like she wanted to crawl onto the wall and become wallpaper. Her eyes were narrowed to slits, but not just because she was high. She looked like she wanted to cry.

"You need to put his ass on papers!" Donna snapped.

"Do you really think the courts are going to give her more than five hundred dollars a month?" I asked.

"What?" Donna asked, looking at me like I was crazy. "Now you're buggin'!"

"What do you mean?" I asked.

"Kenny ain't paying child support," Donna said.

"He says he pays her five hundred a month, plus half of Kiya's daycare," I said.

Donna laughed loudly. "Maybe I should fuck him," she said. "Because whatever he's giving y'all two bitches have got y'all stuck on stupid."

"I'm not stupid!" Alicia finally spoke up.

"And I am not your bitch," I said.

Donna had one more time to call me out my name. The next time it was going to be my foot planted in the crack of her ass.

"Whateva," Donna said, sucking her teeth.

"Look, Kenny's lying," Alicia said, slumping back down on the sofa, "plain and clear."

"Well, we'll see what the judge says," I said, picking the document up off the table. "I hope for your sake you can prove it. If not, I guess your girl here will be raising Kiya while you're bumping coochies in a jail cell." I turned to walk to the door. I turned the knob slower than necessary. I was procrastinating, hoping Alicia would stop me.

"Wait!" Alicia yelled.

"What?" I asked.

"I swear on my daughter's life I don't know nothing about your money," she said.

I turned around, looking at her with clear wide eyes. The desperation on her face led me to believe that she was telling me the truth.

"I swear," she said.

I stared at her, pretending like I was contemplating whether or not I believed her.

"Y'all need to fuck him up," Donna said, before I could respond.

"How?" I asked, walking back over to the chair and sitting down.

"I got some home boys who'll handle him," Donna said, her brown eyes shining. "They can make it look like an accident. No one will ever know the difference."

This broad is crazy! Alicia and I looked at each other. She was probably thinking the same thing I was.

"He's still Kiya's father," Alicia said. "I don't want her growing up without her father."

"Alicia's right," I said. "Murder is a little extreme, but I think I have a plan that will benefit both of us."

"We're listening," Donna said, leaning forward. It was obvious she was the dominate one in their relationship.

"Like I told you before, Kenny got me for twenty grand of my inheritance, but that wasn't all the money I had coming to me. I'm scheduled to get another thirty thousand," I said. I wasn't about to tell the two of them the entire truth. I didn't want them getting greedy and asking for more money than I had originally planned to offer Alicia. "I want a divorce, but if I divorce Kenny he can..."

"Get half of everything." Alicia cut me off.

"Exactly, but if I have evidence that's he's been sleeping around, then the judge is more likely to award him nothing."

"Kenny's a hoe," Donna said, sucking her teeth. "You won't have a problem proving *that.*"

"On the contrary, he's been on his best behavior since I returned from Baltimore," I told her. "I'm sure Alicia can vouch for that." Alicia nodded her head but remained silent. "But if I had physical evidence, such as a videotape." I was silent, giving them time to process the information.

"What's in it for me?" Alicia asked.

"Ten thousand dollars," I said.

"Ten grand!" she screamed, with raised eyebrows.

"Yep."

"Shit, for ten grand I'll do it!" Donna said excitedly.

"I'll do it," Alicia said, rolling her eyes in Donna's direction. "But how do you expect me to get Kenny over here?"

"Not here," I said, "at my house, in my bed."

"He won't let me come by if you're not there," Alicia said.

"He will if he thinks I'm out of town."

"How do I know I can trust you?" Alicia asked, eyeing me suspiciously.

I reached inside my bag and pulled out the bills I had set aside to use as bait to get her to agree. I handed her the crisp stack of Benjamins.

"A down payment," I said. "Twenty-five hundred."

Alicia counted the bills, before asking me," What makes you so sure you can trust me?"

"If you decide to cross me, then I'll have my lawyer file a claim against you." I was lying, I didn't have a legal leg to stand on. However, Alicia didn't know this, and the expression on her face told me so.

CHAPTER 23

I had set the wheels in motion for my plan, which included Alicia. I told Kenny I would be flying out to Baltimore to finalize my mother's will, and that's when Alicia was to come over to my house and seduce Kenny. I had already purchased miniature cameras to set up all over the house.

Octavia's father was a retired private investigator, and had put me on to this place called The Spy Store. They sold cameras small enough to fit in everything from a teddy bear to the crack of your ass. I purchased enough of them to set them up in my living room, bathroom, kitchen, and every bedroom in my house.

I didn't think Alicia would break her end of the deal, but just in case she did, I figured if she and Kenny had sex anywhere in my house, I would catch them. The only way I wouldn't was if they got down and dirty in one of the closets. If they did, then they deserved to get away with it.

Kenny had no idea what I had planned. He was on cloud nine, walking around the house singing and dancing. You would think I had cut him a check from the way he was acting, but I hadn't. However, I had filled his head with promises of the two of us going shopping and vacationing in the Caribbean once my money started coming in. I even went as far as having him go out on a shopping spree. I told him to write checks on his checking account, because in a few days my checks would be deposited in his account. He had no idea that I already had money. He was also clueless to the fact that every check he wrote was going to be returned. I kept all the items I purchased locked in the trunk of my Honda, and the keys to my car on me whenever he was around.

To keep my front up, I got up every morning and got dressed like I was going to work. The truth was that I had actually already quit my job. I planned to find my passion in life once Kenny was out of it.

My plan was in full effect. I told Kenny I had to fly out to Baltimore for the weekend to meet with my mother's attorney. The truth was that I was going to be in Las Vegas with Savoy the whole weekend. I've never been to Vegas, and there was no one who I'd rather experience "Sin City" with more than Savoy.

I made reservations at the beautiful MGM Grand for Savoy and myself. The Celebrity Spa Suite we were staying in was fully equipped with a wet bar, separate living and dining rooms, master bedroom with a king size bed. A separate bathroom, that included a whirlpool tub, separate shower, double vanities, and marble countertops and floors.

After we checked into our room, I slipped into the bathroom to change into my bathing suit. Octavia had helped me pick out a sexy gold two-piece that showed off my new physique. Before my weight loss I would not have dared stepped out in public in a swimsuit, but now I planned to do my thing and show exactly what my mama gave me.

"Umm, umm, umm." Savoy sat on the bed grinning at me, as I walked out of the bathroom.

I put my hands on my hips, and turned slowly on my open toe stilettos. I took small easy steps, while walking backwards. I switched my hips across the room, stepping like a Victoria's Secret model on the runway.

"Work it, baby," he moaned, leaning back on the bed.

I stopped in front of him, and spread my legs shoulder width apart. I tossed my braids to one side, and looked over my shoulder at him. I licked my lips slowly, leaned forward and grabbed my ankles. I shook my hips, causing my ass cheeks to jiggle wildly.

"Damn!" Savoy moaned, his eyes wide. "Keep that up and we won't make it to the pool."

I turned around, and stepped onto the bed with my heels still on. I stood over Savoy, with my legs straddling his body, then slowly squatted, grinding slowly on his chest. Savoy placed both of his hands on my hips, pulling me up towards his face.

"Sit right here," he said, licking his lips.

I positioned myself over his face, and then slowly started grinding my lips against his. Savoy pulled my bikini bottoms to the side, and slid his tongue into my hot spot. I shivered as he made slow rotations inside of me. I stood up, carefully balancing myself on my heels, then pulled my bikini bottoms down, stepped out of them, and tossed them to the floor. I slowly eased myself back down in position over Savoy's face.

"Relax, baby, I got you." Savoy cupped my ass in his hands, holding me up.

I relaxed my entire body while my man went to work. Savoy latched on my clit like it was a nipple, alternating between warm pressure pulling sucks and gentle nibbles. I grabbed a handful of his hair, as Savoy licked down from my clit up into my pussy. He curved his tongue inside of me, while his full lips covered mine. He pulled my hips back and forth until I was rocking back and forth on his face. He rotated his tongue inside of me, and then plunged so deep that he hit my spot.

"Ohhhh!" I screamed, bouncing up and down fiercely on his face. "I'm cumming!"

Savoy moved faster, squeezing my ass harder until his nose, lips and tongue were dripping with my warm sticky fluid. I slid down his body, resting my head on his chest. My heart was pounding, and I was out of breath. I wanted to get up and show Savoy my appreciation, but the oral satisfaction he had given me had me weak in the knees.

"I'll be right back, baby," he said.

I lifted up so Savoy could get up, then snuggled my head into the fluffy feather pillows on the bed. I heard water running in the bathroom, and then Savoy returned with a wet washcloth. He spread my legs with his hands, gently running the warm cloth over the area in between my legs, down each of my thighs. When he completed his task, he returned to the bathroom, then came back to join me on the bed. I smiled watching him as he removed his clothes.

"Ummm, you look good, daddy," I purred.

"Thank you, mama."

I shifted on my side so that Savoy could lie down, and I laid down on his chest. He wrapped his strong arms around me and held me tightly. The two of us laid there for a moment in silence.

"Can I ask you a question?" he asked.

"Anything."

"How can you afford all this?"

I propped myself up on my elbows, so that I could look him in his eyes. "My mother left me some money," I admitted. I didn't go into much detail, and I was hoping he wouldn't press the subject.

Don't get me wrong, it's not that I thought Savoy would turn out to be another Kenny, but I wasn't going to take any chances either.

"You don't have to tell me anything else about it," Savoy said, rubbing my back. "I just wanted to make sure you weren't creepin' around with some thugged out dope dealer, then taking his money and spending it on me." I laughed at the thought. "Seriously," he said smiling, "a brother needs to know if he should be watching his back."

"You don't have to watch your back," I reassured him. "In fact, if anyone should be watching their back, it's Kenny."

"What's up with the two of you?"

"He's been playing me all these years." I said, getting angry just thinking about Kenny.

"He's still cheating?"

"That's only half of it," I said.

"Tell me."

"Let's just say he's not who I thought he was. And if everything goes as I plan, I'll be free of him and our shitty ass excuse for a marriage soon."

"What do you have planned?"

"I'd rather not say."

Savoy frowned, then sat up with his back against the headboard of the bed.

"What's wrong?" I asked, sitting up beside him.

"You say you love me, right?"

"I do love you," I said, confused with where he was going with his statement.

"Then what's the deal with all the secrets?"

"What do you mean?"

"What's really going on, Shon, with you and Kenny?"

"I just told you that..."

"I know what you told me," he said, cutting me off. "You'd rather not go into it."

"I don't want to get you involved," I said gently.

"I'm already involved!" he snapped, climbing off the bed. I watched him as he paced back and forth across the carpeted floor, butt naked with his dick swinging. "Just answer one question for me."

"What?"

"Have you asked him for a divorce?" I looked at him without answering. "Does he even know you want a divorce?" he asked, standing with his arms crossed over his chest. I shook my head no. "That's what I thought." I watched him as he walked over to the armoire where we had stored our clothes, pulled out a pair of oversized basketball shorts, and slipped them on. "Do you even have any intentions of leaving him?" he asked, staring at me. "Or am I the one that's been played?"

"What are you implying?" I asked, getting pissed.

"I'm implying that you're just telling me what I want to hear. Then once I dip, I'll be out of sight out of mind," he said. "Or maybe you just wanted to get back at him for all the years he fucked around on you. Maybe you just wanted to see how it felt to be the one stepping out."

I jumped off the bed with my hands on my hips. "If I remember correctly, you were the one who approached me!" I yelled. "And if I remember correctly, I told you from the jump that I was married."

"And as I remember, your black ass was so damn miserable!" he yelled, turning to face me. "But for someone who is *sooo* miserable, you're still running home to him every fucking night."

"I may be running my black ass home to him every night, but I'm fucking you, Savoy," I said, attempting to reason with him. It didn't work.

"So now we're just fucking?" he asked, his gray eyes narrowing.

"That's not what I meant," I said calmly.

"That's what you said." He slipped his feet into his Nike flip flops then stormed out the room, slamming the door behind him.

I was completely thrown off by Savoy's behavior. He left me standing in the room; naked, alone and horny. I didn't know how to react to his temper tantrum. I decided to call my girl for some advice.

"He's insecure," Octavia said, after I told her about Savoy's temper tantrum.

"Why is he insecure?" I asked. "Savoy can have any woman he wants."

"Not in his eyes," she said, "because at this point, he doesn't have you."

"He has my heart," I said, "and my body." I reminisced on the way Savoy brought me to multiple orgasms. Just thinking about how good he made my body feel brought a smile to my face.

"That may be true, but legally, you're still somebody else's wife," Octavia stated. "And imagine how you would feel if Savoy was the one who was married."

"First of all, I wouldn't even be in that situation," I said firmly. "I don't get down like that."

"Like what?" Octavia asked.

"Messing with other women's husbands." I know I sounded like a hypocrite, but it was the truth.

If Savoy had been married, I would have never let things go as far as they had with him. I know all too well how it feels to have your man cheating on you. I would never want to put another woman through that type of bullshit.

"Maybe," Octavia said. "But I'm saying hypothetically, how would you feel if Savoy had you playing the waiting game?"

I thought about her words for a second. "So how do I make

things right?" I asked.

"Tell him the truth," she said. "That the lying sack of shit you're married to has been using you, and that you're trying to get rid of his ass without having to give him a dime."

"What's my other option?" I wasn't even trying to disclose that type of information to Savoy.

"Don't tell him anything," she said. "And just hope that he'll still be available once you become free."

After my conversation with Octavia, I took a long hot bath and slipped into my crochet knee-length form fitting dress and three-inch open toe heels that tied around my ankles. I pulled my braids high up on top of my head in a neat bun, then applied a fresh coat of lipstick to my lips, and brushed just enough of my Mac face powder over my face to give my skin a flattering glow. After weighing the two options Octavia suggested I use to smooth things over with Savoy, I came up with my own. I planned to use the art of seduction.

CHAPTER 24

An hour later, Savoy walked through the door. His hair and shorts were wet; I assumed he went swimming without me. I was sitting on the sofa with my legs crossed. He looked from my head down to my French pedicure, then back up again before walking out of the room into the bedroom. I thought I would at least get a smile. I took a deep breath, and then followed him.

"I'm sorry, baby." I said sweetly. I watched him as he kicked off his shoes, and slipped out of his shorts.

"It's cool," he said. He stared at me for a moment, then walked into the bathroom and shut the door. A second later I heard the shower running.

Fuck it, at least I tried. I walked back into the living room and sat down on the sofa. I wanted to go out on the town with Savoy, but I had my mind made up that if he was still acting funky when he came out of the shower, I would go out by my damn self.

Thirty minutes later, Savoy walked into the living room looking exotically sexy in a pair of light linen shorts, a matching V-neck short sleeve linen shirt, and Gucci sandals. His twists were pulled back neatly in a rubber band. *Why is he soooo fine?*

"Where are you going?" I asked.

"Out," he responded. It was obvious that he was still pissed off with me.

"Out where?"

"Just out," he said. He picked the electronic door card up off the table before walking to the door.

"So, you're just going to leave me here?" I asked, staring at the back of his head.

"I think it'll be good if I give you your space."

"If I wanted my space, I wouldn't have invited you to Vegas."

"Why did you invite me?" he asked, looking at me.

"Because I want to experience new things," I said. "And I want to experience them with you."

"A new beginning?" he asked.

"Exactly." Maybe he was finally beginning to see things my way.

"Every new beginning has an ending," he said firmly. "How can we look towards the future, if we can't get beyond the past?"

"What do you mean?"

"I can't be with someone that I don't trust," he said. "Or someone who doesn't trust me."

"I do trust you," I said, hesitantly.

"No you don't. If you did, we wouldn't be having this conversation." He turned his back to me, and opened the door.

I thought about all the women he could have been with, and the fact that Savoy, not only wanted to be with me, but that he was in love with me. I began to feel insecure, so insecure that I knew I had to tell him everything.

"Okay," I said, feeling defeated. "I'll tell you whatever you want to know."

He shut the door, before turning around to look at me. His eyes were wide and clear.

"I want to know everything," he said, walking over to me. I slid over on the sofa so that he could sit down. I looked into his gray eyes and smiled.

"I'll tell you everything," I said.

To my surprise, I felt relieved after disclosing all the details of what was going on with Kenny. I told Savoy all about the money I inherited, and my alliance with Alicia.

"Are you sure you can trust her?" he asked, his gray eyes shunned with concern.

"I think so," I said. "Besides, at this point she's my only hope."

"She's not your only hope," Savoy said. "You have me."

"I know, baby, but you can't help me with this one. I have to do this on my own. Besides, what can you possibly do?" I asked.

"You'd be surprised," he said. "You'd be surprised."

I never asked Savoy to elaborate. I didn't need him to. I had my own plan, and I was going through with it. If it didn't work, then I would deal with it when the time came. In the meantime, I planned to have one of the best weekends of my life.

***

After our conversation, Savoy and I decided to go down to Emeril's Restaurant for dinner. Nicolette, our server, took our orders, and then left us sitting at the small cozy table for two.

"What would you like to do after dinner?" Savoy asked

"I don't care," I said honestly. It didn't matter what the two of us did, as long as we were together.

"Clubbin?" he asked.

"It's been awhile since I seen you shake that ass," I teased.

"I don't shake my ass." He smiled. "But I do intend to watch you shake yours."

"Don't worry, baby," I said seductively, "I plan to shake mine for you all night long. And I'm not just talking about dancing," I said, winking my eye at him. Savoy smiled mischievously.

"I'm going to hold you to that," he said.

Nicolette returned with our order. After setting the dishes down, she smiled and told us to let her know if we needed anything else. The food looked and tasted absolutely delicious. I had the pan roasted gulf snapper with herbed potatoes, while Savoy had the Louisiana Cedar Plank campfire steak with mashed potatoes. The two of us consumed our meals, and then sat looking into each other's eyes. We were so caught up in our silence we didn't notice the gentleman approaching our table.

"Two people so in love should have this memory forever," he said. I tore my eyes away from Savoy and looked at the short balding man. He had a camera hanging from his neck. "May I take your picture?" he asked.

"Sure." I smiled, looking over at Savoy. He nodded his head in approval.

"Why don't the two of you move in closer together." he suggested.

I slid my chair around the table next to Savoy's. Savoy put his arm around my shoulder, pulling me close. I lay my head on his shoulder, and smiled proudly for the photographer.

"Say cheese," he said.

"Cheese!" Savoy and I said in unison.

The man snapped our picture, and then looked down at the camera screen and smiled. "Beautiful," he said. "Why don't we get one more?" he asked, staring at me.

I wrapped my arms around Savoy's neck, and planted my lips on his. Our tongues touched, and we kissed like we were the only two people in the room. I saw the flash out of the corner of my eyes, but I continued to kiss Savoy passionately. He was the first one to pull away.

"Wow," the photographer said, letting out a light whistle. "Now that's what I call a woman in love."

I stared into Savoy's eyes, never looking at the man.

"That I am," I said. "That I am."

The photographer showed us our pictures on his digital camera screen. We both agreed that we wanted copies.

"How much?" Savoy asked the man.

"Normally, for a 5x7 five dollars each," he said. "But for you two lovebirds, I'll do a buy one get the second one free."

"We'll take them," Savoy said.

"I'll be right back." The man disappeared through the restaurant.

A few minutes later, he returned with our pictures nicely set in two double sided paper frames, with the word "Memories" stamped on the front cover. Savoy reached into his pocket and pulled out a twenty.

"Keep the change," he said, handing the bill to the man.

"Thanks." The man smiled brightly. "I hope the two of you

enjoy your stay." He then turned and walked away.

Studio 54 was like no other club I had ever seen. It was unbelievable, from the high tech video and lighting, to the live stage dancers and wall walkers. It was also huge with four dance floors and bars, a second level, and several lounges. It was easy for me to see why it was one of the most talked about clubs in Vegas.

After Savoy paid our cover charge, the two of us made our way, hand in hand, across the dance floor to the closest bar. After sitting down, we were approached by a tall, green-eyed bartender. She looked like she had dropped straight out of the 60s, with her hot pink bob-wig and body hugging dress and go-go boots.

"What can I get the two of you?" she asked smiling.

"Two double shots of Hennessey?" Savoy asked, looking at me. I nodded my head in agreement.

"Two double shots of Hennessey coming right up."

Nellie Furtado's *Promiscuous* bumped through the club's sound system. Savoy and I sat whispering and giggling about everything we were going to do to each other once we made it back to our room. We were so caught up in each other we didn't even realize the bartender had returned with our drinks.

"Would you like me to start you a tab?" she politely asked.

"Yes, please." I gave her a quick smile.

I tossed the shot back without hesitation. Savoy winked his eye at me, then followed suit. *Promiscuous* stopped, and Juvenile's *Back That Thang Up* came on. I hopped off my seat and grabbed Savoy by the hand.

"Let's go, daddy," I said.

Savoy followed close behind me as we made our way to the dance floor. I intentionally made sure my ass stayed directly in front of his crotch, and by the growth I felt pressing through his pants, he was enjoying my subtle seduction. The two of us found a spot on the crowded dance floor, and my hips and ass went into complete overdrive. I arched my back, causing my round ass to lift slightly higher and twirked my hips. Looking over my shoulder I smiled, while watching Savoy eye my body like it was an exquisite work of art. I moved to the music, never missing a beat. Savoy placed his hands on my hips and pulled me close. Just as he did, I dropped all the way down to the floor then popped back up.

You would have sworn Savoy was Pinocchio, because the rod in his pants kept growing and growing. Spinning me around to face him, he pressed his lips against mine, and then slipped his tongue in my mouth. My tongue met his with passion. Before I knew it my kitty was purring, and I was nice and wet.

I pulled away long enough to give Savoy my "I want some now" look. He returned my look with a smile, and led me by the hand through the crowd off the dance floor. As we made our way to the door, I took a final look at the amazing club. I decided one day I would return when I had more time, and when I was a lot less horny. As much as I loved the club, I loved the way Savoy made love to me even more.

I looked up, and saw a man standing on the second level looking down on me. He raised his glass, as if he was giving approval of my little show on the dance floor. I waved my hand in his direction before continuing to follow my man out the club.

Savoy and I made it back to our room around 2 am. Once we got through the door, we immediately began going at it. I dropped to my knees and practically ripped his shorts open. I was thirsty, and behind the thin material laid the quencher for my thirst. I pulled his rock hard dick out, licked my lips, and wrapped them around him. I could feel the veins inside Savoy's rod pulsating. He grabbed a handful of my braids and began to pump in and out of my mouth. I grabbed his warm sack and began to massage it slowly. Savoy pumped harder and faster. I began bobbing my head quickly, keeping up with his rhythm. My mouth was dripping wet.

"Oh baby," he moaned.

The sound of his voice turned me on even more. I relaxed the muscles of my throat, took a deep breath through my nose, and then went completely down on his manhood. Savoy twitched as his knees buckled from the pleasure. I literally made him weak in the knees. He let go of my hair and attempted to pull away, but my lips were latched around him like the Jaws of Life. My tongue was playing against his skin like it was a musical instrument.

"Baby, here it comes," he moaned. "You gotta move or else..."

I knew what was coming next, and I wanted it all. I wanted to taste every ounce of my man. I had no idea what I was in store for, but I didn't care. Savoy brought out things in me I didn't know existed. I wanted to try every dirty-freak-nasty thing I could with him. I continued to deep throat him until finally he erupted in the cave of my mouth.

"Shontay!" He screamed my name like a man tortured.

I allowed all of his filling to enter my mouth, then holding my breath I swallowed hard. I was trying new things, but I was not brave enough to taste it, hence the reason I held my breath. After I swallowed two more times, I took him in my mouth again. Savoy was practically begging me to stop.

"Baby...baby...bay...beee," he pleaded. "You gotta...you gotta stop." I let out a small giggle then stood up straight.

"I'll be back boo," I said smiling.

I shook my head, watching him as he hobbled over to the sofa then collapsed. I went into the bathroom to brush my teeth and rinse with mouthwash. When I returned, Savoy had gained his composure and was sitting out on the balcony of our suite. He looked like one of Michelangelo's masterpieces, as he sat stark naked under the moonlight. He smiled when he saw me.

"Mind if I join you?" I asked him.

"Not at all." He smiled. "But there is one condition."

"What's that?"

"Take your clothes off," he said.

In another time and place you couldn't have paid me to go stark naked on the 43rd floor of a hotel, but this time I had no worries or concerns. I was with Savoy, and I felt uninhibited and completely free. Giving him a seductive smile, I slowly slid the dress I was wearing up until my thighs were exposed.

"Take your time," he spoke softly.

Slowly turning on my heels so that my back was facing him, I continued to ease the material up until my firm ass was exposed.

"Like this?" I asked seductively.

"Yeah, baby, just like that."

In my mind I could hear music playing. I moved and swayed my hips back and forth to the imaginary beat. As I rocked back and forth, back and forth, I slowly continued to ease the dress up and over my body. Once I had it completely off, I turned back around to face Savoy. He was sitting straight up with one hand wrapped around his rock hard magic stick.

"See what you do to me?" he asked. He had an animalistic glow in his eyes. He was the hunter and I was ready to be his prey.

"I want you to feel what you do to me," I said, taking small steps in his direction.

We kept our eyes locked until I was standing in front of him. Slowly moving his hands up my legs, Savoy licked his luscious full lips.

"Spread 'em," he ordered.

Tossing my braids to one side, I stretched my right leg out, allowing my heel to rest on the iron railing behind him. Savoy trailed his lips from my ankles, to my calves, to my inner thighs. I was ready. So ready it felt like my moisture would trickle down at any moment. I wanted to grab his head and force him in between my legs, but instead I stood still, allowing him to do his work.

When he reached the crease in between my thigh and hot spot, he replaced his lips with his hands. With one hand, Savoy spread my lower lips, and with the other, he caressed my engorged clit. I tossed my head back and exhaled as one of his fingers slipped inside me. Savoy took his time, making "come hither" motions while his index finger was inside me.

Kenny had fingered me on numerous occasions, but it always felt like he was performing a pap smear exam. He would poke and prod me to the point that it was damn near unbearable. It was nothing like the treatment Savoy was giving me.

Savoy made a small fist with his left hand, and spread his knuckles, gently pulling and tugging on my clit. At the same time he slipped another finger in my kitty. He rotated the two fingers in a stirring motion. I felt the heat growing in the pit of my stomach, as beads of sweat began gathering in the folds of my knees. Leaning forward, Savoy flicked his tongue out, teasing my clit with every rotation.

"Ohhh," I moaned, grabbing his shoulder for balance. I felt like my entire body was on fire.

"Do you trust me?" he asked

"Um hum," I moaned.

"Do you trust me?" he asked again, this time with more authority.

Looking into his beautiful eyes, I nodded my head. "Yes, I trust you," I said.

He gave me a sexy smile, displaying his pearly whites. "Sit down," he said.

I quickly swung my leg off the rail, ready to straddle his lap. Looking at me with an air of mischief in his eyes, he said, "No, baby, I want you to sit up there." He pointed to the rail behind him.

Now granted, I love my man. I really do. However, we were on the 43rd floor, where besides the elevator or the stairs, the only other way down was head first and assed out. He must have sensed my hesitation.

"You trust me, baby?" he asked again.

"Yes."

"Then know that I would die before I hurt you," he said, with sincerity etched in his eyes. "And I would kill before I let another man hurt you." I stroked his face gently with my fingertips.

His words sent a chill down my spine. I know Savoy could have just been feeding me a line, but in my heart I knew his words were true. I stepped away from him, then with his assistance, I eased my bare ass on to the cool railing.

Savoy eased the lounge chair he had been sitting on out of the way, and turned to face me. I grabbed the rail with both hands, as he took each of my thighs in his hands. Despite my better judgment, I casually looked over my shoulder at the scene below. I felt faint from the thought of tumbling backwards off the rail. I could see the headlines: "***Freaky Sex Gone Wrong: Woman* Drops 43 *Floors To Her Death*!**" Okay, maybe I was trippin', but I'm just saying, it could happen.

"Hold on," he ordered. He didn't have to worry about that one, because the last thing on my mind was letting go.

Savoy spread my legs open, and gently lifted me in the air, so that my ass was elevated. I was silently thanking God that I had been working on my upper body, so that my arms were strong enough to hold my weight, at least for a little while. Standing tall, Savoy pulled me up until my open lips met his.

"I got you," he whispered, before covering my lips with his mouth.

Savoy sucked on my clean shaven, purring kitty with fierceness, while dipping his moist tongue in and out. I felt my arms shaking as I struggled to maintain control. He held my thighs tightly, while munching on my goodie bowl. I let my fear go, allowing Savoy to hold me up. He slid his tongue down my wet crease to the crack of my ass, and then began teasing my hole with the tip of his tongue. The pleasure he delivered took me into another world, a world without Kenny, baby mama drama, pain and regret. My heart was pounding a mile a minute, as I felt the blood rushing to my head. I arched my back, my head hanging over the rail.

"Oh, yessss," I moaned, as orgasmic waves erupted throughout my body, one after the other.

I grabbed Savoy's forearms as he positioned my legs onto his shoulders, while stepping away from the rail. My body continued to shake, as he eased me down onto my feet.

Savoy spun me around, then pushed my abs against the rail. Pushing my right leg up in the air, he entered me with force. The impact caused me to gasp loudly. Wrapping his free arm around my shoulders, Savoy held me tightly, while hittin' me from the back. I balanced my weight on my left leg, while grabbing the rail with both hands. Arching my back, I lifted my ass up and began to bounce back and forth on his dick.

"Right there, right there," he moaned, sucking on my earlobe.

I threw it back at him, each time with more force than the first. Savoy changed the pace, and began rotating his hips. I changed my rhythm, following his. Our bodies moved together like two pythons in a heated jungle. I felt Savoy's body beginning to tense up, and I knew much like myself he was about to cum. We continued to move together, climaxing seconds apart.

Chapter 25

After spending the day shopping and sightseeing, Savoy and I returned to our suite to shower and get dressed for another night out on the town. This time, rather than hitting a club, we opted to see a performance of Cirque Du Soleil and then dinner at Wolfgang Puck.

Cirque Du Soleil was mesmerizing. I watched in awe as the featured acrobats flipped and tossed each other from huge chandeliers suspended high in the air, while striking intricate posses. The dramatic fluorescent lights and orchestra music, combined with the vibrant costumes that fit like body art, only added to their captivating performance. During one act of the show, the center of the stage turned into an in ground pool, which the performers used to play out scenes under water. I was so entranced by the show I could have stayed and watched all night. However, a sista was hungry, so we left to hit the restaurant.

Wolfgang Puck was located next to the Cirque Du Soleil Theater, which was another fabulous thing about Vegas; the shops, hotels, casinos and restaurants were all convenient. Inside the restaurant, Savoy and I sat inside the private glass enclosed dining room, enjoying sautéed Maine crab cakes.

"Are you enjoying yourself?" he asked, looking across the table at me.

"Of course I am." I gave him a sweet smile. "I'm with you."

He smiled, then reached across the table and took my hand in his. "Where do you see yourself in five years?" he asked.

I had never thought about where I would be in five years. Truth be told, I had no idea where I would be in six months, I was just hoping and praying it was free from Kenny.

"I'm not sure," I said honestly. "I'm just taking it moment by moment."

His facial expression displayed that he was thinking about my answer.

I took another bite of my crab cake, and asked, "And where do you see yourself?"

"Let's see," he said, "by that time I hope to have completed at least ten new residential developments. In addition to the residential developments, I hope to have tripled my net worth and expanded my business. I'd like to have offices in Los Angeles, Florida, Alabama and Maryland. I want to have my foundation for the homeless and my shelter for battered women off the ground as well."

I was impressed that he had actually set his goals, and by the look in his eyes, he would accomplish many, if not all of them.

"That's wonderful, Savoy." I smiled, giving his hand a light squeeze.

"That's not all." He took a sip of his ice tea then stared at me. "I also want kids," he said, "at least four."

When I heard him say he wanted children my heart sunk. At that moment it hit me that maybe Savoy had been making plans, plans that didn't include me in his future.

"You'd make a wonderful father." I was being 100% genuine. I knew any child or woman that had Savoy in their life would be extremely blessed.

"And you'd make a wonderful mother." He smiled. I assumed he had forgotten that I was unable to bear children.

"Thanks, but I can't…"

"We can adopt," he said, cutting me off.

The thought of Savoy and myself being parents together made

my heart flutter. In my current situation, I knew the last thing I should be doing was planning a family with a new man before I got rid of my old one, but that's exactly what I sat there doing.

"Just hear me out," he said, leaning forward. "We could first adopt here in America, then go to Africa, Asia, China, or wherever you want. Our home would be a melting pot!" He smiled.

"I love that idea," I said, smiling also.

"Really?" he asked, sounding surprised.

"Yes, really!" I leaned across the table and gave him a peck on the lips.

"There is one more goal I hope to accomplish."

"There's more?" I asked, thinking that what he already wanted to accomplish was more than enough.

"Yes," he said.

The look in his eyes turned serious, as he reached across the table and took my other hand.

"What is it?" I asked impatiently. He was making nervous.

"At some point and time I plan to make you my wife." *Oh, shit. Did he? Is he? Was that just a proposal?* "I'm not asking you now," he stated, as if reading my thoughts. "There is still a lot we have to learn about each other, and I know there are some things that have to be taken care of." I knew he was referring to Kenny. "However, at this moment I can see us growing old together," he stated.

I respected and loved the fact that he was being realistic about our situation. Instead of telling me what he thought I wanted to hear, he kept it real.

"Savoy, I love you, and I would love to see just how far we can go," I said.

He showed his appreciation by pressing his thick juicy lips to mine. I reciprocated by slipping my tongue in his mouth. We shared a long passionate kiss until our server returned with our meals. Savoy had the rib eye steak with Tuscan potatoes and brandy wine sauce, while I enjoyed the organic chicken with garlic potato puree and honey glazed carrots. After we devoured our meals, we headed back to our room for desert.

CHAPTER 26

My weekend in Vegas went by far too quickly. Before I knew it, Savoy and I were kissing goodbye and headed our separate ways. He was off to the construction site for the Ambiance 2, and I was headed home to start my divorce proceedings.

It was Monday, and I knew Kenny would be at work, leaving me time to pull my hidden cameras, and review his and Alicia's sex tape. I was confident that Alicia had not let me down, and that she had kept her end of our bargain.

The Yellow Cab I was riding in pulled up to the curb in front of my home. The driver was unable to pull into the driveway due to my Eclipse and a brand new cocaine white Escalade blocking the drive. I paid the cab driver and climbed out of the cab, with my bags behind me. I walked from one side of the vehicle to other admiring the details. *22-inch custom wheels, electronic mud runners, wood grain interior, leather seats, and dealer tags.* I was so engulfed in admiring the ride, that I hadn't focused on the fact that my soon to be ex-husband was still home. Could he possibly be inside screwing one of his tramps? The mere thought of physically catching Kenny in the act made my nipples hard. I quickly made my way to the front door and let myself in.

Inside, my living room was spotless. It smelled like a fresh bottle of Pine-Sol. Kiya's toys were nowhere to be found, and there were fresh track marks where someone had vacuumed. I was shocked, but not half as shocked as I was to find Kenny sitting on the sofa alone, waiting on me. I was quite disappointed that there wasn't any fucking action going on. I would have been happy to catch him getting some head, sucking some toes, anything. It would have made my morning to be able to throw his ass out at that moment. However, there was nothing. I would have to wait until I retrieved the video, or knowing Kenny, the videos before I made my move.

"Good morning." He smiled.

He was wearing freshly creased khakis and a button down Sean John shirt. His face was neatly edged, and he had a fresh Caesar cut. If I hadn't grown to despise him so much, I might have actually thought he was attractive.

"Whose car is that in the drive?" I asked, skipping the pleasantries.

"It's mine." He smiled.

"Yours?" I asked, pushing my bags into the living room closet.

"Yep."

"How?"

I knew Kenny didn't have a dime to his name. So how did he manage to purchase a brand new vehicle? Last time I checked, even if you wrote a check, the dealership called to verify funds.

"Well, it will be mine," he advised me. "I told my boy at the dealership I would be back this week to pay cash." *What the hell?* "So he let me bring it home for the weekend." He was smiling like a cat in a room full of mice.

"You told him you would be paying cash," I stated, in disbelief.

"Yep." He grinned, standing to his feet. "You know they don't accept checks without verifying funds." I watched as he walked over and stopped in front of me. "And I knew my baby would take care of it for me." He laughed lightly. I didn't know who his baby was, but whoever she was, I knew she wasn't me.

"And who is your baby?" I asked sarcastically.

Stroking my cheek gently with his fingertips, he smiled. "You, of course!" This time I was the one who laughed. "Real talk, baby," He smiled. "I told him we'd have his money by the end of the week."

"We...I...haven't even gotten my first check yet," I lied.

"It's all good, baby," Kenny spoke, with confidence. "I *know* the truck will be mine before the week is up." *Is he trippin'?* There was no way on God's beautiful green Earth I was going to buy him a truck. Hell, he couldn't get a Huffy from me.

"Shouldn't you be at work?" I asked, changing the subject.

"I'm off today." He smiled. "I'm 'bout to ride out." I watched him snatch the keys to the truck off the coffee table. "I'll be back in the morning," he said, walking to the door. "Mama and I are going to spend the day in Tunica."

"Tunica?" I asked.

"Yeah, now that *we're* rich we can afford to splurge!" he said, flashing me a 1000 watt smile. *What is up with all the French? We this and we that! We my ass!* "Baby, I would have invited you, but I know things between you and Mama aren't the best. But that is soon to change."

He was right, because soon he and his mama would be out of my life. He gave me a peck on the cheek then bounced out the door. I slid over to the window and watched as he hopped in the truck, cranked up the system, then backed out the driveway, with his head bobbing back and forth. I was in a total state of shock.

Kenny was in la-la land, making plans to spend my ends. He was definitely in for a rude awakening. The good thing about his arrogance was that he didn't have a clue about what I had done to his bank account. This became dreadfully honest when I found receipts totaling $3,000.00 for clothes and shoes he had purchased by writing checks, checks that were going to bounce at any moment.

I waited just to make sure he didn't return to the house. After thirty minutes had passed, and I was confident the coast was clear, I began running through the house, pulling all my surveillance equipment. The sales rep at the Spy Store, not only sold me the cameras, but taught me how to convert the film onto DVDs by having the cameras connected to my laptop wirelessly. My palms were sweating while I waited for what seemed like days for the footage to finish downloading to the disc. Once the DVD was completed, I ran into my bedroom, popped the disc in my DVD player, and sat down on the bed.

The first day of my trip started with Kenny sitting around the house doing nothing. He made a couple of phone calls, drank a few beers, ate, shit, and went to sleep. I was holding my breath, praying that Alicia came through. On day two she did. The footage showed Kenny on his cell talking to Alicia. I couldn't hear what she was saying, but his conversation went like this:

"Naw, she gone."

"Yeah, she's in Baltimore."

"I don't think that's a good idea."

"I love my wife, and well, you and I we have history."

"I don't think it would be respectful for you to be here without her approval."

For a moment I felt a hint of guilt. This only lasted a brief moment.

"What about Kiya?"

"Okay, Alicia, but I'm going to call Shontay, just to make sure it's alright."

"Yeah."

I watched as he pressed the end button on his cell, then proceeded to dial another number.

"Hey, Tay, it's me," he said "Alicia wants to come over to talk about Kiya. I told her I had to speak with you first. I don't know why I'm getting your voicemail, but call me back if that's a problem. Love you."

I hadn't realized Kenny had called while I was in Vegas, maybe because I had my phone off the entire weekend, except when I called Octavia. I made myself a mental note to check all my messages later.

Re-directing my attention to the DVD, I watched as Kenny sat watching TV, until twenty minutes after their phone call, when Alicia arrived. She actually looked a little less ghetto on video. She was sporting yet another ponytail that hung down to her ass, and a short button down sleeveless dress. The first few buttons were open, revealing she was braless.

As soon as she walked through the door, she started her seduction by attempting to kiss Kenny. He pushed her away, stating that if she came to talk about Kiya she needed to talk, otherwise she could walk. Alicia appeared shaken by his comment, but it didn't stop her from trying. Her next move was kissing Kenny on the neck, while attempting to rub his crotch. Kenny responded by grabbing her wrist and pushing her away.

"Alicia, I'm not playing with you," Kenny said loudly. "If you got something to say, say it. Otherwise get the fuck out!"

"Why you acting like this?" Alicia sounded hurt. "What, you don't want me no more?"

"I love my wife."

"Since when?" Alicia snapped. She put one hand on her hip. "You been fucking me for how many years?" she screamed. "Now all of a sudden you want to play the happy husband?" Alicia was losing her cool quickly.

"Alicia, you need to go." Kenny opened the door, and stepped back.

"Baby," Alicia said calmly, reaching out to stroke his face. I watched as Kenny stepped back, and grabbed her wrist. "Kenny, you're hurting me!" she whined.

Her whining got her nowhere. Kenny held his grip around Alicia's wrist, while pushing her out the front door. He locked the door behind her, then went to the kitchen and returned with a beer.

A few seconds later, his phone rang. It was Alicia. From what I could make out from his portion of the conversation, he advised Alicia that the only thing they had to talk about was their daughter, and that he wanted nothing else to do with her. Then he hung up. I didn't know what to think. Kenny didn't even allow Alicia to get to first base. I was hoping that the rest of the footage showed some form of infidelity. I was stunned when it didn't.

After Kenny kicked her out, Alicia must have called at least twenty times, and each time Kenny shot her down. Finally, the calls stopped. The rest of the night, Kenny sat at home alone. My heart was filled with disappointment. I couldn't believe what I had witnessed. Alicia was there, and Kenny shot her down like a nuclear missile.

The footage from the next day was even more disappointing than the day before. Kenny didn't leave the house, nor did he talk on the phone. He had absolutely no contact with the outside world. He cooked, cleaned the house, and studied the Bible. I had no idea he even owned a Bible. I saw the video, but I still had to hear it from Alicia, plus I had to make sure she didn't sell me out to Kenny by mentioning our agreement, or the fake document I had shown her. I retrieved my cordless and called Alicia's home.

"Hello." Alicia sounded annoyed on the other end.

"Alicia, it's me, Shontay."

"Hey," she said.

"I saw the tape," I said, getting straight to the point. There was no need for small talk.

"I tried." She said, sounding nervous.

"I know you did."

"Kenny's on some more shit now," she said.

"What do you mean?"

"He says he wants to make it work with you." She let out a small laugh. "We got a daughter together, and we've been fucking for ten years, but he wants his marriage to work." Sarcasm was oozing from her voice.

"It's all about money," I said

"Naw," she said. "He's been using you for years, and never, not once, has he ever turned me down. He's on some more shit," she repeated. "Look, you can keep that money, but I can't go to jail." *Jail?* I had completely forgotten I had threatened to have her arrested. "I promise you, I didn't take your money."

"Don't worry about it," I said, feeling guilty.

"Seriously, Shontay," her voice was cracking, "Kenny lied. I don't know anything about your money."

"Did you tell Kenny about my plan?" I asked.

"No!" She sounded convincing. "I promise!"

"Did you tell him you know about the signed confession?"

"No." I didn't know if she was lying or telling the truth. However, I would soon find out.

The sound of keys unlocking my front door startled me.

"Look, Alicia, I gotta go," I said, rushing to grab all my surveillance equipment. "We'll talk soon."

I hung up abruptly, as I heard Kenny calling my name. I grabbed everything and threw it under the bed. What was he doing back so soon? Tunica was at least a five hour drive.

"Shontay!" he called again.

"Coming!" I yelled. I scurried out of the bedroom, shutting the door behind me.

Kenny was standing in the living room holding a box. The box was wrapped with a big red bow. He was smiling, as I approached him.

"I thought you and Etta were going to Tunica." I tried not to sound nervous.

"We are," he said, walking over to the sofa. I watched him as he sat down, placing the box on the coffee table. "I told her I had to take care of you first. You're my wife," he said. "You come first."

"What's up?" I asked, rubbing the back of my neck. I was trying hard not to fidget, but I was nervous as hell.

"I bought you something," he said, pointing to the box. "Open it."

I slowly eased over to the sofa, and sat down next to him.

"What is it?" I asked, staring at the box like it was diseased.

"Open it, baby." He smiled. "I really think you're going to love it."

I was still thinking about my conversation with Alicia. I was distracted. So much so I couldn't even focus on the gift Kenny had so kindly used my money for, or the imaginary money he thought I was giving him.

"Baby." The sound of his voice brought me back to reality.

"Yes?" I asked.

"Are you okay?" Kenny stroked my cheek. "You look troubled."

"I'm fine," I said softly. I picked the box up and sat it on my lap. Pulling on the ribbon gently, I watched the bow fall.

"You know I had forgotten what our vows stood for," Kenny

said standing. I listened as he walked around the coffee table and stood looking down on me. "Love, cherish," he spoke "In sickness, in health." He cuffed his hands in front of him. "For better or for worse." He was having his own personal rededication ceremony. "For richer or poorer." He continued. "Till death do us part." I stared in his eyes. "I get it now, baby," he said softly. "I get it."

"Kenny, I…"

"Don't talk," he said. "I just want you to think about us and all we've been through. All I put you through. Yet you forgave me over and over again," he said, shaking his head. "I hope one day I can be half as kind as you."

I guess reading the Bible did something to him, because I couldn't believe my ears. It was as if Kenny had just been born again.

"This is to our future," he said, pointing at the half open package on my lap. "I love you, baby."

I pried the tape open on all four sides, and then removed the box top. My gift was wrapped in pretty purple shimmering tissue paper. I folded the paper back, to reveal a beautiful cherry wood picture frame. Etched across the top in calligraphy was the word "Forever". I looked at the pictures behind the glass, and my heart began to melt. I held the frame tightly, while looking up at Kenny. He smiled.

"You like it?" he asked. My mouth was dry, as tears began to gather in the wells of my eyes. "They're beautiful, aren't they?" he asked. "My favorite is the third one from the bottom."

There were five pictures in the frame. I didn't have to look at which one he was referring to. I knew the scene like the back of my hands. The pictures were memories. Memories I hadn't forgotten, beautiful and wonderful memories. They were memories of my trip to Vegas with Savoy. The first one was of the two of us checking into the MGM. We were holding hands. The second one was of the two of us at Emeril's posing for the mystery photographer. The third was of us dancing at Studio 54. The fourth showed the two of us making out at Wolfgang Puck, and the last was of the two of us kissing while walking the strip. There was a knot forming in my throat. I swallowed hard, but the knot wouldn't move.

"How did you know?" I asked lowly.

Kenny tossed his head back and laughed. "I'm just that good." He snickered. "Naw, I hired a private investigator. Had him follow you and your Ziggy Marley wannabe." He laughed. "What's his name?" he asked. "Savoy, right? Good job, Tay" He applauded "Oh, and kudos on recruiting Alicia." The tears rolled down my cheeks as I dropped my head. "Oh, don't worry," he said, "she didn't tell me." As bad as my situation was at the moment, I found some comfort in knowing Alicia hadn't ratted me out. "That's what I like about Alicia," he said, pacing back and forth, "she sticks to her word." He stopped pacing, looked at me, and laughed wickedly. "Unlike some people I know."

"You fucking cheated on me," I yelled, jumping up, "and had a baby outside of our marriage. And you have the audacity to talk about sticking to your word?" I questioned.

How dare Kenny play the victim? After everything he put me through, he had the nerve to want to play the victim?! I was a victim. Hell, even Alicia was a victim.

"You're right." He laughed. "But you forgave me. Now I'm willing to grant you the same favor," he said, rubbing his hands together. "On one condition."

"What's that?" I asked, knowing very well he wasn't getting shit out of me.

"I want half of everything," he said. "In addition to that, I want you to take care of the checks I've written and I want my truck." *Who does he think he is?*

"You're outta your mind," I said.

"Okay, so we'll let the lawyers handle it," he said nonchalantly.

"Go ahead." I was furious. "You still ain't getting shit!"

"I've got proof you were unfaithful," he stated. "Right there on film. Oh, and on DVD."

"What DVD?" I was completely confused.

"Shit, baby, you're a star!" Kenny smiled. He reached in his back pocket, and pulled out a disk. I stood silent as he loaded the DVD player, and hit play.

My stomach did a somersault, as I watched Savoy and myself having sex on the balcony of our room at the MGM. I could tell from the angle that the person making the DVD had been somewhere in the building across from the hotel.

"Damn, Tay," Kenny grabbed his crotch, "I didn't know you had that in you! Baby, if I had known you were into hanging off rails and shit, I would've had that ass up in the air a long time ago!"

I pushed pass him, walking over to the DVD player, I hit stop then eject.

"Don't worry, baby, you can have that one." He laughed. "I got other copies."

"What did I ever do to you?" I asked, my tears starting again. "Why are you being like this?" There was a pregnant pause between us.

"Karma, baby," he said, giving me a look of disgust. "Karma." *What Karma? He did all the dirt and I was being punished!*

"Listen," he said, taking a deep breath, "you want out…I want out. Let's settle this. Pay me."

"Go to hell!" I screamed.

"Someday possibly," he said seriously, "but not today."

"I hate you!" I was shaking. There was a mixture of pain, anger and fear flowing through my blood. At that moment the thought of killing him ran through my head.

"I know you don't mean that." He laughed. "You're just upset right now. I'm going to give you some time to think," he said.

"There's nothing to think about," I said, wiping my tears away. "You're not getting a dime."

"We'll see about that," he said. "I got you on DVD screwing your man's brains out. I got pictures. I got trumped up documents, with a confession I didn't provide. By the way, that shit is illegal," he informed me, as if I didn't know.

"Well, I got proof you forged my name on a check made out to me." I cut him off. "Oh, and your daughter is proof that you're a cheating hoe."

"You're right." He laughed. "But here's the thing, you stayed with me after you found out about Kiya. After we reconciled, you were the one on tape getting their ass ate out," he stated. "You want to go to war, Tay?" He questioned. "Just remember you got a whole helluva lot more to lose than me."

He was right. Kenny didn't have shit, and that which he did have was mine. If I didn't play my cards right, I could be stuck taking care of him for the rest of his sorry life.

"I can see you have a lot to think about," he said. "I'll give you some time." He walked to the door, but before opening it, he turned and looked at me. "By the way," he said, "the Lexus dealership said *our* new whip came in early." He smiled, displaying all his teeth. "I can't wait to take a ride, babe." He opened the door. "Oh, and that ass looked real good on tape, real good." He licked his lips then walked out the door.

My life was spiraling out of control, and Kenny was holding the wheel. I slid down to the floor, crying uncontrollably. I thought I had Kenny where I wanted him, but I was wrong. He had me, and there wasn't a thing I could do about it.

***

After I finally regained my composure, I called my best friend. She was at my home in less than ten minutes. Octavia and I sat on my sofa looking at each other.

"What am I going to do?" I asked her.

"I don't know, Tay." She had compassion etched in her eyes. "But you gotta tell Savoy. Kenny knows who he is, and there's no telling what he's capable of," she added. She was right. I couldn't put Savoy at risk.

"I know from personal experience, hiding things from the man in your life can be deadly."

I had almost forgotten not long ago Octavia had been trapped in her own love triangle. When she and Damon met she was single and loving it, but somewhere along the line, she fell for Damon. However, it didn't stop her from hooking up with a dope boy named Beau. When Octavia tried to cut Beau off, he flipped out and started stalking her. Their fling almost cost her, her relationship with Damon and her life. In the end, Beau showed up at their home, and the triangle ended with Damon killing him in self-defense.

"Did I mention he has us on video?" I asked sadly.

"Who?" Octavia asked.

"Me and Savoy."

"Doing what?" Octavia looked puzzled.

"The nasty," I said, ashamed.

"Where?"

"The hotel balcony." I looked at her, as she processed the information. "Yep," I laughed. I was laughing to keep from crying. "Ass up, hanging off the railing."

"Weren't you on the 43rd floor?" Her eyes lit up.

"Yep."

"Dang, Tay," she chuckled, "you *are* a freak!"

This made me laugh because I knew my BFF, and she was not the one to talk.

"Takes one to know one." I laughed.

"Birds of a feather…"

"Flock together!" I finished her statement. We shared a laugh.

"And what is up with the brothers these days and the damn videotape?" She asked, rolling her eyes.

Much like myself, Octavia had her own sex tape that had been secretly recorded. Beau had videotaped the two of them getting down, and had sent a copy to Damon.

"I remember when men used to act like men," she said. "They respected the game."

"Not anymore," I told her. "These days, some of them act like straight punks."

"I know!" Octavia said, nodding her head. "Videotaping a chick and shit. They could at least ask first!" she added. We both laughed.

After our laughter subsided, things turned serious again.

"I can't let Kenny take half my money, Tavia," I said sadly. "I'm not giving him a dime."

"I understand that," she said, grabbing my hand. "And I wouldn't give him a dime if I was in your shoes."

"What would you do?" I asked.

"Call my attorney," she said.

"Shit, for her to say she told me so? She warned me from the very beginning," I informed her.

"Well next, I would call my back up plan." Octavia shrugged her shoulders.

"And who is your back up plan?" I was curious.

"My daddy."

"Sexy Charles." I said it jokingly, but between me and you, Octavia's Daddy really is fine.

"Don't make my mama cut you." Octavia laughed.

"Girl, I may appear stupid with everything that's going on now," I said truthfully. "But trust me, I'm not crazy." I laughed.

Octavia didn't share my hidden personal put down. Instead, she pulled me to her, allowing me to rest my head in her lap.

"You're not stupid," she said. "You made a bad decision by loving and marrying a sorry sack of shit. We've all made mistakes," she said, "but the trick is to keep pushing and looking for better days."

"How?" I asked, allowing my tears to flow freely.

"By putting the ball back in your court," she said. "Kenny just made his move, now it's time for you to make yours. If he doesn't want to play fair," she continued, "then we'll just have to change the rules."

"Tavia, I have a feeling that this isn't going to end well," I said honestly.

"You're right," Octavia agreed, "it's not going to end well." There was a moment of silence between us. "It's not going to end well," she repeated, "for him."

CHAPTER 27

After Octavia left, I took a long hot bath, then slipped into a pair of satin pajamas. I climbed into my bed, and called Savoy. I told him everything that happened with Kenny that day, and how my plan with Alicia had failed.

"It's not over yet," he said.

"I know, but it seems hopeless," I said.

"Baby, there's more than one way to skin a cat." There was something different in his voice. I couldn't put my finger on what, but it was something.

"Tay, we'll get through this," he said. "I promise you."

"Savoy, I don't want you to get caught up in my drama." I loved him too much to ruin his life. What happened with my life was one thing, but I couldn't hurt the people I loved.

"I'm already involved," he said "And I'm not going anywhere." His words made me smile. "As a matter of fact, I don't want you there," he said. "I would rather have you here with me."

The thought of lying in his arms made my heart smile and my kitty tingle. However, I refused to be run out of my own home.

"I would love that, baby," I said sincerely "But I have got to face Kenny head on."

"Shontay, things are going to get worse before they get better.

You don't deserve that type of pain. I want you here with me," he begged "Please, baby."

"Savoy, this is my home."

"I'll build you a new one," he said. "Hell, I'll build you two. Just please, baby." He continued to beg. Savoy sounded so sexy begging. Plus I didn't want to be alone, so I agreed.

"Okay, baby, but just for tonight," I finally said.

"Okay." His voice held a mixture of relief and disappointment. "That will do for now."

"I love you," I said, trying to lighten his mood.

"I love you too."

"I'll be there in a little bit."

"See you then."

After we hung up, I hopped out of bed and grabbed my overnight bag. After I packed a few things, I slipped out of my pj's and into a pair of fitted velour pants and a tank top.

Savoy pulled me through the door into his arms. I buried my face in his bare chest, inhaling the scent of Irish Spring. *Thank you Lord.* I thanked God because, through all my drama, He allowed me to meet such a beautiful man. Kissing my forehead lightly, Savoy held me tightly.

"Don't let go," I whispered.

"Don't worry, I can't." In one sweet swoop, he picked me up in his arms and carried me inside.

CHAPTER 28

I woke up the next morning with a smile on my face and dread in heart. I was happy to be with Savoy, but dreaded facing Kenny. I stretched slightly, not wanting to wake Savoy. He had his huge arms wrapped around me. He held me the entire night, never letting me go. I propped myself up on his chest, watching him as he slept. Even with his mouth half open, and the hint of drool at the corners of his lips, my man was fine. Savoy wiggled a little then slowly opened his eyes. Wiping his mouth with one hand, he smiled sweetly.

"Good morning, beautiful," he said.

"Good morning, daddy," I purred.

"How did you sleep?"

"I always sleep well when I'm with you." I was being truthful. I had slept like a baby in Savoy's arms.

"The feeling is mutual." He leaned forward and gave me a peck on the lips.

"Are you hungry?" I asked him.

Smiling seductively, Savoy squeezed my ass. "I'm always hungry," he replied.

"You are so nasty." I giggled. I pulled my legs up until I was straddling him.

"Put it right here," he instructed me, pointing to his lips.

"Gladly." Before I could assume the position, the phone rang.

"You were saved by the bell." He laughed. I rolled off of him so that he could retrieve the cordless handset.

"Morning, bro," he said. "We're good. How is Octavia and Jasmine?" I knew he was talking to Damon when I heard Octavia and my goddaughter's names. "I was about to get my morning meal until you called. You already know." Savoy chuckled. "Dame says hello," he told me.

"Tell him I said morning," I said.

"She said morning. Breakfast?" he asked, looking at me. I nodded my head in agreement. "Give us fifteen. Alright, one." Savoy ended his call with Damon. "Octavia is almost done with breakfast." He looked disappointed. "I guess our playtime will have to wait. But we always have the shower." He gave me his bad boy look.

Laughing, I rolled off the bed onto my feet. "I'll see you in there," I said.

Octavia had prepared bacon, scrambled eggs, pancakes, homemade biscuits, grits and sausage links. It was amazing how domesticated my girl had become. There was a time when a man couldn't get her to pour him a glass of ice tea.

The four of us sat around Octavia and Damon's breakfast table enjoying our meal.

"Baby, you get better and better," Damon said, smiling at Octavia.

"Are you referring to my cooking or something else?" Octavia asked, giving him a seductive smile.

"Both, baby, both!"

"You too are some damn freaks." Savoy laughed, wiping his mouth.

"No you didn't!" Damon looked shocked. "Baby, I called this brother about breakfast, and he was talking about he was just about to have his morning meal." Damon snitched.

Octavia looked from Savoy to me, then back to Savoy. "That's a shame," she said, shaking her head. "Y'all wake up trying to do the nasty."

"I know you didn't." Savoy looked at her. "Baby, tell me why one morning I woke up, and Mr. and Mrs. Whitmore here were butt naked in the Gazebo with a bowl of whip cream." I looked across the table at Octavia. Her honey brown eyes were big as fifty cent pieces.

"Damn freak!" I teased.

She stood and started collecting our empty plates. "First of all, it was melted white chocolate, and second, we thought Savoy was gone." I laughed.

"I came out the guesthouse with my gun." Savoy laughed. "I thought it was a rabid bear or something. All I heard was GR-RRRRRRRR…GRRRRR." He mimicked. "It turned out to be Damon!" We all cracked up at the same time.

"I told you I have allergies." Damon blushed. "There was a tickle in my throat. I was just trying to clear it!" He stood to assist Octavia.

"Sure," I teased. I stood to help the two of them.

"Sit down!" they ordered at the same time. I did as I was ordered.

"They feel some kinda way about people and their kitchen," Savoy whispered. "I found that out the first night I was here."

"We heard that," they said in unison.

I watched the two of them washing dishes together. I looked at Savoy, wondering if one day I would share that type of love and connection. He looked at me and smiled.

"I tried to convince Tay to stay here until things with Kenny are resolved," Savoy said.

"I think that's a great idea!" Octavia said, looking over shoulder. She and Damon finished the dishes, and then returned to the table to join Savoy and myself.

"I would love to be here," I said honestly. "However, I can't run from my problems."

"It's not running, Tay," Octavia said, running her fingers through her hair. "It's making sure you're safe and secure."

"Thank you," Savoy agreed.

"I'm worth more to Kenny alive than dead," I said. "I doubt he will try anything."

"But you never know," Savoy reminded me.

"True," Octavia agreed.

"Shontay's right," Damon finally spoke.

"What?" Octavia looked at him sideways. "Baby, we don't know what Kenny's capable of!" The look in her face indicated her disapproval. Damon took her hand in his, and kissed it gently.

"Hear me out, Boo," he said. Octavia took a deep breath then exhaled. "If she moves out, Kenny has more ammunition," he reasoned. "We have to make sure that the cards are played in Tay's favor."

"Can't we do that with her here?" Savoy questioned. "Dame, I just got a bad vibe," he added.

"I do too," Octavia agreed. I looked at Damon. He smiled his winning smile.

"Do you all trust me?" he asked.

"Baby, of course I do," Octavia said, squeezing his hand.

"Me too," I added

"Do you?" Damon asked, looking at Savoy.

The two of them stared at each other briefly. The tension was so thick you could cut it with a knife. I looked at Octavia, who shrugged her shoulders indicating she sensed it too.

"Of course I do," Savoy finally answered. "You're my brother." Damon smiled slowly.

"Everything is going to be alright," Damon said. "Despite the power Kenny thinks he has, he's about to be dethroned."

CHAPTER 29

Octavia and I decided to have a girl's day out, while Damon and Savoy were off to the Ambiance 2 to look over the progress. Octavia's grand opening was quickly approaching, and the guys wanted to make sure there were no issues holding her back. We all agreed to hook up later in the day for dinner.

I hadn't returned to my home yet, and Kenny had yet to contact me. I figured after some much needed girl time, I would go home to see what was waiting for me. In the meantime, I planned to enjoy the day with my best friend and goddaughter. Our first stop was by the Lexus dealership to pick up my new car. I was more than excited to see everything to my liking.

"I love the color!" Octavia squealed, looking at the fresh paint job. "It's hot."

"Isn't it?" I asked, smiling like a kid with a new toy.

"Yes ma'am."

"You don't think it's too much?" I questioned.

"You're asking the woman who has two Mercedes, a Land Rover, and a Hummer in her garage?" She laughed sarcastically.

"Okay, when you put it that way." I laughed, running my fingers across the hood of my new ride.

"You deserve it," she added. "After taking care of Mr. Dumbass all these years, you deserve the finer things in life. And I'm not just talking about the car, Tay," she said. "You deserve Savoy, and anything else you want or need." I gave her a faint smile. "What's wrong?" She had concern stamped in her voice.

"What if all of it slips away?" I asked, tearing up. "What if Kenny makes sure that I end up with nothing?"

"He doesn't have the power to make or break you," she said soothingly. "At this moment, Kenny is just a bug waiting to be squashed." I laughed. "So what do you say we swing by Zonda's so you can get those micros freshened up." Octavia wrinkled her nose, looking at the top of my head.

I knew my braids didn't stink, but it was time for me to get them touched up, due to my hair growing since I first had them done.

"Works for me." I smiled.

"Then we'll take lil mama to her grannies house." She peeked through the back window of her Mercedes at Jasmine, who was sleeping peacefully in her car seat. "Then the two of us shall go shopping." She smiled her winning smile. "We still have to get our attire together for the grand opening of Ambiance 2."

"That's right," I stated, as if a light bulb just went off in my head. "With everything that's been going on, I totally forgot we had a major event coming up."

"Yes we do." She grinned. "And the two of us can be no less than fabulous."

"That shouldn't be hard."

"Of course not," Octavia placed one of her well manicured hands on her hip, "because when you're as fine as we are, some things just come naturally."

***

It was a good forty-five minute drive to the Ellis home, but the time passed flawlessly while riding in my new vehicle. I parked behind Octavia's Mercedes, inhaled the sweet new car smell one more time before getting out.

Octavia's parents' home was situated on six beautiful green acres of land. From the outside, their four bedroom red brick rancher looked historical, with its beautiful classic columns and wrap around porch. The shutters were painted a soothing emerald green, and they were the kind that you could pull together to cover the window or push open to reveal it. The house was surrounded by a cute white picket fence, tiny well manicured shrubs, and three big weeping willows. From the outside, the home gave off a cute Mayberry vibe.

The inside was completely updated with granite counter tops, glamour baths, and stainless steel appliances. Octavia's father had built the home for himself, but later remodeled the inside when he and Octavia's mother remarried. Octavia said her mother liked modern appliances and furnishings, but she also loved the antique look. Her father gave her the best of both.

Before we could reach the front porch, Charlene came bouncing out the front door. She wore a long sky-blue off the shoulder cotton dress, and black open toe wedge heels. Even in her fifties, Octavia's mother was beautiful. Her brown skin showed no signs of wrinkles or those unsightly crows' feet. Her brown sugar complexion seemed to glow. She gave the two of us a sparkling white smile, and extended her arms out to Octavia.

"Give me my grandbaby," Charlene said.

"Dang Mama!" Octavia whined. She gently handed Charlene the convertible baby carrier that held a sleeping Jasmine inside. "I'm fine. And you?" Octavia asked, pouting slightly. Charlene gazed down at her sleeping granddaughter, then turned her attention to her daughter.

"I'm sorry." She smiled again. "How is my baby?"

"I'm fabulous." Octavia gave Charlene a big smile, and leaned in to kiss her cheek.

"Good."

"How are you, Shontay?" Charlene asked, giving me a look filled with compassion and concern.

"I'm fine, Ms. Charlene," I said.

"I was very sorry to hear about your mama," she said sincerely.

I gave her a small smile, while attempting to fight back tears. I had been so caught up in my drama with Kenny, I hadn't thought about spreading my mother's ashes, or even much about my mother at all. In a way it was a good thing, but in another, I felt somewhat guilty.

"Thank you." I smiled half-heartedly, as she leaned in and kissed my cheek.

"Where's Daddy?" Octavia asked

"He's out back frying a few catfish he caught this morning."

"Eww, sounds good." Octavia rubbed her flat belly. "But Tay and I have a shopping date."

"There's also hushpuppies, cole slaw, macaroni and cheese and," she gave me a loving smile, "my famous peach cobbler."

I loved Charlene's homemade cobbler. It was no surprise to me that Octavia went into the restaurant business herself, because her family could and loved to cook. My stomach started to grumble from the thought of eating the meal the Ellis had prepared. Octavia cocked her head to the side, and looked from me to her mother.

"If I didn't know any better, I would swear you and Daddy were trying to keep us here," Octavia said.

Charlene batted her long black lashes, and gave us her signature smile. "Would I try and bribe my only *two* daughters with food?" Her emphasis on the word two made my heart flutter.

"Yes you would!" Octavia laughed.

"Did it work?" she asked. Octavia and I looked at each other, and nodded in agreement. Charlene smiled triumphantly. "Wonderful." She turned on her wedge heels, still carrying Jasmine, and then went through the front door. Octavia and I laughed, as we followed behind her.

After Charlene laid Jasmine down in the princess theme room they designated as Jasmine's bedroom, the three of us went out to the outdoor kitchen to see Octavia's father, Charles. He stood over the deep fryer removing golden brown catfish fillets. I smiled immediately. I can not and will not deny that I have, and probably forever will have, a crush on Charles. Looking at the tall, handsome chocolate man, I further confirmed my crush was forever.

Charles looked up at the three of us approaching and smiled, his honey brown eyes shinning brightly.

"Hey Daddy!" Octavia cooed, throwing her arms around her

father's neck.

"Hey, baby girl." He turned his head to give her a light peck on the cheek. "How you doing?" he asked, stroking Octavia's cheek lovingly.

"I'm good," she said.

I stood back a little, letting them enjoy their father-daughter moment. Charlene walked up to the place where Charles had sat the pan of cooked fish and picked it up.

"I'm going in to check on the rest of the food." She flashed me a smile, and then headed back towards the house.

"Tay!" Charles grinned, removing the apron he was wearing. "Come give me a hug." I smiled, and strolled over to the place where he and Octavia were standing. He gave me a fatherly embrace, then stepped back to look at me. "You look good," he said. "You lost some weight."

"Yes sir." I smiled proudly.

"Good deal." He smiled, holding one arm out for Octavia, and the other out for me. "Let's take a walk," he said.

Octavia and I each took one of his arms, while looking at each other suspiciously. Charles led us from the outdoor kitchen, down through the beautifully manicured lawn, to a white rose covered gazebo. The breeze was cool but not cold, a subtle reminder that fall was approaching, and soon I would have to change up my wardrobe. We strolled along with an uncomfortable silence hovering over us. We settled onto the bench inside the gazebo before anyone spoke.

"What is it, Daddy?" The look in Octavia's eyes showed that she was worried.

"I'm fine, baby girl." Charles patted her hand, and relief washed across Octavia's face. "This is about Tay." He darted his eyes in my direction.

"What about me?" I asked nervously.

"I hear there are some problems with you and Kenny." Charles looked at me with raised eyebrows.

I shot Octavia a look, asking if she had filled her parents in on my marriage issues. She shook her head, answering my unspoken question. Neither one of us responded to Charles statement. There was a pregnant pause between the three of us.

"I'm listening." Charles looked from me to Octavia then back to me. I stared into the calmness of his smoldering eyes and exhaled.

"Well…" I began, before pouring my heart out about my current situation and the complete and utter mess that I was currently in. I left out the part about the DVD due to embarrassment, but I did fill him in on my relationship with Savoy.

***

Once Octavia, Charles and I returned to the house we filled Charlene in on the drama.

After lunch, the four of us sat around the dining room table recuperating from our meal.

"So what's the plan?" Charlene asked, looking at Charles.

"I don't have one yet."

"Our girls are always getting themselves into messes." Charlene shook her head as she stared across the table. She looked from Octavia to me.

"Mama, we don't ask for trouble," Octavia said, sucking on her teeth.

"I know, I know," Charlene said, waving her hand in the air.

"And the thing with me and Savoy just kinda happened." I was being honest. I had no intention of things getting so hot and heavy with Savoy, but it was too late now. I was completely in love with him, and there wasn't any changing that.

"I know, sweetie." Charlene reached across the table and patted my hand. "I just wish the two of you could have been a little more discreet."

"Mama!" Octavia's eyes were wide.

"What?"

I watched Octavia as she crossed her arms across her breasts. "Weren't you the one out at the movies, rollerblading, and taking trips to Tunica with your *then* ex-husband, while your *then* husband was away caring for his depressed daughter?" she asked.

Charlene ran her fingers through her feathered bob, and cleared her throat. I looked at Charles, who was trying hard to keep from smiling. Before Charles and Charlene got remarried, the two of them had a very public affair while Charlene was still with her ex-husband, Bill.

"That's different," Charlene said, giving Octavia her famous *don't try me* look.

"How?" Octavia asked.

"Because I said so!" Charlene stated firmly. I looked from Octavia to Charlene and giggled.

Octavia rolled her eyes, but didn't say a word. It was amazing that at twenty-eight years old Octavia knew not to try her mama.

"I need some time to think about how we're going to handle this," Charles said, changing the subject.

"I appreciate all of you wanting to help, but I have to handle this on my own," I said sincerely. I loved all of them for wanting to rescue me, but I knew it was my mess, and that I had to handle it alone.

"Did we sound like we were giving you an option?" Charlene asked. She gave me the same look she had just given Octavia.

"No ma'am," I said.

"Well alright then," she said, rising from the table. "Charles will figure out the best solution. The two of you," she pointed at me then at Octavia, "will keep your butts out of trouble."

"Mama, if Shontay…" Octavia began.

"Case closed." Charlene cut Octavia off quickly.

"But Ms. Charlene..." I began.

"I said *case closed*!"

I immediately closed my mouth. I watched as Charlene gave Charles a quick peck on the cheek, then walked around the table, kissed Octavia on the forehead, and then kissed my forehead as well. She turned on her wedge heels, and slowly switched out the kitchen. The three of us sat silent for a brief moment.

"Daddy, what have you done to her?" Octavia whispered, leaning forward in her chair. "Ever since you two got back together, Mama has been off the chain!"

Charles laughed, rubbing his hands together. "I guess I bring out the best in her." He smiled.

"You bring out the *something* in her," Octavia teased. "So you're going to try and help Tay?" she asked, getting serious.

"Of course I am." He looked at me, and smiled gently. "You've always been a good friend to Octavia, I thank you for that."

I smiled back, looking at the handsome man. I had so many bad things and bad people in my life that it was hard to believe that people like Octavia, Damon, The Ellis, and Savoy existed. It was even harder to believe they were a part of my life, and that they loved me just as much as I loved them.

"Thank you," I said.

Charles nodded without saying a word. Now that he was treating me like his other daughter, maybe I could stop drooling over him. I stared across the table, looking at his chocolate features. *Naw, I doubt it!*

"Daddy, I have one question for you," Octavia said.

"What's that, baby girl?"

"How did you and Mama know something was up with Kenny and Tay?" Octavia had asked the question that had yet to cross my mind, but now that she put it out there, I too was curious.

"Your mama overheard a couple of women talking about it."

"Where?" Octavia and I asked at the same time.

"The Hairtip."

"The Hairtip?" I asked, confused as to why someone, anyone, would be discussing me at the Hairtip.

The Hairtip was a local salon where Octavia got her hair done regularly. I went there, but it had been a while due to my new obsession with Zondra and her technique for doing braids. I could have gotten my hair braided at the Hairtip, but the last time I went I felt somewhat out of place, like people were staring and talking about me. I guess my feelings were justified.

"Alicia," Octavia mumbled.

"What about Alicia?" I asked curiously.

"I completely forgot she gets her hair done there." Octavia gave me a look, letting me know she had been withholding information from me. "Mona told me last year while I was there for one of my appointments," Octavia advised. "I didn't tell you because…well."

"It's okay," I reassured her. I knew my girl was trying to protect me, so I wasn't trippin'.

"Do you think Alicia told someone at the salon about the offer?" Octavia questioned.

"Could be," Charles answered. "That would explain how Kenny knew."

"I don't know." I pondered over the possibilities. The more I thought about it, the more it seemed feasible that Alicia could have told someone, and they told someone who told Kenny.

"We may never know," Charles said.

Jasmine had been asleep the majority of our visit. When Octavia and I were ready to leave that had changed. Charlene kindly volunteered to keep Jasmine all night. After calling Damon, just to verify he was cool with it, Octavia gratefully obliged. Octavia was one of the best moms I knew. She would only leave Jasmine for a few hours, and rarely had she allowed Jasmine to stay all night anywhere.

"I don't want to inconvenience anyone," she'd say. I think she was so attached to Jasmine she just couldn't let go for long. I'm sure the only reason she had agreed to let Jasmine stay tonight was because she wanted to keep an eye on me. Octavia confirmed my suspicions after we kissed Jasmine and her parents' goodbye.

"You want to go get a couple of drinks?" she asked, as we walked to our cars.

"I'd better get home," I said gloomily.

"You're right" She smiled. "No need to delay the inevitable." I nodded my head in agreement. "I'm coming with you."

She climbed into her Mercedes and shut the door before I could protest. I shook my head, but inside I was secretly thankful she was so stubborn. I was nervous about being around Kenny alone. Not for myself, but instead for him.

Chapter 30

I heard the music pumping from the stereo before I got out of my car. I also felt the anger coursing through my veins. I waited by my car door, while Octavia climbed out her car with her Louis Vuitton handbag in hand. I watched as she admired the Escalade hogging the driveway.

"What is it with assholes and Escalades?" she asked sarcastically. I laughed lightly, remembering her stalker, Beau, had driven an Escalade.

"Wish I knew," I said, walking to the front door with Octavia so close she almost stepped on my heels.

I opened the front door, and the scent almost knocked me on my butt. My already accelerated blood pressure went through the roof. Kenny was sitting on the sofa in *my* house getting high. He looked up at me with glazed eyes, then when he saw Octavia his eyes widened.

"Well, well, well." He smiled, taking another pull from his half smoked blunt. "Octavia."

"Kenny." Octavia said his name like it left a bad taste in her mouth.

I looked at Octavia, her eyes were lowered in small angry slits. She clutched her bag to her side like it was her life preserver. I pulled my eyes from her, marched over to the stereo and turned it off.

"Nice to see you, Tavia." Kenny smiled, eyeing Octavia. I watched his eyes scan from her head down to her French pedicure.

Laughing, Octavia gave him a fake smile. "Wish I could say the same," she said.

"Let's go in the kitchen," I said to Octavia, but kept my eyes on Kenny. He looked like a black python the way he watched Octavia's every move. I watched him lick his lips, as he continued to stare her down.

"You're looking good, Tavia." He smiled. He leaned forward, putting the blunt out in the ashtray sitting on the table in front of him. "Real good," he said. "That body bounced back from the baby." He continued on as if I wasn't even there. "Did you come over to show me just how well that body bounced back?"

Octavia stopped in her tracks, still clutching her bag to her side. It wasn't until then that I realized why she had such a threatening grip on her purse.

"In your dreams." She chuckled.

"Oh I've had them." He laughed. He looked at me with raised eyebrows. "Sorry, boo, I figure we might as well be honest. We've been lying to each other for far too long." He looked back at Octavia then to me. "To be *honest* I've had quite a few dreams. Would you ladies like to help me fulfill them?"

I wanted to scream that I hated him and wanted him to die, but I knew that now was not the time. Octavia placed her hand on her hip, and cocked her head to the side.

"If I remember correctly, you barely had enough for one." She smiled a smile that oozed with arrogance. "Yet alone for two." I laughed.

I had forgotten Octavia had the displeasure of seeing Kenny naked when the two of us busted him on one of his cheating sprees. Kenny looked pissed off by the open put down of his manhood. He stood abruptly, his eyes glazed and red from his being high.

"Besides," Octavia further pushed him, "once you've been upgraded, it's hard to go back to the *small* things in life."

"Why don't I show your stuck up ass just what I can do," Kenny snapped, breathing heavy. Octavia appeared unaffected by his obvious anger.

"And why don't I show you what I can do," Octavia said. I watched her as she slowly slid the zipper on her bag open, and slid her hand inside.

"I think I'll take you up on that offer," I spoke quickly. I had to defuse the situation before someone, mainly Kenny, got hurt. "Tavia, why don't you just go wait for me in the car?"

"No way." She spoke to me, but continued her stare down with Kenny.

"Just to give me a few minutes to pack," I said. This caught both of their attention.

"Where the fuck you going?" Kenny barked. "You spending the night with Ziggy?" It was amazing that his attention had been taken off of Octavia so quickly.

"Who's Ziggy?" Octavia asked, her hand still inside her purse.

"He's referring to Savoy," I said.

"I know you didn't." She laughed. "You could learn some things from Savoy."

"Oh yeah?" Kenny snarled. "Like what?"

"Like how not to be a little bitch," she spat, "who preys on women because he doesn't have enough nuts to go out and get his own." Kenny didn't retaliate, so she winked her eye then turned on her heels. "I'll be right outside." She gave me a smile, and sashayed out the door.

Kenny mumbled some profanities, before turning his attention back to me. I stared into his cold dark eyes. I knew what I had to do. I was tired of arguing, and tired of others feeling like they had to come to my rescue.

"Fine," I said firmly. "You win."

I came out of my home with my suitcase in one hand, and the urn with my mother's ashes in the other. Octavia was posted by the door, still clutching her bag. She looked at me in a way that told me she overheard my conversation with Kenny. I was ready for her to yell, scream, or even shake some sense into me. She didn't. She smiled.

"Let's get out of here," was the only thing she said.

"Okay," I mumbled, feeling half defeated.

We walked in silence to our separate vehicles. I didn't look back, I knew I was making the right decision. I knew money and pride were not worth losing or hurting the people who I loved. I also knew that as wonderful and loving as my best friend was, she was also hot headed. If Kenny tried her, she wouldn't hesitate to protect me because she loved me. I knew inside her beautiful Louis Vuitton bag she had her hand on her gun.

After telling Damon and Savoy that I had agreed to pay Kenny off, there was a thick fog of tension surrounding the four of us. Savoy and Damon felt I should have stood my ground and fought Kenny all the way. Octavia being the friend that she is; stood by me, although I knew she felt the same. I could hear it in her voice when she called Charles and told him that he didn't have to worry about working on a solution. I was so stressed that I dismissed myself to the guesthouse without dinner or socializing. I took a shower then climbed into bed. I was truly drowning in self-pity. Savoy waited for approximately an hour before coming to join me. We didn't talk, he just snuggled in close to me and held me in his arms.

CHAPTER 31

It was unseasonably cool for an early October day, so I decided to wear my new purple sheath Ann Taylor dress with matching mid knee blazer and a pair of purple stiletto pumps. I looked sexy but I felt like a complete pile of crap. I couldn't stop replaying the way things had gone down with Kenny. He finally won and there wasn't a thing I could do about it. I called my attorney's office and set up an appointment. I knew, much like my friends, my attorney would be disappointed too, but it was what it was. Now that Kenny had what he wanted, he was more than happy to sign papers. I rode to the bank feeling like I had the weight of the world on my shoulders. I was actually going to withdraw the money to pay for the truck.

I had gone to my preferred bank branch, and the line was practically out the door. I was in a mood, so I left and drove another thirty minutes to the University Drive branch. I hated the University Drive branch because I always saw someone I knew and didn't want to be bothered with. Today was no exception.

In the parking lot I ran into Michelle from the daycare. Her hair still looked a hot mess. She told me what felt like a hundred times that she missed me. Then she not so nonchalantly asked what I was up to, and why I had quit. I told her for personal reasons and that I was in a hurry.

I stood in line, staring at nothing in particular until I heard a somewhat familiar voice. I turned my head to see who the voice belonged to. I saw the woman, but couldn't put my finger on where I knew her from. She was wearing a navy blue pantsuit and blue pumps. She was standing in the doorway of one of the corner offices speaking with an elderly couple. I figured maybe I had seen her at my branch, but something kept telling me that wasn't how I knew her. I watched as she shook the couples' hand, and then escorted them out the office.

I turned my head so she wouldn't catch me staring, at the same time the teller called next. I moved slowly to the counter, and then casually looked in the direction of the office. The woman was inside sitting behind a desk. I was so caught up in trying to figure out who she was that I hadn't heard the teller speaking to me.

"How may I help you?" she asked again, looking annoyed.

I glanced up into her pale blue eyes just long enough to ask, "Who is she?" I nodded in the direction of the office.

"Our branch manager, she said sharply.

"What's her name?" I asked.

"Donna Briceson," she replied.

"Donna Briceson," I repeated robotically. *Could it be?*

"Ma'am, can I help you with something?" The teller continued to get snappy. Little did she know she had already helped me. I ignored her, and stared in Donna's direction. *It was!*

"Thanks," I mumbled, turning and hurrying out of the bank.

I was halfway to my car when I dug in my purse to retrieve my cell phone. I quickly dialed Alicia's home number. It was sad, but yes, I had my husband's baby mama's number memorized. It rang and rang and rang, but there was no answer. I went to my contacts on my Blackberry, and found Kenny's name. I went in to view the numbers I had stored under his name. I had gotten Alicia's cell phone number out of Kenny's phone, so that I could compare it to our phone bill and keep up with how often he was calling Alicia. Thinking about it now, I realized I should have filed for a divorce ages ago. No one should have to go through so much drama. I dialed *67 then dialed the number. It was one thing for Alicia to have my home number, but it was a different story with my cell.

"Hello?" I didn't respond. "Hello? Look, Alicia," Donna snapped, "stop playing on my damn phone!" Then she hung. I knew it was her, but I wanted to be extra sure.

I walked back into the bank, and then redialed the number. Sure enough, Donna Bricemore flipped open her cell and I heard her practically yell, "Hello?" I hung up quickly, and hauled ass out of the bank. I made it back to my Lexus and quickly climbed in.

I suddenly felt as beautiful as I looked. I knew it could all be a coincidence, but my heart told me better. Considering her role at the bank, I was willing to bet Donna was the one who helped Kenny cash my check. I was also willing to bet she was the one who told him about my proposition to Alicia. Kenny had hired a private investigator to follow me and Savoy in Vegas. I decided that it was time for me to do the same.

Hey Tay," Octavia said, answering on the first ring.

"Call Charles," I said.

"You changed your mind?"

"No, not yet," I said honestly. "But I have some new info."

"I'm listening."

I brought Octavia up to speed on my current discovery. Then I made the drive back to my preferred branch of Regions. I withdrew every dime of my money, closed my account, and then drove across the street to Wachovia and opened all new accounts.

CHAPTER 32

Over the next couple of weeks, four important things happened. One, I paid off the checks Kenny had written. Two, I bought him the Escalade. Three, I hired a very bubbly and eager realtor by the name of Stephanie to help me sell my house. I was not going to let Kenny have it, and he was not going to let me live there in peace, so we came to a mutual agreement that I would put the house on the market and we would split the profit. Four, but definitely not the least important, Charles confirmed my suspicions. Kenny and Donna were seeing each other. He even gave me copies of pictures, he had taken of the two of them leaving and entering Donna's apartment. I was still banking on the fact that Alicia knew nothing about it. I decided it was time for me to confirm that suspicion as well.

Alicia agreed to meet me at Starbucks. I didn't want to risk the chance of Donna, or worse, Kenny catching me at Alicia's. Plus, Octavia insisted on being on stakeout. She was parked across the street in the event that anything went wrong.

Alicia was waiting on me when I arrived. She looked extremely tired. She wore her hair up in a curly ponytail. It wasn't blond or any other bold color, it was black and it actually complimented her. I took a seat across from her, and gave her a small smile.

"Hey," I said.

"Hey." She smiled.

"You took your gold cap out," I said.

"Yeah." She looked nervous.

"I think you look better without it," I said sincerely.

"Thanks." She lowered her eyes.

It was at that moment that a new thought crossed my mind. Alicia was vulnerable, almost childlike, without her friends around. She looked like a woman who had been scorned and broken.

"Where's Donna?" I asked casually.

"I'm not sure." She fidgeted with her fingers, then finally added, "I haven't seen her in weeks. We had a big fight, and she told me to leave her alone."

"Alicia, are you aware that Donna and Kenny have been sleeping together?"

Her eyebrows raised, but she didn't look surprised. "I knew they were," she said. "The three of us…" She didn't have to finish her sentence, but I already knew.

"How did the three of you hook up?" I asked.

"Kenny wanted a threesome, and we were willing."

"So you knew Donna, and introduced her to Kenny?"

"Yeah, Donna and I met like a year ago."

I let her words sink in for a moment. I knew that Donna had been Kenny's connect at the bank, which linked the two of them together much longer than a year.

"I have proof Kenny and Donna knew each other way before you met her," I spoke softly.

I reached into my bag and pulled out the surveillance photos of Kenny and Donna together. Looking at Alicia, I slid the photos across the table. She hesitated before picking up the pictures one by one. She studied the photos carefully, then finally looked at me. There were tears in her eyes, but those tears didn't hide the anger and betrayal in them.

Alicia let out a small nervous laugh, shaking her head. "They've been playin' me," she said. She stared off into space, then looked at me with eyes so frightening I would have run if I didn't know her. "Every dog has his day," she said. "Every bitch does too."

"How did it go?" Octavia had her pink University of Alabama baseball hat pulled snuggly down over her eyes.

"It went well," I said, climbing into the passenger side of her Range Rover.

"Fabulous." She smiled, starting the vehicle. "Operation shakedown is in full effect." I looked at her then burst out laughing.

"Operation shakedown?" I asked her.

Octavia pushed the brim of her hat up so that I could see her honey brown eyes. "Do you have a problem with the name of the operation?" she asked, popping her lips.

"No, no," I teased. "I love it, but it's very obvious you've been watching too much *CSI*."

"Sad but true." She laughed. I giggled along with her, as I put my seatbelt on. Octavia slowly pulled away from the curb.

"So you told her everything?" Octavia asked.

"Yep, and she wasn't happy."

"Did we really expect her to be?" Octavia was right. I don't know what reaction I was expecting from Alicia.

"No," I said.

"So you gave her the package?"

"Yep." I stared out the tinted windows, gazing at nothing in particular.

"Are the two of you friends now?"

"Not at all." I looked over at Octavia. "I have all the friends I need." She took her eyes away from the road just long enough to flash me her beautiful smile.

"Well, I think it's really nice what you're doing for her," Octavia said.

"Yeah, but she's doing something for me too," I said, feeling guilty.

I was giving Alicia something, but she was also giving me something in return. Did that really make me any better than Donna or Kenny?

"You're not like them." Octavia said, as if she had been reading my mind. "You would help Alicia even if she didn't do it."

Octavia was right. I would help Alicia even if she decided she wanted nothing to do with "operation shakedown". However, I didn't have to worry about Alicia's participation. The look in her eyes told me she would help in any shape, form or fashion to bring Kenny down. I had provided her with enough ammunition; the pictures of Donna and Kenny, and enough motivation...money. She was on board, and something told me she was more willing than any of us to bring them down.

"So how are you?" I quickly changed the subject.

"I'm good." Octavia smiled.

I had been so caught up in my own drama that I hadn't taken the time to see how things were for my best friend.

"And married life?"

"Damon is wonderful." Her voice seemed to radiate. "I love being a wife. I love being a mother."

"But?" I asked, knowing there was something she wasn't saying.

There was silence, as Octavia merged onto I-565, headed towards her home. "Damon has been talking about having another baby," she finally said.

"Yeah, but I thought you wanted more kids too." I remembered a previous conversation where we had discussed her having at least two or three more kids.

"I do," she said. "Well, I did."

"What changed your mind?" I watched as her lips curled up into a small smile.

"Jazz," she said. "I had no idea I would fall so in love with anyone," she said. "But I did when I had her."

"That makes sense."

"Plus I want my career back," she added. Octavia still owned Ambiance, and now she would be running Ambiance 2. I was completely confused as to why she felt she lost her career. I looked at her with my eyebrows raised. "Yes, I have the Ambiance and Ambiance 2." She sighed. "But I miss being in my restaurant on a daily basis. I miss being at the forefront."

Now I understood. Since having Jasmine, Octavia had only made appearances at her establishment. Before, she was there six days a week.

"So go back," I said. "You can be a mother and still have your career."

"Yeah, but I'll feel like a total and complete jerk if I dump Jasmine in daycare," she said exhaling. "I know Mama would be happy to watch Jasmine, but she and Daddy just got in a good place."

"And you don't want to inconvenience them," I finished.

"Right."

"What about a nanny?" I suggested. Octavia paused, and looked at me. I could tell she was considering it.

"That might work," she said. Instantly it sounded as if her mood had been lifted.

"She'd have to be licensed in CPR," I said. There was no way just anybody could take care of my goddaughter.

"And Christian," Octavia said.

"But not too holy," I added.

"Yeah, we can't have her condemning us to hell because of our minor flaws."

"And she'd have to have excellent references."

"Pass a background check," Octavia threw in.

"Mature," I added.

"And ugly," I darted my eyes in her direction. "What?" she asked innocently. "I've read the stories about affairs with the nanny." She laughed lightly.

"Damon only has eyes for you," I reassured her.

"Maybe, but I'm not willing to take any chances." I nodded my head in agreement.

"Okay, so we know what we need," I said, laughing lightly. "Now we just have to find her."

"Just one more thing," Octavia said. We pulled up to the iron gate outside her home. She hit the automatic opener on her sun visor.

"What else could there be?" I asked.

Sitting back against the driver's seat, she looked at me. Her eyes were wide with concern. "I have to convince Damon," she said.

CHAPTER 33

Fall had definitely fallen. It seemed in a twinkling of an eye the leaves had gone from green to burnt orange and beautiful shades of red. The temperature had dipped to the mid-sixties, and the nights were as low as the forties. I didn't mind. I had Savoy and his perfect body to keep me warm.

Stephanie had located a buyer for my home, and closing was set for November 18th, which was just a month away. The terms and conditions of my divorce had yet to be worked out with my attorney because I hadn't filed yet. I was waiting because I was counting on things turning in my favor.

I stood looking at my reflection in the floor length mirror. I smiled. My braids were pulled high on top of my head, which were held in place by several crystal covered bobby pins. The ends were curled in tiny spiral curls. I turned to the left then to the right, admiring my reflection in the mirror. The purple silk spaghetti strap ankle length gown hugged my body, highlighting every curve. I had put a couple of pounds back on, due to stress and not running everyday, but I was still wearing the dress. I vowed after everything was over, I would start working out again.

My gown was a gift from Octavia. She had purchased it from a local boutique, but it was still a designer, so I was willing to bet money that she paid a pretty price for it. I wore open toe stilettos the same color of my dress. They had slim crystal-encrusted straps going across the toes and around the ankle. The shoes were also a gift from my BFF. Around my neck, I wore the locket my mother had given me. The dress, the shoes, not even the one-carat diamond studs Savoy had given me, could compare to the locket hanging from my neck.

I applied a thin layer of my Mac Lustre lip gloss, and quickly grabbed my purple silk wrap and purple clutch off the bed. I hurried out of the guest bedroom, down the hall, and walked down the winding staircase. Octavia had insisted that I get dressed in one of the guest bedrooms in the main house rather than the guesthouse.

"It's too far to walk," she complained. "And I don't want anything getting on the bottom of that dress."

Octavia stood at the bottom of the staircase, waiting for me. She looked like a beauty pageant contestant, minus the over the top make-up. Octavia's make-up was natural looking. She had just a hint of bronze eye shadow on her lids and glossy pink lip gloss. I knew it was also Mac's lip gloss because we had purchased it together. Her dress was gold silk and strapless. It hugged her body as well, and was also ankle length. However, the bottom of her dress flared out like a fishtail. Her shoes were gold open toe stilettos that tied around her ankles with gold ribbons. She wore her naturally long hair pulled straight back in a neat ponytail. Around her arms she too wore a silk shawl, however, hers was gold to match her dress. The light seemed to bounce off her diamond chandelier earrings and matching diamond necklace.

"Hellooo sexy," she teased, letting out a low whistle.

I stepped off the bottom stair and onto the marble floor. Putting my hand on my hip, I did my version of a runway model's turn.

"You look fabulous." She smiled.

"Thank you," I said, returning her smile. "You look pretty hot yourself." She put her hand on her hip, shifting her weight from one leg to the other, shaking her hips.

"Thank you, thank you," she said, batting her long eyelashes.

We giggled and teased each other for a few more seconds before heading out the front door to the waiting chauffeured car. Damon had rented a stretch Mercedes limo to transport Octavia and myself to Ambiance 2.

He and Savoy had left a few minutes earlier so they could make sure everything was running smoothly. I have to say the two of them looked like two GQ models in their black tuxedos. They each wore mid-length jackets and silk shirts and ties. Damon wore a gold shirt and tie to match Octavia's dress, and Savoy wore purple to match my dress. Savoy's twists had grown long enough for me to secure them neatly with a rubber band. He looked like a black king, and I was glad he was mine.

After settling into the limo, Octavia and I poured ourselves glasses of champagne. We were quieter than normal, and I imagined she was thinking about the same thing I was.

"Where's your ring?" she asked, looking at my bare ring finger.

I had completely forgotten the gold band I had stuffed in my handbag earlier. Let's be honest, I hadn't worn my wedding band since what seemed like forever. I popped my purse open and retrieved the ring. Sliding it on my finger, I stared at it for a moment like it was diseased. It felt uncomfortable. I had wrapped a ring guard around it earlier. It was too big because of the weight I had lost when I first met Savoy, but this wasn't why it was uncomfortable. It was uncomfortable because it no longer meant what it once had to me.

"It's going to be fine," Octavia said. I looked up into her shining eyes.

"I know," I said. "I know."

"Are you okay?" she asked, genuinely concerned.

It was amazing that this was her big night, but she was worried about me. The things we had planned for this night could possibly tarnish her reputation, or even worse destroy it, but yet I was her main concern. I knew what I had to do. There was no turning back now.

"I'm fine." I forced myself to smile. I held my crystal champagne glass in the air, and said with as much enthusiasm that I could muster, "Cheers."

"Cheers." Octavia smiled, raising her glass as well.

I relaxed against the leather seat and let the soft jazz coming from the car speakers ease my mind. I thought of Savoy, and a smile crept across my face instantaneously. Octavia noticed the change in my disposition.

"What are you thinking about?" she asked, staring at me.

"Savoy." I smiled.

"You really love him." She was making a statement more than asking a question.

"I do." I smiled happily. "I really do."

"I'm happy that he makes you happy," she said sincerely. "You deserve to be happy."

"Thanks, Tavia," I smiled, fighting back tears, "for everything."

"Anytime." She flashed me her winning smile, as we arrived at our destination.

Damon had gone all out for Octavia's grand opening. There was velvet red carpet outside leading to the entrance of the restaurant. Valet parking, and even members from the local press outside. Damon stood among them smiling, while being bombarded by questions. The driver held the door open, as he assisted Octavia and myself out of the car.

There was a VIP entrance, where those guests who had been sent personal invites entered without waiting. For the general public there was a line formed on the sidewalk. The turnout was unbelievable. I slipped through the VIP entrance as planned, leaving Octavia outside with her husband to discuss her latest business venture with local reporters.

Inside, the restaurant was breathtaking. The main floor held row after row of gold linen-covered tables on one side of the room. While the other side of the room, housed several black velvet covered booths. There was a huge elevated dance floor in the back of the room. There were Grecian columns throughout, and each table and booth housed its own antique lantern with an eternal candle glowing. The main lights were up bright, but I knew that once dimmed, the atmosphere of the restaurant would be extremely intimate.

I walked through the crowd until I spotted Savoy. He was surrounded by City Councilman Richard Showers and Mayor Loretta

Spencer. As if he sensed my presence, he looked up and our eyes locked. He smiled then nonchalantly glanced towards the elevator. I nodded, confirming I understood his unspoken request. Smiling, I politely nudged my way to the elevator, stepped inside, and hit the number 2 to go to the second floor. The elevator went all the way up to the roof, where there were also tables set up for rooftop dining. However, the roof had been closed for the opening.

The second floor held the glass private dining room, lounge, and another dance floor. Octavia's office was also located on the second floor. Octavia called the floor the Red Zone, and I saw why. From the carpet to the fluorescent lights, practically everything was red. The only exception was the private dining room, which had low white lights. On the tables there were white linens and white votive candles burning. The red outside the room, reflected off the glass, causing a dramatic spectrum of color. It was truly beautiful.

I glanced around to make sure none of the guests saw me, and then slipped behind the double wooden doors of the office. Inside, Octavia had a private bathroom, cherry wood furniture, and a 32" flat screen TV. I eased down in one of the two high back wooden chairs in front of the desk and waited patiently.

Seconds later the door opened, and Savoy entered looking sexy as ever. He locked the door quickly, and stretched his arms out to me. I jumped up quickly, almost running into his arms. He held me tightly. I snuggled my nose into his neck, inhaling the smell of his cologne. I loved the way he smelled. On a normal day, under normal circumstances, I could've named the fragrance. But at the moment, I was having a memory lapse. I also had what felt like a field of raging butterflies in my stomach. We stood there holding each other until he finally pulled away.

"You look beautiful." He smiled, and I swear my butterflies floated away.

"Thank you." I smiled sweetly.

"You are really wearing that dress." He gave me a sexy smile that sent heat gushing down my thighs.

If I hadn't had other things to worry about, I would have forgotten the event and had him naked in less than sixty seconds.

However, I had to allow my mind to take control over my body. We would have to wait.

"If I haven't told you already," I said, taking his hand in mine, "I love you."

Savoy reached out and stroked my cheek with his fingertips, causing my skin to tingle.

"I love you too, baby." He leaned in, kissing me softly on the mouth. The kiss was short, but sweetly sexual.

"See you later." I smiled nervously.

"Yes, baby," he said, smiling in return, "later." He opened the door slowly then stuck his head out.

Once he confirmed the coast was clear, he motioned for me to exit. I stepped out of the office, and headed back towards the elevator. Savoy closed the door behind him, and veered to the right, I presumed to take the stairs.

Downstairs Octavia and Damon smiled, looking like the poster children for the perfect marriage. I admired how well the two of them worked together, Damon giving credit to Octavia for her continued success with the Ambiance, and Octavia giving credit to Damon for finding her the perfect architect when he recommended Savoy. When Octavia's eyes landed on me, she politely excused herself from the group she and Damon were entertaining.

"Did you see your man?" she asked, with her eyebrows raised.

"Yeah, we just left your office," I said.

"No, not that man," she said, "*that* man." She directed her eyes to one of the booths in the far left corner. I followed her glance, and sure enough, wearing a dark suit, red shirt and red tie was Kenny.

"He actually showed up," I mumbled.

"Yes, ma'am," Octavia answered.

I watched Kenny as he sat in the booth moving his head to the soft jazz blowing through the room. He was sitting alone with a frosty champagne bucket, a bottle of champagne and two glasses.

"Did he come with her?" I asked, not taking my eyes off of him.

"Nope," Octavia advised me, staring at him too. "Alone."

I finally managed to pull my eyes away from Kenny to look at her. "Maybe we should..."

"Not a chance." Octavia flashed her brown eyes at me. "Operation shakedown is still on."

Has she lost her damn mind? "What if she told him?" I stared at her with disbelief. She looked like she was considering the possibility.

"It doesn't matter," she said bluntly. "We're not backing down."

I exhaled deeply. I knew Octavia was right, we had to finish what the two of us had started.

"You're right," I finally admitted.

"Great," she said, sounding relieved.

"Now put your big girl thongs on and go over there and play nice with your husband." I laughed at her poor choice of words. Not because of the whole "big girl thongs" thing, but because of her use of the word "husband".

"I'll try, but what about ole' girl?" I asked her.

"Don't worry, we got her covered."

I didn't bother questioning Octavia with the details. Instead, I took her at her word, and slowly headed in the direction where Kenny was sitting.

"Hello Kenny." My voice was so shaky I barely recognized it.

Kenny stared up at me, and a small smile instantly crept across his face. My palms suddenly felt wet and sticky. *Breathe. Just breathe.* I took a deep breath through my nose, and then slowly exhaled through my slightly parted lips.

"Wow!" Kenny let out a low whistle. I watched his eyes, as they traveled from the top of my head down to my pink French pedicure. "You look…" He didn't complete his sentence.

Instead, he picked up the half empty champagne glass sitting on the table in front of him, and finished his drink in one gulp. Sitting the glass back down, he stared at me. The look in his eyes confused me. It wasn't the look he had been giving me the last few weeks when our paths crossed, or even the look he gave me when he informed me that he was only with me for my money. No, this wasn't that look. It was something more.

The music abruptly changed, and *Always and Forever* began to play.

I quickly scanned the room, and Octavia's eyes met mine. She stood on the dance floor with her arms wrapped around Damon's neck. The two of them swayed slowly to the music. Other guests followed the host lead, and stepped out on the floor and began to dance.

"This used to be our jam," Kenny said, laughing lightly. I frowned at Octavia from across the room.

The lights were low, but she confirmed she saw my expression when she simply nodded her head.

"Tay?" Kenny said.

"Yeah, yeah it was," I returned my attention to Kenny, "a long time ago."

When Kenny and I first started dating, *Always and Forever* was *our* song. I didn't know where Octavia was going with having the DJ play it, but I knew it had something to do with us keeping up our façade.

"You wanna dance?" Kenny asked.

Is he serious? I wanted to scream hell no! Instead, I forced myself to smile.

"Sure, why not," I said.

He slid from behind the booth, and slipped his hand into mine. I allowed Kenny to lead me out onto the dance floor, not far from where Octavia and Damon were. Kenny pulled me into his arms, securing his arms around my waist. We were close, too close. I put one hand on his shoulder, and one on his chest, trying to regain some of my personal space, however I failed terribly. I could feel his heartbeat. It was loud, strong and rapid. I looked into his eyes, and they were dark but calm. He looked at me with a half smile on his face. I waited for some snide remark or degrading comment to come, but they never did.

The silence and closeness between the two of us was almost unbearable. The familiarity I found being in his arms made me nervous. I didn't like feeling so comfortable with him. This was the man who had hurt me over and over again. This was the man who had used and emotionally abused me. Why was I so calm? Why wasn't I beating on his chest, causing a scene? Why wasn't I telling him he was the lowest, most disgusting form of a human being ever created? We continued to stare at each other. I tried to find the words that would express the hatred that I wanted to feel for him at that moment, but there were none.

"Did you ever love me?" The question escaped my lips before I realized it.

Kenny never took his eyes off of me, as he answered, "I did." His voice was soft, almost sweet. I waited for him to elaborate, but he didn't.

"So what happened?" I asked calmly.

I didn't always have money. I wanted, no needed, to know when things went wrong. He was silent for a moment. I figured he was trying to gather his words.

"Sometimes in life we have to make choices," he began "Sometimes the choices are made for us."

"What does that have to do with us?"

"We were cursed from the start," he said. I tried to make sense out of what he was saying. Did he mean he didn't have it in him to be a good man?

"So you knew from the first day that you didn't want me?" I felt tears swelling in my eyes.

I swallowed hard, trying to force the lump in my throat down. I felt like I was going to break down at any moment. I took a deep calming breath. I refused to let him see me cry.

"I loved you." His voice was soft, but it sounded sincere. I didn't question him any further.

One, because I couldn't fight my tears back any longer, and two, because I could see Octavia out the corner of my eye. She was no longer in her husband's arms. She was waiting for me. I knew it was time to take care of business.

"Excuse me." I stepped back, breaking our embrace. "I have to go."

Kenny stuffed his hands in his pockets, and nodded his head. I quickly walked in Octavia's direction, never looking back.

CHAPTER 34

There was nothing complex or even remotely extraordinary about the plan. It was simple. I invited Alicia to the grand opening. I had also explained that Donna would be attending. Octavia had made sure Donna received a VIP invite. Donna confirmed she would be attending when she sent back her reply card.

Once they arrived, I was to confront Donna with the pictures of her with Kenny, as well as bust her on being the one who assisted Kenny with cashing my check. My goal was to have Donna confess to having an affair with Kenny way before my relationship began with Savoy. I thought the worst that could or would happen would be that she and Alicia would get into a lover's quarrel and make a scene at the restaurant. I was wrong.

Octavia had sent Amel to keep Kenny company at the booth he was sitting in. Amel was a pretty girl, so I knew that holding Kenny's attention wouldn't be hard for her. Then factor in the fact that Kenny was getting his drink on, I figured he would be trying to get Amel back to her place in little to no time. Amel had been instructed to call Tavia if Kenny moved from the booth.

The Ambiance 2 had two back entrances. One that led to the back of the restaurant, designated as the employee entrance. The other was designated just for Octavia. Her office housed a hidden passageway that opened to the exit. You could either go downstairs to exit on the street or upstairs to the roof. Savoy called the passageway the safe exit.

When Alicia arrived, Octavia's bouncer, Tarik, was supposed to escort her through the employee entrance and up to the office, where Octavia and I were waiting. Donna was to be escorted through the same entrance and escorted to the office as well, but somehow the plan changed, and Octavia and I were not educated on the change.

Octavia and I sat in her office in silence, waiting for Alicia's arrival. My nerves were bundled tighter than the braids in my hair. I was so nervous, that when Octavia's phone rang, I felt like my body was going to climb from underneath my skin.

"Hello," Octavia said. "What? What kind of commotion?" My heart began to jump in my chest. I was holding my breath. "No!" Octavia practically screamed the word. "I'll handle it," she said calmly.

She pressed the end button on her Blackberry, and quickly stood up. I followed her lead and rose to my feet as well.

"What happened?" I asked.

"Karen, my cook, was out back on break," she began to explain, "and she heard a commotion coming from the roof."

"What?" My question sounded more like a statement.

"Two women arguing," she said.

"I bet it's Alicia," I mumbled, taking a guess in the dark.

"And Donna." Octavia looked cool, calm and collected. I, on the other hand, felt like I was going to have a panic attack.

"Why would they be on the roof?" I asked.

"Who knows," Octavia said, walking towards the door.

"Should we get Damon and Savoy?"

Octavia spun on her heels to look at me. "Hell to the no!" she said, raising her voice. "So we have to hear their lecture on how we kept this from them?" She raised her eyebrows, looking at me like I was the swamp thing. I exhaled deeply. She was right, the last thing I needed was a lecture. We were responsible for Alicia and Donna's appearance, and we would have to be the ones to handle it.

"Let's go," I said.

I could hear the two of them shouting before Octavia and I reached the steel door to the roof. The night wind hit my skin like a thousand tiny little cold pins. The goose bumps raised on my skin instantly.

"You think you can just use me and get away with it?" Alicia's voice was sharp. "I know everything."

I noticed that she was no longer wearing a weave, and her jet black hair hung naturally at her shoulders. She wore a black satin spaghetti strap evening gown that complimented her figure. She looked nice, classy even.

"You know what I tell you!" Donna yelled.

"Keep your voices down," Octavia barked, moving towards the two of them.

I looked at Donna. She stood with her hands on her hips, wearing a beautiful strapless sea blue sequin gown that went down to her ankles. The side was opened by a long split that ran up to her thigh. She held a small gold sequin clutch in her hand. Her short hair was gelled straight back. She looked like she should have been a runway model instead of a liar and a thief.

"Who the fuck are you?" she snapped, looking at Octavia.

Octavia crossed her arms across her breasts. "I'm the owner of this establishment," she snapped back. "Most importantly to you at this moment," she said, putting her hand on her hip, "I'm Shontay's friend."

Donna's eyes darted to me. She looked like she wanted to laugh but then, as if a thought had suddenly clouded her thoughts, her expression changed. Her lips were tight as she looked from me to Octavia then to Alicia.

"What did you tell them?" Donna questioned, moving towards Alicia. She looked like she wanted to choke her.

"She didn't tell us anything," I finally spoke up. "I have my ways." Donna laughed.

"You have your ways?" She laughed again. "This from the woman who didn't know her husband had a child." She rolled her eyes at me. "You have got to be the most pathetic out of you three bitches." She pointed her skinny finger around at each of us.

"I know she didn't!" Octavia looked like she was ready to kick Donna's ass. I stepped in front of my girl before she could make her attack. "You better watch who you call bitch," Octavia spat, looking around me at Donna.

"I'm not the one who is going to prison for forgery and theft," I stated, staring at Donna. The cockiness left her face. "That's right," I laughed this time, "I know that you and Kenny helped yourselves to *my* money. I know you told Kenny about my offer to Alicia," I continued on. Donna's face was cold. I had hit the nail on the head.

"The two of you were lovers before we met," Alicia jumped in. "He had you approach me."

"Who told you?" Donna asked, looking at Alicia then me.

"He did," I lied. "It's amazing who he'll sell out for a few dollars." This part wasn't a lie. "Why do you think I bought him the truck?" I asked.

"'Cause he...he caught you cheating," Donna stuttered.

"Wow!" I giggled. I gave her my best poker face. "You'll believe anything he says! Kenny and I are back together." I flashed her an award worthy smile, then held up my ring finger.

"Bullshit!" she spat. "You're lying!"

"She's not." Alicia came to my defense. "Kenny told me so himself."

"We were just together last night." Donna sounded like she was trying to reason with herself. "You moved out," she said, looking at me.

"No sweetie," I said, tossing my head back. "I took a break, to give Kenny time to tie up some loose ends."

"By loose ends, she means you," Octavia cut in. She stepped up beside me, and crossed her arms across her breasts. "Now who's the pathetic one?" she asked, sucking on her teeth.

"And...you... knew about this?" Donna stuttered, looking at Alicia.

"Yes," Alicia said firmly. She looked at Donna then shook her head. "I loved both of you," she said. "But you betrayed me. Now payback is..."

"A bitch." Octavia helped her.

"Yeah, a bitch." Alicia agreed.

"You're all lying," Donna mumbled. "He would never betray me."

"Helloooo," I said, sounding more confident than I really was. "I'm wifey with the money."

"And I'm the one with his daughter," Alicia added.

"And you…" I was searching for the right words, "well, you're the piece of ass who sacrificed her career and freedom for someone else's husband," I said.

"And baby father," Alicia added.

Donna ran her fingers through her hair, then turned her back to us. She walked to the brick ledge and placed both hands palm down. She turned to face us.

"Kenny told you?" she asked.

I parted my lips to answer her with another lie, when the steel door flung open. I turned on my heels to see Kenny staring at the four of us. He looked from one to the other. We all were silent, as he did physical inventory with his eyes.

"Kenny." Donna sounded out of breath.

"What's this?" His words were slurred. It was obvious he was drunk.

My palms were sweating again. I knew I had to stay in character. So, without thinking, I turned and batted my eyes at Donna, gave Octavia a nervous smile, then walked over to Kenny. *Lord, Jesus, please help me.* I stared into Kenny's glazed eyes then smiled. Reaching out, I stroked his warm skin with my fingers. He didn't pull away or scream at me not to touch him.

Instead, he tilted his head slightly, so that his cheek was resting in the palm of my hand. My heart fluttered. Leaning in close to him, I pressed my lips to his. The scent of alcohol made me gasp just a little, but I didn't stop. That's when it happened.

He responded by moving his lips and kissing me in return. His hands wrapped instinctively around my waist, pulling me into his embrace. I could feel his heart beating. His breath was heavy, but strong. He slipped his tongue into my mouth, and although

I wanted to push him away and run, I reciprocated, allowing his tongue to play against mine. The kiss lasted only for a moment, but the effects of it would last a lifetime. I pulled away, trying hard to slow my breathing. He looked at me, and without any words being spoken between us, he gave me a real smile.

"I'll see you downstairs," I whispered.

I looked at Octavia, and her mouth was wide open. She undoubtedly thought I had lost my mind. Using only my eyes, I gestured for her to follow me. She nodded. I shot a glance at Alicia, who looked at peace, and I could have sworn she was suppressing a grin. Donna was a different story. Under the moonlight, she looked pale and broken. I knew that my mission had been accomplished. I had made her a believer. I held my head high as I swung the steel door open. Stepping out of the cool breeze, I entered the stairwell with Octavia right behind me. When I heard the door slam shut, I exhaled.

"What was that about?" Octavia asked, stepping up behind me.

"Freedom" I said nonchalantly. "Freedom."

We had just made it to the first flight of stairs, when I heard the shots, followed by a woman's voice. My flesh crawled from the heart wrenching scream.

CHAPTER 35

At that moment, the earth felt like it had stopped moving. Octavia and I looked at each other, neither one of us moving. In an instant Damon was there, followed by Savoy.

"Are you two alright?" Damon asked, in a frantic voice.

"Yeah, we're fine." Octavia spoke for the both of us.

"Shontay?" Savoy said soothingly. I looked into the ocean of gray in his eyes.

"Yes," I said.

"Stay here," he ordered.

The two of them looked like they were moving at the speed of light, as they rushed past us and up through the door leading onto the roof. I knew, even before Savoy came rushing back down past Octavia and myself. I knew before Octavia and I grabbed each other's hands and went to see what had occurred. How did I know? My heart told me.

It felt like the breath was being pulled from my body. The scent that tainted the air was rancid and thick. I coughed, trying hard not to choke on the bile rising in my throat.

Kenny looked like he was sleeping. His body was stretched out, as he lay in a pool of blood. The blood was coming from the wounds in his chest. I felt my stomach jump then tighten into a pain driven knot. I couldn't move.

Beside him, Donna looked like a fallen angel. A small smile was stretched across her pretty face. If it hadn't been for the small trail of blood trickling from her left temple, I would have thought she was dreaming. I wanted to scream, but I couldn't. I could hear Octavia's voice and feel her hand in mine, but my mind and body felt disconnected. I remember Damon being there. He was standing by Alicia. She wasn't hurt, but there were tears streaming down her face. Had she done this? No. No. This wasn't how it was supposed to happen. It wasn't supposed to end like this. I felt my body shaking back and forth, back and forth.

"Tay!" Octavia's voice bolted through me.

My mouth popped open as I gagged and choked, trying to fill my lungs with air. "What happened?" I cried. "What happened?"

"She shot him," Damon answered. "Then she shot herself."

"Shot? How…" I babbled then I saw it.

The small black killer lay in Donna's semi-opened hand. It looked small, but the damage it had caused was bigger than life. I looked at Alicia, she stood unmovable.

Damon was with her, speaking to her softly. "It's alright," he said. "Everything is going to be alright. You have to be strong for Kiya," he said.

At the sound of my stepdaughter's name, my knees gave way, and I felt the levee to my tears break. I cried hysterically. Frantically, Octavia was there beside me, rocking me in her arms.

"It's okay," she whispered. "It's okay." I couldn't respond.

My tears drowned out the sound of her voice, drowned out the sounds of sirens piercing the night, drowned out everything. I cried for the deaths. I cried for the lives that would be affected. Most of all, I cried for Kiya who had been innocent in all of this. I cried because she would never touch, see, or have her father again.

The scene at Ambiance 2 was like a scene from a movie. There were police and reporters everywhere. All the guests had been ushered out onto the streets. I sat in Octavia's office being consoled by a grief counselor by the name of Anne. I looked at the older white woman. Her face was kind and loving. Her pale blue eyes reminded me of the sky after a rain, they were slightly cloudy, with a hint of dim light to them. She was trying to comfort me. I was the widow she said. My world had been shattered. She felt like I needed her, but I didn't. I wanted her to leave me alone. I wanted to scream go to hell, but didn't. I just listened to her go and on about counseling and resources to help me through my trauma, until she finally finished and excused herself.

The detectives had already questioned me. They concluded I had nothing to do with the deaths. In their eyes, I was not a person of interest. I was the pitiful broken widow, whose husband had been murdered by a disgruntled lover. They were wrong. I had played my dirty role in the confrontation that led to the murder-suicide. I was just as guilty as Donna.

Octavia was also questioned and dismissed, along with Savoy and Damon. Savoy stated he and Damon had heard Alicia's screams, and that they immediately headed towards the roof to see what had transpired. They found Alicia shaken, and Kenny and Donna dead. Savoy had left the scene to go call for help. Damon's story was almost identical to Savoy's, with the exception that he stayed behind to comfort Alicia. Alicia, however, was still being questioned. Octavia explained all of this to me when she returned to her office to join me.

"What did Alicia say happened?" I asked, still half dazed.

"After we left, Donna pulled out her gun and shot Kenny in the chest," she said quietly. "Alicia said Donna then turned the gun on herself."

"Why were they on the roof?" I asked.

"Alicia said they bumped into each other upon arrival." I was silent. I knew there was no way they should have arrived at the same time.

"Donna confronted her about being there, and Alicia retreated to the roof to try and escape her." I looked at Octavia. Her expression told me she knew that was a lie, but it was a lie neither one of us would expose to the authorities.

"Why was K…" I choked on my attempt to say his name.

Octavia took a deep breath then exhaled. "Amel stated Kenny

had left the restaurant," she said. "Amel watched him get in his truck and drive off."

"He came back?" I asked.

"Yes, he received a text from Donna," Octavia said.

"She told him she was here," I concluded.

"Yes, and told him to meet her on the rooftop." I tried to process the information. It didn't add up. Yes, Donna could have text Kenny and asked him to meet her, but why would she if Alicia was there and they were arguing?

"Did anyone else witness anything?" I asked. Octavia shook her head.

"No, from what the detectives explained, the other guests witnessed nothing."

"So, the only one who really knows what took place…"

"Is Alicia," Octavia finished. I sunk farther down in my seat. "Shontay, you have to get ready for what has to happen next," she spoke softly.

"More questioning?" I asked.

"No," she said gently. "At least I don't think for us."

"What?" I was mentally and emotionally exhausted. I didn't have the strength to guess or attempt to know the answer.

"Facing Etta," she said, looking at me.

CHAPTER 36

The next week went by in a daze. The headlines were blunt and the case, for the most part, was open and shut. Kenny was killed during a lover's quarrel. His lover had then turned the gun on herself. The gun was registered in Donna's name. Speculation circled that Donna was involved in embezzlement, and a list of other fraud charges. After the news that Kenny was not going to leave his wife, the woman went crazy and created a crime of passion.

Alicia's life was spared, but no one knew why. I was not, nor had I ever been, a suspect. So, to the outside world, I was just another victim of an affair gone wrong. I later discovered Kenny had a fifty thousand dollar insurance policy, but the beneficiary was his mother, which ruled me out from any participation in his demise due to insurance.

The night of the murder, I couldn't bring myself to call Etta, so Octavia did it for me. I remember hearing the woman on the other end of the phone screaming like someone had reached inside of her and ripped out a part of her soul.

Octavia, Damon and Savoy were treating me like a fragile china doll that could break at any moment. Inside I felt like I could break. I was still sleeping at Octavia's home, but rather than sleeping in the guesthouse with Savoy, they moved me to one on the spare guest bedrooms. Savoy and I spoke to each other, but there were no intimate moments between us. The love was still there, but he understood I needed time to mourn, even though I was mourning the loss of a husband with whom my marriage had long been over.

I hadn't seen or spoken to Alicia. Damon suggested that this was a good thing, in the event that detectives were watching her, the two of us didn't need to appear to be too close. I was an emotional wreck. The few pounds I had put on, quickly disappeared with what felt like ten more.

By the time Kenny's body was released to me, I was so overcome with guilt I didn't know where to begin with planning his memorial service. Octavia held true to her title as my best friend, and coordinated everything for me. I was grateful for her loyalty and love. She even went as far as to buying me a new black dress for the service. I still had unanswered questions, but I pushed these aside. It was time for me to bury my husband.

Octavia had arranged for a simple gravesite service. Etta hadn't protested. Octavia said she was quite cooperative, especially after Octavia explained she and Damon would be the ones footing the service. I hated to think Etta was happy to keep her money to herself, but that's the impression I was given.

The day of Kenny's funeral was a rainy day, which only made my depression worse. The temperature was around the early fifties, which meant it was extremely cold. Octavia sent a car for Etta to ride in, due to Etta refusing to ride in the same limo with me. I didn't care. Etta and I disliked each other, and nothing, not even the passing of Kenny, could make us forge a bond.

At the gravesite, Damon stood beside Octavia under one umbrella, while I stood on her other side with my own umbrella. Out of respect for Etta, Savoy opted not to attend the service. I longed for his shoulder to lean on, but I knew he was right in his decision. Etta stood across from us next to Octavia's Pastor. A handful of Kenny's friends and old co-workers gathered behind us. In the distance, I saw Alicia holding an umbrella standing alone.

Pastor Davis repeated a simple Verse from Psalms 118. "I shall not die," he said, "but live, and declare the works of the Lord. The

Lord hath chastened me sore; but He hath not given me over unto death. Open to me the gates of righteousness: I will go into them, and I will praise the Lord. This gate of the Lord, into which the righteous shall enter. I will praise thee: for thou hast heard me, and art become my salvation." He concluded with an Amen. We each said Amen as well.

After offering Etta, and then myself condolences, Pastor Davis kissed Octavia goodbye and departed. He was followed by the other visitors at the grave.

"Are you ready?" Octavia asked, looking at me.

"Give me a moment," I said.

Nodding her understanding, she tucked her arm through Damon's, and they headed to the car. Etta stood still, not moving for a moment. Then her eyes drifted from her son's grave and met with mine. She said nothing, as she turned and walked away.

I stood alone in the rain, allowing the umbrella I was holding to drop down to my side. The rain had just begun to hit me, when someone came up beside me, blocking the cool water. I turned slightly and saw it was Alicia.

"He loved you." She said it so softly, it was practically a whisper.

"I loved him," I said.

"So did I," she said. "I thought we would be married one day. He promised," she said.

"It was my fault it happened." I hadn't admitted to anyone that I felt like I was to blame for the way things went down with Kenny and Donna, but at that moment with Alicia I let it go.

"No it wasn't," she said quickly. "We each played our part. But in the end, the only one responsible was the one with the gun." I turned to look at her. Her eyes shined like stars.

"Alicia, what really happened?" She stared out into the open, appearing not to focus on anything in particular.

"Karma," she finally answered. I exhaled loudly.

"I wonder what karma has in store for us."

"Hopefully forgiveness," she said. "Peace."

"Happiness," I added. We looked at each other; there was a pregnant pause between us. "How is Kiya?" I asked.

"She's okay," she said. "She's too young to understand." We were both silent for a second. "I'm going away for a little while," she said.

"Where are you going?"

"I have family in Los Angeles. I think it'll be good for Kiya and me if we had a fresh start."

"I'm going to miss her," I said. Kiya came into my life on a whim, and now she was leaving on another one.

"We'll be back to visit," Alicia reassured me. "And you can visit us as well." I returned her smile.

"I'd like that," I said.

"You shouldn't feel bad." Alicia's smile quickly changed. Her face was strong and serious. "You didn't deserve to be treated the way he treated you. The way I treated you," she added, sounding guilty.

"I forgive you," I said.

"Thanks for everything," she said.

"Do you or Kiya need anything else?"

"No," she said quickly. "We'll have a very good start."

I raised my eyebrows, but didn't ask her to elaborate. I had given Alicia ten thousand dollars, but I didn't know how long ten thousand would actually last in Los Angeles. I shrugged my curiosity off, and assumed Alicia knew something about Los Angeles that I didn't, or maybe her family was going to help her out.

"I should be going," she said. "Take care of yourself." I nodded then smiled.

"You as well." She turned to leave, but stopped. "Do me a favor?"

"What's that?"

"Tell Etta that I'm leaving," she said. I rolled my eyes.

"Is there anything *else* I can do? Donate a rib?" I asked. "Stop world hunger?" Alicia laughed lightly.

"No, just that."

I took another deep breath. "Are you sure?" I asked.

"Positive." She chuckled.

"Okay. Okay."

We both turned, and walked away in opposite directions. I reached the warm limo, and slid in beside Octavia.

"Everything okay?" she asked. I looked from her to Damon. They each had looks of concern on their faces.

"Everything is going to be just fine," I said smiling.

By the time we made it back to Octavia and Damon's, I was exhausted. I hadn't truly slept since the incident at Ambiance 2, and sleep was calling me in more ways than one. Yet there was so much left for me to do. I couldn't continue to let Octavia handle my business for me; it was time for me to restore order in my life. I knocked on the guesthouse door lightly.

"It's open." Savoy's voice sounded like a sweet melody to my ears.

I opened the door, and stepped in, pulling the door shut behind me. Savoy was stretched out on the bed watching television. He was barefoot and wearing denim jeans. I looked at his bare chest and longed to lay my head there. His smile grew as he looked at me.

"Hi." I smiled slowly.

"Hey." I walked over to the bed and took a seat on the edge, turning so that I could look at him. "How are you?" His voice was gentle and concerned.

"I'm better, much better," I said.

"Good." There was a thick fog of tension filling the air.

"I've missed you," I said lowly.

"I've missed you too." We both smiled. I looked aimlessly around the room. I noticed his bags were packed and were sitting in the corner.

"You're leaving?" I felt tears welling in the pockets of my eyes.

"Yes, I have to get back to Atlanta and my business." His voice sounded full of regret.

"When...when were you going to tell me?" I stammered. I felt alienated and hurt.

"I don't know," he said, shrugging his shoulders. "I didn't want to put you under any more stress."

Okay, yes, I had been a zombie lately. True, I hadn't been the best girlfriend, friend, or anything since Kenny's death. However, I didn't want Savoy leaving without so much as a notice.

"I'm sorry for shutting you out," I said.

"It's okay," he said sweetly, "as long as you're okay." A single tear trickled down my cheek.

"I don't want to lose you, Savoy," I cried.

Sitting up he pulled me by the arm into his embrace. "I'm not going anywhere," he said, holding me close. I rested my head against the soft hairs on his chest. The scent of Giorgio Armani filled my nostrils. I had missed his scent and the strength of his arms.

"Then why are your bags packed?" I mumbled sarcastically.

"But I'm not going anywhere you can't go," he reassured me. He kissed the top of my head. " You're welcome to come see me, when you're ready," he said. " Until then, just remember that miles are just stepping stones," he said.

"I love you, Savoy."

"That's good, because I love you too."

I snuggled closer to him. I was enjoying the warmth he provided, after being in the chilly rain. I closed my eyes and let go of my worries. The sleep I had been fighting for days finally claimed me.

CHAPTER 37

The closing on my home was quickly approaching, and I had numerous things to do to get ready. For one, I needed to purchase a new home. I wasn't 100% sure that I still wanted to stay in Huntsville, so that was one I could wait on. Packing, however, was another story. My house was completely furnished, and I wanted no part in the memories attached to the furnishings. I called Goodwill and let them take every chair, table, and bed I had. I also had an entire wardrobe that I couldn't wear, due to my weight loss. I sent those as well.

Packing my things meant that I would also have to pack Kenny's. I boxed up his clothes, shoes and jewelry, and then with the assistance of my BFF, I loaded them into the Escalade. I found a few pictures of Kenny with Kiya tucked inside his dresser drawer. Kiya looked only a few months old. They were taken before I knew she existed. I assumed he had hidden them, and then forgotten they were there. I stuffed them into my jacket pocket.

The possessions Kenny had on him the night he was murdered had all been destroyed at the morgue, per my request, all with the exception of his wallet and cell phone. I told the police they could keep the cell phone, I didn't need or want to know who else my husband had been sleeping with. Inside his wallet there was nothing but his license and three one hundred dollar bills. I took the wallet and packed it with his other items. It took us eight hours to get everything packed and removed. The things I wanted to keep were already at Octavia's home.

I donated my Eclipse and Honda to a local program called Cars For The Less Fortunate. They took used cars and repaired them so that families in need could have a vehicle to get back and forth to work. Both my cars were in excellent working condition, so I knew that whoever got them would be lucky. There was nothing left for me at the home. I cranked up the Escalade, backed out, and left without looking back. Octavia followed closed behind me, as I led the way to Etta's house.

From the outside, Etta's home looked deserted. There were pots of wilted brown plants cluttering the porch. I figured the recent frost we experienced had taken their lives. The grass had grown up to the point where, if you stepped onto it, it would cover your ankles. I knew these were signs of Kenny's death. If he had been living, he would have made sure his mother's yard was maintained.

Etta opened the door on the first knock. She wore an orange fleece housecoat with matching slippers. Her eyes drooped from the enormous bags under her eyes. I knew the bags were not just a sign of aging, but a sign of a mother's mourning. Etta and Kenny had the same dark chocolate skin and dark black eyes. Etta's hair was completely gray. She had countless orange sponge rollers and pink pins wrapped around her hair.

She stepped back so that I could enter. The house smelled like liniment and boiled collard greens. I hadn't been to Etta's home in over seven years. There were no shared family gatherings or family dinners during the course of my marriage to Kenny. Thinking back now, I realize just how dysfunctional our families had been.

Inside Etta's home looked completely upgraded. I figured Kenny was the one to thank for this. She had a brown leather living room set, oak coffee and end tables, and even a large flat screen television. The one thing that hadn't changed was the mirage of pictures covering the walls and the two bookshelves in the room.

"Sit down," she said, motioning towards the leather recliner. I nodded, and carefully eased down in the chair. Etta stood looking at me.

"I brought his things," I said, "and his truck." She nodded her head. "Would you like me to unload the boxes?"

"No," she said quickly. "I'll get it myself." *Silence.*

"Alicia asked me to advise you that she's moving to Los Angeles." *Silence.*

I fidgeted nervously with my nails. I didn't know which was worse, Etta snapping on me, or the fact that she was saying nothing at all. At least if she had popped off, it would have been a two-way conversation.

"Oh," I blurted, "I almost forgot" I reached into my pocket and pulled out the pictures of Kenny and Kiya. "I figured you might want these." I held the pictures up. Etta walked to the bookshelf and pulled out a dusty photo album. She walked over to me and handed me the album.

"Put 'em in there," she said roughly. "I gotta go check on my greens."

I watched her turn and walk out the room. *Awkward.* I found empty spaces in the back of the photo album, and slid the pictures behind the protective clingy film. I debated on bolting for the door while Etta was gone, but I didn't want to be rude. I stood and placed the photo album back in the place where Etta had removed it.

On the shelf there were several framed pictures, and quite a few books. I scanned the titles. *The Holy Bible, Their Eyes Were Watching God, To Kill A Mockingbird.* She even had a few urban titles, including one of my all time favorites, *The Coldest Winter Ever* by Sister Souljah. I was baffled. I had no idea Etta was a reader, and that we actually had some of the same taste in books. Just one of the many things I didn't know about my mother-in-law.

I picked up one of the wooden frames, and brushed it against my jeans to knock some of the dust off. The picture behind the glass was old and slightly discolored. It was of a young Etta. She wore fitted bell bottoms, a fitted sleeveless shirt, and had a huge afro. She was leaning against an old school Lincoln. Etta was actually pretty in her earlier days. I replaced the frame then picked up the next one. It was Etta again. She had on the same outfit as she did in the last photo, only this time she was smiling and hugged up with a handsome young man. I studied the photo carefully. I heard Etta re-enter the room, but didn't acknowledge her presence.

"My brother was a good man," she said. I pulled my eyes from the picture, and watched her as she shuffled over to the sofa and sat down. "Ashad was our family pride and joy." She began to reminisce. "He believed in standing up for what was right. I believed he would one day lead a movement all on his own. But he was quick to be distracted." She looked at me with pain in her eyes. "Kenny was just like him, quick to drop everything for a pretty face and a big ass," she mumbled. I sat the picture back down on the bookshelf, then turned and looked at the old woman. "When he brought you home, I had a feeling," she rambled on. "But I wanted to be sure. Then he told me who your people were." She looked at me, her face was expressionless. I listened in silence. "Josie was loose." She laughed. "I figured like mother like daughter." I didn't like her talking about my mother, but I also knew choking the life out of her was not the answer.

"Don't you dare talk about my mother," I said angrily.

"Your mother is the reason my brother is dead."

"Ashad's death was caused by the men that beat him," I snapped.

"He died defending her." Etta wiped a single tear from her cheek. "She was a tramp, always in some man's face." She shook her head. "She liked the money and cars."

"She loved Ashad," I said defensively. "She suffered from her decisions. She regretted the things she did," I continued.

"I hated her," Etta said, rubbing her hands together. "I felt if Ashad had just stayed away from her."

"I'm not saying my mother made the best choices," I said calmly. "But hating her didn't bring your brother back."

"I tried my hardest to get Kenny to leave you alone," she said softly. "But he said you were different."

"But you didn't want to give me a chance."

"Because of Josie," she confessed.

"You were the reason he kept the letters from me?" I concluded.

"And the phone calls?" She nodded.

"But he still told me about the hospital," I said it more to myself.

"He was torn," she said. "But he did the right thing. I put a lot of pressure on my son." She looked at me with tears in her eyes. "Pressure that I'm sure drove him to making a lot of bad choices. Running with all those fast ass women." She continued. "Smoking and drinking." She shook her head.

"He was going to leave you," she said. "Because I wanted him to."

"Then he found out about my money," I concluded. She nodded her head. There was a brief moment of silence between us.

"Kenny made his own choices," I finally said. "Things could have turned out differently."

The anger I felt before had dissipated. I now felt pity and sorrow for Etta. Years of hatred for my mother led her to hating me, and wanting to sabotage my marriage. In the end, she was broken and lonely.

"He could have chosen a different path," I said, "with or without your influence."

"But a son's loyalty to his mother runs deep."

"Your influence on your son may have been negative," I said.

"But he still had a choice."

"What happens now?" she asked weakly.

I thought for a second. "We forgive," I said positively. "And we live."

Epilogue

SHONTAY

A small bead of sweat trickled down my face, as I continued to pound my feet in the warm white sand. The sand tickled my toes, and I enjoyed the cushion and freedom it provided me, allowing me to run barefoot. The soothing sounds of the Caribbean Sea filled the air around me. I inhaled. The scent of saltwater, mixed with Armani, tickled my nostrils.

I looked to my right to see Savoy running right next to me. In the moonlight he looked like a warrior, confident and strong. The light illuminated the tiny droplets of sweat glistening on his bare chest. The two of us slowed our strides as we reached our rented villa.

I stopped running, and slowly slid my feet out into the sand until I was in a lunge position. I watched Savoy do the same. I smiled, looking at him. After so much heartache and pain in my life, it felt good to have a new beginning.

After making peace with Etta, well Henrietta, I decided that it was time for me to live on my own terms and conditions. The guilt surrounding Kenny's death still shook me from time to time, but the love I felt in the present overshadowed it.

I decided that day that I couldn't let Savoy leave me behind. I figured we both could use a vacation, so I chose beautiful Belize. When we arrived, we rented a private yacht and had an intimate-private memorial just for my mother. I spread her ashes along the Caribbean, and finally told her to rest in peace.

"A dime for your thoughts," Savoy said, walking up to me and pulling me into his arms.

"I can show you better than I can tell you," I said seductively.

Smiling, he bent down and pressed his lips to mine. His lips ignited a burning in me that I hoped would never end. I didn't know where we would be tomorrow or the day after that, but I didn't care. I was living in the moment, and at that moment, the only thing I wanted and needed was him.

OCTAVIA

I opened my eyes slowly, allowing a small yawn to escape my lips. After an intense and passionate lovemaking session with Damon, I had slept like a Queen. *Lord, I love my husband.* Running my hand over the Egyptian sheets, I felt around for his warm body, but instead came up empty handed. I rolled over onto my side and saw that his side of the bed was empty. Pushing my hair out of my face, I sat up and looked at the crystal alarm clock on the night stand. It was only 2:00 am.

"My poor baby is probably up for diaper duty," I said aloud.

I tossed the sheet aside and climbed out of bed. I was completely naked, but I opened my bedroom door and slipped out into the hallway. My first stop was the nursery. I figured Damon had slipped out of bed to check on Jasmine. I carefully opened the nursery door, and poked my head in. Damon was nowhere to be found. I quietly tiptoed up to the bassinet, and saw our beautiful daughter sleeping peacefully. I couldn't help smiling at the sight of her.

"Mommy loves you," I whispered.

I turned and tiptoed back out of the room. I pulled the door closed behind. My next step was downstairs to the kitchen. As I walked down the winding staircase I could hear Damon's voice.

I continued making my way to the kitchen, while listening to his conversation.

"No, its fine," he said. "I'm glad you called. Well, I'm glad the two of you made it safely. Right. Call me if you need anything. Goodbye."

I was now standing in the doorway of our kitchen. Damon was wearing nothing but a pair of silk boxers. He stood holding his cell phone with his back to me.

"Who was that?" I asked.

Damon slowly turned around. At first his eyes locked with mine, then his eyes traveled down, scanning my naked body.

"Savoy," he said, focusing on my exposed breasts.

"They made it safely?" I asked.

After everything that had taken place, I feared that another tragedy might occur. I was being irrational, I know, but my nerves had been a mess since the shootings. Although the incident had not bruised my reputation, patrons were still flocking to both of my establishments; I couldn't shake my intuition that there was something missing from the story.

"Yes, they did." Damon smiled. He finally stopped gawking at my girls and brought his eyes back up to mine. He moved slowly until he was standing in front of me. "So *we* can go back to bed now," he said sexily.

I smiled and wrapped my arms around his neck. In one swift movement, Damon had me in his arms. Leaning down, he kissed my lips softly.

"I love you, Mrs. Whitmore," he whispered.

"I love you, Mr. Whitmore." I held onto my husband's strong shoulders, as he carried me back to our bedroom.

Inside our bedroom, he laid me down on our bed, where the two of us indulged in round two of our lovemaking.

I was awakened to the sound of my cell phone ringing. I quickly slid from under Damon's strong arms, and rolled over to my side to grab my Blackberry off the nightstand. I looked at the Caller ID, and saw it was Shontay. I looked at my alarm clock and saw it was 6 am. I figured she and Savoy was getting ready for their daily run.

"Hey Tay," I whispered, sliding out of bed.

I didn't want to wake Damon, and it was obvious from the smile on his face that he was sleeping very peacefully. I slipped into our private bathroom and shut the door.

"Hey boo!" Shontay seemed unbelievably happy. I smiled at how perky she was. It was long overdue.

"I wanted to let you know we made it," she said.

"I know," I said.

"How did you know?" she asked. "Let me guess, mommies intuition?"

"No." I giggled. "Didn't Savoy talk to Damon?"

"Not that I know of," Shontay said. "This is the first time either of us has picked up a phone."

I knew it was early, and that I had just had wonderful sex with my husband, which always makes me a little weak. However, I know what Damon had told me earlier.

"Octavia?" I had totally zoned out while Shontay was still talking.

"My bad," I said, slightly confused. "I haven't gotten my nap out. What were you saying?" Shontay laughed on the other end.

"Nothing, sweetie, go back to bed." Little did she know I was no longer in a sleeping mood.

"Okay," I said, faking a yawn. "Call me soon."

"I will," Shontay said enthusiastically. "I love you."

"I love you too."

I pressed the end button on my Blackberry and slipped back out of the bathroom. Damon was still sound asleep. He looked completely at peace while I, on the other hand, was filled with confusion. I had never had a reason not to trust my husband, and to my knowledge he had never lied to me. We were always open with each other. Even when he had his very intimate dream about Jada Pickett-Smith, he shared it with me. In fact he went into very graphic detail. So, why would he lie to me now? I didn't know, but I knew I was about to do something I never thought I would. I was about to go through my husband's phone.

I slowly tiptoed over to his nightstand and snatched his Blackberry up off the marble top. I also grabbed the baby monitor. If Jasmine woke up, I didn't want her to wake Damon. The last thing I wanted to do was get caught snooping before I had some valid accusations to throw at him.

Damon didn't move an inch, so I dipped back into the bathroom. I pressed the green call button to retrieve the call history, but was unable to do so due to the phone being locked. Why did he have his phone locked? I was curious, but I wasn't trippin. Instantly I tried the last four numbers of Damon's social security number, which was incorrect. Next I tried the day and month the two of us got married, this too was incorrect. I paced back and forth across the marble floor, trying to think of what could possibly be the pass code. I looked at the white plastic baby monitor and it hit me.

I knew Jasmine provided me with too many characters, so our daughter's nickname was the next best thing. I used the corresponding letters to spell out Jazz, and was relieved to find out this was the password. I peeked out the bathroom, just to make sure Damon was still dreaming about me or Jada, and was happy to hear him snoring.

I pressed the green call button and the call history popped up. The last call received was at 1:50 am, and lasted for only ten minutes, but it was from a number I didn't recognized. My heart rate began to increase, as countless thoughts ran through my head. Was it another woman? Was Damon cheating on me? How much time will I get for killing the two of them? I finally decided to stop torturing myself, and I called the number.

She answered on the first ring. *She was probably waiting by the phone for my husband to call her!* "Hey Damon." Her voice sounded somewhat familiar. I wanted to scream, *this isn't Damon, you home wrecking bitch*, but I decided against jumping to conclusions.

"This isn't Damon," I said calmly.

"Octavia?" She said my name like she knew me.

"Who is this?" I snapped.

"Alicia." *Aww, hell naw!* So it was a home wrecking bitch on the other line. Okay, maybe I was being too irrational. Alicia had changed more recently, at least Shontay said she had, but still why was she now calling *my* husband?

"Why are you calling my husband?" I said, with attitude.

"Octavia, nothing is going on between us." She sounded like she was making a plea. It was a good tone for her to use, because if I didn't receive an explanation that convinced me that she was not creepin' with my husband, she would definitely be making some pleas to me. Like for me not to kick her ass.

"As I remember, my question was, why are *you* calling *my* husband?"

She exhaled deeply on the other end. "Octavia, I think you should ask Damon." *Did I ask her what she thinks?*

"That's fine and dandy," I whispered, sarcastically. "However, I'm asking you." There was silence on the other end. My patience was growing thin with Alicia. "Tell you what," I began, "why don't you tell me what your connection is to my husband, before I catch the next plane out to Los Angeles and bring my father, the *detective,* with me?" I was making a threat, but if Alicia didn't answer my question, my threat would soon be a well fulfilled promise. "I'm waiting," I said firmly. "Or should I be booking reservations?"

"No," she finally exhaled. "I'll tell you everything"

To Be Continued

ABOUT THE AUTHOR

Mz Robinson is a native of Huntsville, Alabama. As a child, writing poetry became one of her many hobbies. It wasn't until much later in life, that she reconnected with her love for writing and began to pen short stories. After falling in love with the characters she created, she turned one of her short stories, into her debut novel: What We Won't Do For Love. She took a break from writing to pursue other career opportunities, but deep in her heart writing was always her passion. Five years later she signed her first contract with G Street Chronicles. When she's not writing, Mz. Robinson enjoys reading and spending time with her family. She is currently hard at work on her fourth book and other projects.

The Love, Lies & Lust Series begins here

Octavia Ellis is a sexy and independent woman who plays it safe when it comes down to relationships. She lives by one rule: keep it strictly sexual. Octavia is living her life just the way she wants. No man. No issues. No drama. When she meets the handsome Damon Whitmore, everything changes. Octavia soon finds that Damon has become a part of her world and her heart. However, when temptation comes in the form of a sexy-hardcore thug named, Beau, Octavia finds herself caught in a deadly love triangle. She soon learns in life and love, there are no rules and she's surprised at what she herself, will not do for love.

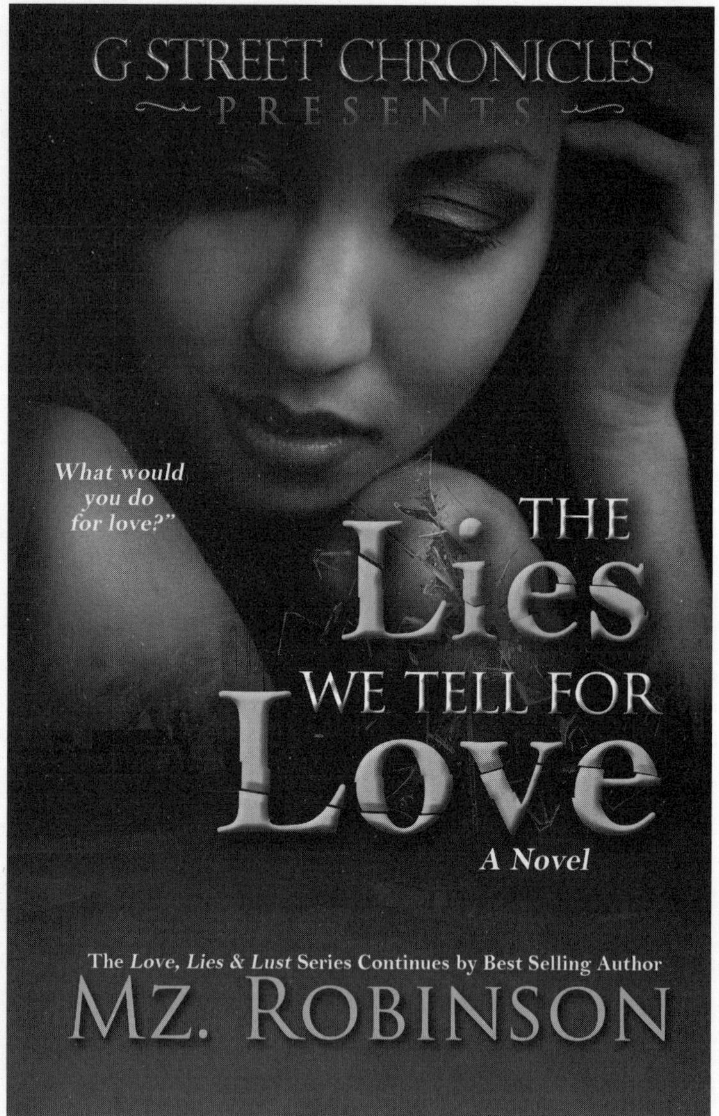

Coming Soon

The Love, Lies & Lust Series Continues

"What would you do for love?"
"How would you handle the discovery that your marriage was built on lies?"

Damon Whitmore is a true go-getter who will stop at nothing to get what he desires. His wife Octavia was no exception. When Damon first saw Octavia he knew he had to have her. He went through great lengths until his mission was accomplished. Now, two years later, he and Octavia share a wonderful and lavish life together. Damon exceeded all of Octavia's expectations while managing to keep his secrets of deceit and manipulation hidden but what's done in the dark eventually comes to light and Damon's lies are slowly beginning to unravel.

When a face from Damon's past re-surfaces, Damon finds himself facing a life alerting dilemma that could cause him to lose the very thing he fought so hard to build—his family with Octavia. Damon refuses to lose and he'll stop at nothing, including murder, to keep his family in tact.

Octavia Ellis-Whitmore never thought she would be a one man woman. Living by a no strings attached policy, she kept her encounters with men strictly sexual. When she met Damon everything in her world changed. Octavia opened her heart and fell hard for Damon. Octavia is now living and loving her life to the fullest. However, history has a way of repeating itself and temptation has a way of finding Octavia. When things at home begin to get rocky, Octavia finds herself struggling between remaining true to the vows she pledged to Damon and exploring her feelings for a new and mysterious stranger—a stranger who has a startling connection to Damon and his past.

As the drama unfolds, lies and secrets will be exposed and lines will be crossed on both ends. How far will Damon and Octavia go to protect each other from the other's transgressions and how many will fall victim to the lies that have been spun in the name of love?

Essence Monroe went through great lengths to escape her sordid past and the lovers in it. Using extreme and deadly tactics she re-invented herself and now she's well on her way to a promising future. Not only is she engaged to Andrew Carlton, one of Atlanta s most sought after athletes, but she's slowly creating a name for herself in the fashion industry. Essence is a former bad girl - gone good and she's living a life that others can only dream of. That is until Essence's life is shaken, when she discovers that someone knows her secrets. Essence must revert to her bad girl ways, in order to protect herself and the man she loves. While she's focused on keeping her skeletons buried, there's another woman focused on taking her place by Andrew's side. Not only does the mysterious woman want to take Essences man but she wants Essence life for her very own. In the end there can be only one winner and no one is prepared for the outcome.

G&L Enterprises is the biggest marketing firm in the country. Each year thousands of intern applicants apply with the hope of securing a position with the illustrious firm. Out of a sea of applicants, Asia is bestowed the honor of receiving an internship with G&L. Asia is beautiful, ambitious, and determined to climb her way up the corporate ladder by any means necessary. From crossing out all in her path, to seducing Parker Bryant the CEO of G&L, Asia secures a permanent position with the marketing giant. However, her passion for success will not allow her to settle for second best. Asia wants the number one spot, and she'll stop at nothing, including betraying the man responsible for her success to get it. Asia, is taking corporate takeover to a whole new level!

PRESENTS

Visit www.gstreetchronicles.com
to view all our titles

Join us on Facebook
G Street Chronicles Fan Page

City Lights
A-Town Veteran
Executive Mistress
Essence of a Bad Girl
Two Face
Dealt the Wrong Hand
Dope, Death & Deception
Family Ties
Blocked In
Drama

The Love, Lust & Lies Series by Mz. Robinson
What We Won't Do for Love
Married to His Lies
Coming Soon
The Lies We Tell for Love

"Coming Fall 2011"
Still Deceiving
(part 2 of India's Dope, Death & Deception)
Trap House
Chasing Bliss

"Coming 2012"
Drama II
69

Name: ______________________

Address: ______________________

City/State: ______________________

Zip: ______________________

ALL BOOKS ARE $10 EACH

QTY	TITLE	PRICE
	Married to His Lies	
	What We Won't Do for Love	
	City Lights	
	A-Town Veteran	
	Beastmode	
	Executive Mistress	
	Essence of a Bad Girl	
	Family Ties	
	Blocked In	
	Drama	
	Two Face	
	Dope, Death and Deception	
	Dealt the Wrong Hand	
	Shipping & Handling ($4 per book)	

TOTAL $ __________

To order online visit

www.gstreetchronicles.com

Send cashiers check or money order to:

G Street Chronicles

P.O. Box 490082 College Park, GA 30349